THE ULURU CODE

ERNEST DEMPSEY

ISBN: 9781944647124

**Get Ernest Dempsey's Best Selling Novel and
two introductory novellas FREE.**
Become a VIP reader and get the free
ebooks at http://ernestdempsey.net/vip-
swag-page/ or check out more details at the
end of the book.

Prologue
Milbrodale, New South Wales
Australia, 1893

It couldn't be coincidence.

At least that's what Robert Mathews told himself.

He peered over the top of his theodolite with suspicion, rechecked his position, and then looked through the instrument again.

"That doesn't belong there," Robert said under his breath.

A tall, lanky black man stood nearby with arms crossed, watching curiously. His name was Charley, and he'd been assisting Mathews with his research. At present, he was trying to understand what had the anthropologist so befuddled.

Mathews craned his neck to make sure his angle was right and then stood up straight. He turned to Charley, who'd taken off his wide-brimmed hat and was wiping sweat from his forehead. Even though Charley was an Aborigine and had lived in the area his whole life, the blazing summer heat was clearly taking its toll.

"What you make of that rock over there, Charley?" Mathews asked in his sharp Aussie accent.

Charley shrugged. "Looks like a rock, Bob."

Very few people called Mathews *Bob*. Most called him *Robert* or *R.H.* Oddly, Mathews liked the fact that his friend used the shortened version. He felt it sort of symbolized their unique friendship.

Mathews had been studying the Aboriginal tribes as an outsider when the two met. Charley was a half-caste and a native of Broke, not far from Milbrodale. Thanks to Charley, Robert's learning of their culture, customs, and history was greatly accelerated. The man Mathews paid to be his assistant had become a trusted friend.

A gust of wind rolled across the grassy hillside leading up to the rock formation. Specks of dust kicked into the air, forcing the two men to shield their faces with their forearms. A moment later, the wind was gone.

The rock he'd noticed was about fifty feet down the hill, tucked away in a stretch of tall grass. He'd probably walked right by it a few times and not even realized it. From his current vantage point, it stood out against the backdrop.

Mathews stepped out in front of his theodolite and raised a hand to his forehead, shielding it from the bright sunlight. *That rock was put there by someone. But why?*

The thought pulled at his mind. He'd not really noticed the stone before because all his focus was on the cave drawings of the ancient Aboriginal creator god called Baiame.

Since Mathews had been a surveyor in his previous career, he'd thought it might be interesting to do a little work on the surrounding area to see if there was anything worth noting. "How did I not notice that before?" he said to himself, a habit of his when deep in thought.

He turned to Charley again. "Let's give it a look, Charley."

The other man gave a curt nod and joined his friend. The two walked across a patch of dirt and back onto the path leading down the hill. When they were almost perpendicular to the rock, the two veered off the trail and waded through the long grass until they reached the anomaly. The rock was much darker than the surrounding sandstone, and it jutted out of the ground to a height just shy of four feet. It barely stood out over the tips of the grass. Still, its displacement had caught Mathews's eye.

"Just a rock, Bob. What you thinking?" Charley asked. He put both hands on his hips and glanced over at Mathews with probing dark eyes.

Mathews squatted next to the rock and ran a hand over it. "It's a different kind of rock than that over there." He flicked his head back toward the cave. "It didn't come from around here."

"What you mean, it didn't come from here? What's it doing here then?"

Mathews's head shook from one side to the other. "Not sure, mate. But it didn't come from here. See how the color of this sandstone is different than that?" He pointed at the rock formation above.

Charley looked up at the cave entrance and then back at the little rock near Mathews's feet. "Sure. I suppose maybe a little more red to it."

"Precisely. That subtle difference is probably why no one has noticed it before."

"We didn't notice it when we walked by it before."

"Indeed. To the untrained eye it looks like it's just another random rock."

Charley peered at his friend. "You sayin' my eye isn't trained?"

Mathews chuckled. "I said we both missed it, mate."

Charley's lips parted in a friendly smile. "I know. I was just messin' with you."

"You're a dag one, aren't you?"

Charley shrugged. "I try." He motioned to the rock. "So what you figure, Bob? If that rock isn't from here, who put it here and why?"

Mathews leaned closer to where the ground and rock merged. He turned around and took a brush from his tool belt and started scraping away some of the dirt. He worked for a few minutes while Charley looked on with intense curiosity.

The native had seen his friend do that sort of thing a hundred times or more. Over the course of their friendship, Charley had performed the same kind of work in several locations. At the moment, he wasn't sure what Mathews expected to find under a stone that was easily half a ton.

About five minutes passed when Mathews, sweaty from his work, stopped and sat up straight. "That's what I figured," he said.

"What?" Charley didn't see anything unsual.

Mathews took a rag from his back pocket and wiped the sweat from his brow. He shoved the kerchief in its place and pointed at the rock. "That rock only goes down a few inches into the ground."

"So?" Charley asked with a shrug.

"So that means it's much more likely it was put here than indigenous."

"You know, mate, I think the heat might be getting to your head. Let's go back to the cart and get something to drink. Your fascination with this rock is starting to worry me."

"No, I'm fine." Mathews shook his head. "Someone put this here for a reason. Maybe it was ceremonial. There are lots of stones like this all over the world that were put in places just for sacred meaning or for some kind of ritual."

"That would make sense. This is a very sacred place to the native people."

"Right. But what if it's something else?"

"Like what?"

"I dunno," Mathews said. He put his hands out to the side. "What if the people who put it here buried something underneath it?"

Charley's dubious expression said it all. "Seems like an awful lot of work to drag a rock like that from somewhere else just to hide something."

Mathews nodded. "It does. You're right about that."

He glanced around the area. No one else was around. He looked farther down the hill at the two horses. "You know, I don't think it will hurt anything if we just take a look underneath."

Charley held up a hand. "Now wait a minute, Bob. You're talkin' about destroying something that might be sacred to my people."

Mathews tilted his head to the side and shot his friend a sarcastic glare. "Five minutes ago you didn't know this rock was here. Now you're saying it's sacred?"

"You make a good point," Charley said. "But still."

"Come on, Charley. Where's your sense of curiosity? Don't you want to know if there's something underneath there? It might be a relic from your people's past."

"Or it might be something we shouldn't bother."

Mathews put his hands on his hips. "If I'd dug that rock out of the ground two days ago when you went for supplies, you would have never know the difference."

He made a convincing point. Good enough that Charley finally caved.

"Okay, fine. But we have to put it back. If that is a sacred rock, I don't want my ancestors getting angry at me about it."

Mathews grinned. "We'll put it back exactly where it was. Now, let's get the horses."

It took almost forty minutes for the two men to harness two ropes around both the jagged rock and the horses. The latter proved to be the more troublesome chore. Both horses weren't keen on standing on the slope and had to be settled down three times before the men could finally get the ropes the way they wanted.

Using gravity to assist the horses seemed like the obvious decision. Putting the horses downhill from the rock would make their job easier. If Mathews's assessment of the stone was correct, it wouldn't take much for the animals to pull it over. He hadn't thought through the part about putting the rock back where it was. Mathews had no intention of telling Charley that yet. They could figure it out later. Right now, he wanted to know what—if anything—was under the stone.

"Ready, Charley?" Mathews said to his friend.

Charley was standing fifteen feet away, tending the horses. "Ready, Bob!"

"Okay, go ahead!"

Charley clicked his tongue, and the animals started clomping forward. The second they did, the ropes slid over the top of the rock and fell to the ground. Charley saw the ropes dragging through the grass and stopped the horses with a gentle, "Whoa."

Mathews sighed. "Well, that didn't work."

"Maybe it's my ancestors telling you to leave their rock alone."

"Or maybe I just need to pin the rope in place. Back the horses up, and let's try it again."

Charley's head turned back and forth, but he did as requested, moving the animals backward until Mathews had enough slack to loop the rope around the rock once more. He lifted his foot and pressed the boot heel hard into the rope, pinning against the stone.

"Okay, try it again. We'll see if this helps it stay in place."

Charley raised an eyebrow at the idea but said nothing. The idea of his friend somehow ending up on the ground was humorous enough to let him try.

"Ready?" Charley asked.

"Yep. Go ahead."

Charley clicked his tongue again, and the horses started moving just as they had before. This time the rope held, and within seconds the big rock toppled over onto its side with relative ease.

"Whoa!" Mathews shouted. He almost sounded ecstatic, though Charley wasn't sure why.

The stone's fall had kicked up a small cloud of dust, and Mathews waved both hands around to dissipate it. "Well done, mate," he said to Charley who'd left the horses and rushed over.

Mathews joked with him. "For someone so concerned about this being sacred, you sure seem interested to see what's under it."

"Might be a curse waiting for you, Bob. I'm hoping it's a funny one. Nothing too hurtful. Maybe you get kangaroo ears or something."

Mathews snorted a laugh and kept waving his hands around. It didn't take long for the breeze to pick up and blow away the dust, leaving a clear view of the impression the big rock had left in the ground.

"Doesn't look like there's anything there, mate," Charley said. He didn't try to hide the disappointment in his voice.

Mathews let out a long sigh. He put his hands on his hips. "No, it sure doesn't. Well, it was worth a look. I guess now we need to figure out how to get this thing back in place."

Charley's eyebrows lowered. "You're not gonna dig or anything like that? How do you know there's nothing buried in the ground right there? It might be a marker or something."

Now Mathews was certain Charley didn't care if the site was sacred or not. Maybe he'd changed his tune at the thought of a potential treasure.

"We could go a little deeper," Mathews said. "I'll be real careful. Just let me get a few things."

He turned to walk back to the cart when something caught his eye and froze him in place. He stared down at the exposed bottom of the rock, mesmerized. "Charley?"

"Yeah?" Charley stepped over to where his friend was standing and followed his gaze until he saw it too. "What's that?" he asked in a hushed tone.

At first, Mathews didn't answer. He took a cautious step toward the rock and then bent down on one knee. "I'm not sure, Charley. Looks like some sort of Aboriginal drawings."

He took out his brush and started to wipe away some of the excess dirt, but Charley stopped him. "Wait, Bob." He put his hand on his friend's shoulder. "What if you rub it off?"

"I won't. It's carved into the rock. So even if the paint comes off, we can still get a rubbing."

The explanation seemed to convince Charley, and he removed his hand from Mathews's shoulder.

Mathews held the brush delicately in one hand. His fingers fought off nerves that would have caused them to tremble. He'd never discovered anything like this before, and there was no way he wanted to mess it up.

The bristles flicked back and forth against the rock's surface. With each pass they pulled away more and more dirt until the entire image was in view. When he finished, Mathews took a long breath and then let it out slowly.

He stood up and stared at his handiwork.

"You ever seen anything like this?"

Rows of circles, arranged in columns, were etched into the stone. Each circle contained two smaller circles. Next to the grid was a line pointing in two directions. Beside that was an image of a boomerang under the center of three upside down Vs.

Charley lifted the hat off his head and scratched his temple for a moment. "I seen circles like that before but never that many of them on one rock. Not sure what the line means, but there are heaps of boomerang drawings around here. It was part of our ancient culture. This close to the Baiame Cave must mean it's god's boomerang."

Mathews heard everything his friend said but didn't respond. Instead, he kept his thoughts moving forward. "Each circle represents a day." He squatted down again and looked closely at the engraving. "There are forty-five circles here, which means forty-five days."

He was telling Charley something he already knew. Ancient Aborigines had used circles as representations of the sun to keep track of the passage of time.

"Yeah, but forty-five days for what?"

Mathews was already ahead of the question. He tapped the handle of his brush against the line in the rock. "From what I understand, a line like this can often mean a direction. If someone left it here, it could mean that whoever drew it wanted to remind someone which way they should go."

He stood up and stepped over to the impression the rock had left in the dirt. Mathews tilted his head sideways. He glanced at the rock and then again in the dirt, putting the puzzle pieces together in his mind.

"If I'm guessing correctly, when we pulled the rock out of its place, the arrow would have been pointing in that direction."

Charley stared where his friend was pointing. "Northwest?"

"Good. Glad to see we were thinking the same thing. It can get a little disorienting out here at times."

"Not much out that way," Charley said as he peered in that direction. "Just hills and trees."

"No," Mathews agreed. "Not much at all. But think bigger. If someone were to walk for forty-five days in that direction, what would they find?"

"Those things probably indicate mountains or hills of some kind," Charley said, pointing at the inverted Vs.

"Ripper, Charley. You're right. Those would have to be some kind of mountains or something."

Mathews stood up and walked past the horses to the cart parked in a little clearing of dirt. He flipped open a leather pouch sitting in the front and pulled out a folded piece of paper. Charley joined him as Mathews spread out the map on the back of the cart.

The old surveyor had a keen eye for reading a map. It came with the territory from his previous career. He ran his finger along the map, retracing it twice to make sure he figured the direction correctly.

"If someone were to walk at an average of a little over three miles per hour for forty-five days, they would travel around sixteen hundred miles. Give or take."

"How'd you come up with that?" Charley asked with wide eyes.

"I figure walking a day, so about twelve hours. Then you get something like thirty-six or so miles a day. Times forty-five, not hard."

"You did all that in your head?"

Mathews grinned. "I can teach you how to do that too, mate. Although that is a lot of mileage to go on foot. They must have used animals of some kind. That many miles wouldn't have been manageable." He returned his attention to the map. "So if we say around sixteen hundred miles to the northwest..." He reached over and took out a compass and made a circular line around the area in question.

He leaned over the map and looked closely. No towns intersected the line, but there was something even more interesting on the paper that was closer to his drawing than anything else.

"Crikey," Mathews said. He glanced back up the hill at the rock lying on its side. Then he looked at the map once more. "It can't be. Why... How would they..." His voice trailed off.

"What?" Charley prodded. "What you going on about?"

Mathews said nothing. He just stared down at the point where his finger had stopped. Next to it was one word.

Uluru.

Chapter 1
Sydney, Australia

Annie shuddered at what she'd just done.

Maybe no one noticed, she thought.

Annie Guildford had worked at the museum for nearly thirty years without ever breaking anything. Being meticulous and overly cautious had served her well over the length of her career. Her immaculate reputation was well known around the tight circles of museum curators both in the city and throughout the country.

Now that could be thrown out the window.

She'd been taking inventory of some items in the storage vault as she did on a yearly basis. If she was honest, Annie often wondered why they did it annually. Very few things were added to the collection in storage. Most of the new stuff was put on display or sent around the country for exhibits.

She stole a quick glance toward the only door in and out of the room. No one had seen or heard what happened. How would they? She was the only one working after hours. Reminding herself of that eased her paranoia. A few deep breaths, and she was okay.

Still, there was the issue of the desk.

Annie bent down and looked underneath it.

The item in question was an antique oak desk that dated back to the early part of the twentieth century. She wasn't even sure why the museum was holding onto it, thinking it might be better suited for an auction house or perhaps the office of a writer who enjoyed antiques. The stain had faded over the decades, but the desk remained in good condition. Well, except for the fact Annie had broken it, or so she at first suspected.

A piece of wood dangled from the underside of the desk near its front. When she'd looked initially, it appeared she'd knocked a piece loose. Now she realized it wasn't an ordinary piece of wood like all the others composing the desk. This one was hanging from internal hinges.

It was a false door.

She stood up and looked around again, making sure the room was vacant. Annie shook her head. "You're the only one here. Remember?"

Her eyes involuntarily searched the room once more as she crouched down on her knees and tilted her body to stare up at the anomaly. It was too dark under the desk, so she pulled out her cell phone and turned on the LED light. The bright, sterile glow cast on the desk's underbelly revealed what she'd suspected. Whoever owned this desk had installed a fake panel.

But why?

She rolled onto her back and slid under to get a better view. Holding the phone up to the hanging panel, she shined the light into the cavity. It was difficult to see at first, but there was definitely something inside. Carefully, Annie pushed herself up enough so her head was against the bottom of the desk and her eyes were nearly level with the opening.

Annie got her first view of the object within the desk. It was a rolled up piece of paper. She reached out her hand to take the scroll, but something clicked from the front of the room near the door. Her hand snapped back to her side, the other quickly dimming the light by pressing it to her blouse. Her heart pounded in her chest, beating faster with every breath. She swallowed hard and tried to mute her breathing but felt like it echoed through the room.

After a few minutes that seemed like hours, she crawled out from under the desk and took a quick look around. Still empty. She had no idea what had made the noise, but as far as she could tell, she was alone. Her eyes darted back and forth until she was convinced. Then they drifted back to the mysterious desk.

With another swallow she got back on her hands and knees and crawled back to the spot under the desk. She wasted no time. She pointed the light into the hole with one hand and reached up with the other.

Wait, stupid. This is potentially a hundred-year-old piece of paper. You know better than that.

She scrambled back out from under the desk and walked over to a workstation against the wall near the door. She picked up a pair of white gloves sitting on the table and slipped them on. Annie had been handling delicate items for a long time. She wasn't about to get sloppy now. Plus the walk to the door gave her a chance to do one more survey of the room.

Still alone, she thought. Maybe she was going a little crazy after having been by herself in the vault for so long. Some fresh air would do her good. First, though, was the matter of the paper in the desk.

She strode back to the antique piece of furniture and slid underneath again. Once more she put the light's beam directly into the cavity. With the other hand she reached up and gently rolled the paper with a gloved finger until it rested on the edge of the hole. Then, with a steadfast patience, Annie pinched the paper as lightly as possible and pulled it down out of the desk. It wasn't until she held it in her palm that she realized she'd been holding her breath.

She sighed and took a few deep breaths as she stared at the strange object.

A minute later she was back over at the work table. She warily pried apart the paper and began rolling it open. Annie had to be careful not to do it too fast. If the page had collected any moisture during its time in the desk, the surface could stick together and tear. Since the document had been hidden for the better part of a century, she assumed whatever it was must be important. Tearing it was not an option.

This wasn't the first time Annie had worked with old paper. She'd done it dozens of times over the years, though usually under the watchful eye of experts. The techniques were ones she'd learned from her predecessor. He'd been a gruff man and stubborn to a fault. When it came to taking care of valuable antiquities, however, he was like a father with his firstborn. He worked with a sort of fear hanging over him, as if he screwed something up the world would come to an end.

Annie had taken on those traits through constant observation. As she finished peeling back the paper and pressing it against the surface of the table, she breathed a sigh of relief. Again she'd been holding her breath, although consciously this time.

She stared at the nonsensical writing on the page. Her eyebrows stitched together as she tried to understand what it could be about.

Journal Entry 73,

Charley took ill about a month ago. We haven't been able to do any further investigation on the treasure for nearly three weeks. It appears that he has taken a turn for the worse, and I do not believe he will survive the next few days.

My heart aches to see my friend in such pain. He's been a loyal assistant and comrade throughout this strange journey, a journey I fear is at an end.

I cannot go on without him. It wouldn't be right. After all, the treasure we seek belongs to him and his people, not me—an alien in this land. I'd hoped we'd find it before he passed. I even had the idea of going it alone in an attempt to bring it back to him. His condition, however, grieved me, and I didn't want to leave his side.

So here, at the end of the journey, I must abandon this quest. It pains me to have come so close only to have to walk away.

I have left the clues in place for whoever may find this note. When I gave my speech to the Royal Society, I omitted anything that has to do with the treasure. While they are a decent group of people, there is corruption among them. Were one of the bad seeds to find the clues to the treasure and decode them, I fear the great reward would fall into the wrong hands. As I've said before, it belongs to the Aboriginal people.

If you, dear reader, make the decision to embark on this treacherous journey, remember that. Should you find the treasure, it must be given to the Aboriginal people. I realize there are many tribes, but at their core they are one.

I leave you with this, if you are considering the task. It began with Baiame and a foreign stone, turned and unturned. From there, forty-five suns to the northwest in the northern chasm of the three. Rivers mark the way where light turns dark.

R.H. Mathews

Annie blinked rapidly as she finished the passage. Who was R.H. Mathews? And what was this treasure? From his description, it sounded significant. There were several references to Aborigines and the treasure belonging to them. As far as she could recall, she'd never come across any relics from their culture—nothing of financial value, anyway. Everything she'd seen was more valuable from a historical perspective.

While Annie did have a vague grasp on Aboriginal history, it was hardly her field of expertise. Her mind raced. She had to know someone who might know who this Mathews fellow was, or perhaps knew something about this treasure.

Her thoughts stopped on one name. He was a long shot, but she figured if any of her friends knew anything about what was in this letter, it was him. More importantly, she could trust him. If she were to tell her coworkers about this, who knows what they would do? Better to keep it confidential for now.

She pulled out her cell phone and snapped a quick photo of the paper, careful to make sure the words were clear enough to read. Then she sent it to her email.

Next Annie slid into the desk chair at the computer on the table and logged into her email, found the one she'd just sent, and then typed a quick message to her friend. She copied the image attachment into the email and then hit send.

She let out a short sigh and then shut down the computer. It was time for her to leave. She'd stayed longer than normal anyway. Her eyes darted back to the paper on the table. She'd need to secure that.

Annie stepped over to a shelf where they kept several compressed plastic files. She'd used them before for delicate documents just like this one. Essentially, the files would seal off the inside from external air, thus preserving the paper for considerably longer than if it were just sitting around.

She was lucky the Mathews document wasn't in worse condition. Now that it was in the hands of an expert, she would take better care of it. She carefully slid the paper into the folder and pressed the edges down to complete the seal.

Annie had already decided where to hide the thing. She floated over to a filing cabinet where dozens of similar documents had been stored and slid it in right behind the letter *M* on the divider. That way she would know exactly where to find it when she came back. And should anyone question her about it, she could claim she'd done as she was supposed to and kept it where it belonged. Annie wouldn't be accused of thievery.

She closed the filing cabinet and then walked over to where she'd left her keys on the work table. She hoped her friend received the email by morning. Curiosity was getting the best of her.

Whatever the Mathews paper was about, one thing was certain: Annie wouldn't be getting any sleep until she had some answers.

Chapter 2
Adelaide, South Australia

"You gotta be kidding me!" Reece Skelton stared at the television screen in disbelief. "How you gonna let him run all the way down the field like that?"

The television announcer commented on how easily the player made his way through the defense.

"Thank you, yes, we all saw what just happened. Idiots."

He shook his head and reached for the bottle of VB sitting on the end table next to his chair. The second he wrapped his fingers around the cool brown bottle, he realized it was empty. "Of course."

Reece got up and took the bottle to the kitchen, dropped it in the rubbish bin, and opened the fridge to get a fresh one. He opened the new bottle and tossed the cap into the bin with the others and returned to his usual spot.

"Since you blokes aren't gonna help me out today, I guess I could get some work done," he said to the television. "I guess that's what I get for cheering for a bunch of rabbits."

He set the beer down on the nightstand and picked up the laptop from the lounge cushion next to him.

Reece ran his own adventure tour business. Most of his runs went from Adelaide up to the north, and they usually consisted of Americans. They all wanted to see the famous Ayers Rock, known to the locals as Uluru. Of course, Reece always threw in a few extras with his trips. A few picturesque mountain ranges, some pretty waterfalls, a little mountain biking and kayaking from time to time—depending on the fitness level of his customers.

Lately, things had gotten slower. That was highly unusual for this time of year. Reece knew what was to blame.

The internet was chock full of adventure tour guides hocking amazing trips to all parts of Australia. He'd been offered the opportunity to join one of the bigger internet groups, but by doing so he knew he'd have to stick to a more rigid set of rules.

Reece Skelton didn't care too much for rules.

As a result, he'd slowly been squeezed out of the adventure tour game. His last jaunt was two weeks ago. And he didn't have another one scheduled for two more weeks. That was nearly a month without a paycheck. The last time he checked his bank statement, the news hadn't been good either. He had enough saved up to get him through a couple of months of bills. After that, he might actually have to do something he detested even considering.

He'd have to get a real job.

Worse, he might have to go work for one of his competitors. Not that they weren't nice guys. He'd been friends with some of them for years. It was the thought of having to tuck tail and fold up shop that really got under his skin.

The laptop screen glowed to life. Reece took another sip of beer before clicking on the little mail icon at the bottom of the desktop. He looked out the living room window as a late morning breeze rattled the wind chimes on his front porch. Five new messages popped up in the queue. Three were from creditors. One was from a prospective customer, apparently based in the UK. The fifth was from his old friend Annie Guildford. The subject line said it was urgent, and since he hadn't heard from Annie in a while he figured he may as well check it out first.

He checked the time it was sent and immediately felt a bit guilty for not having read it sooner. She'd sent it the night before at a fairly late hour. It came from her work email, which caused him to wonder what in the world she was doing on the job so late. Then again, it was Annie. She was more tied to her work than anyone he knew.

Reece clicked the email and started reading. It was only a few paragraphs long, but he could sense her urgency in the wording.

Annie said something about finding an old journal entry from a guy named R.H. Mathews. She claimed she'd found it in an antique desk in the museum vault but didn't know who the guy was or what the message meant.

Reece clicked on the attachment and narrowed his eyes to get a better view of the writing. It was a tad difficult to read, but he could make out well enough to get the gist.

"Aboriginal treasure?" he said. "Oh, Annie, someone's taken you for a galah again."

In the years Reece had known Annie, he'd learned she could be quite gullible when it came to practical jokes.

As he continued reading, however, his tune changed. "Baiame?" he said to himself. "I wonder if that's referring to the cave drawings."

He scratched his head for a moment then unconsciously took another sip of beer. He couldn't make much sense of the riddle at the bottom of the journal entry. Reece had a few Aboriginal friends, but they weren't around at the moment. They'd be of no use. And besides, if this thing Annie sent was legitimate, sharing it with one of the tribesmen might not be a great idea. They might not take kindly to someone like him poking around their heritage.

Reece racked his brain to come up with an answer to the riddle, but nothing clicked. He looked at his beer and realized part of the problem could very well be the alcohol slowing his brain. "Nah." He shrugged it off and took another swallow.

The television was still on in the background, and a commercial for a vacation to the United States appeared. The man was saying something about visiting the incredible countryside the States had to offer.

"That's it," Reece said. "The Americans. They'll know what to do with this. I bet ole Tommy will eat this up."

He pulled up a new email and started pecking away at the keys. Five minutes later, he had an email addressed to Tommy Schultz and sent it on its way. Reece was sure to include the bizarre attachment he'd received from Annie and asked his American friend what he could make of it.

Jokingly, he'd ended the email with a "Come on down and check it out if you've got time." Reece felt certain there was no way Tommy would just drop whatever he was doing and make the ridiculously long flight to Australia. The man was busy. Reece understood that, which is why he thought it was a funny joke.

His computer made a swooshing sound that signaled the email had been sent successfully. Reece shook his head as he stared at the other four new emails. "Not right now," he thought. "I'm enjoying my afternoon."

The wind chimes banged together again on the porch, drawing his eyes out the window.

Reece lived on the outskirts of the city. Some people called it the country, but he was barely beyond Adelaide's suburbs. Not far to the north of his property, oil had been discovered. The area was turning into a regular boomtown but luckily hadn't stretched as far south as Reece's property. Where he was situated, things were still quiet, which was why seeing the black Range Rover approaching down the long driveway was such a strange sight.

Reece set the laptop back on the couch where it was sitting before. He took another sip of beer and placed the bottle on the end table, keeping his eyes on the approaching vehicle.

"Who do we have here?"

He stepped closer to the window with his hands on his hips. "Looks like my luck is starting to turn around."

The black SUV was one of the higher-end models. He recognized that right away. With expensive cars came customers who had money to spend, money he needed.

He moved close to the window and stared out as the vehicle rolled along the gravel, kicking up a cloud of dust as it neared. Whoever they were sure seemed in a hurry. Probably Americans from the northeast of the country. Those types were always anxious to get things moving.

Reece crossed his arms and watched as the SUV rounded a short turn and headed toward the house. He was about to wave to the occupants when the vehicle ground to a sudden halt. At first his frown was one of puzzlement. It soon turned to one of panic as the back window opened and a gun barrel poked out.

The muzzle blazed, pouring an onslaught of hot metal through the windows, door, and walls. When the magazine ran out, the shooter immediately reloaded and fired again, repeating the process two more times until the home was a tattered shell of its former self. The driver stepped on the gas. The tires spun and kicked up gravel. As quickly as the SUV had appeared, it was gone.

Reece lay motionless on the floor.

Chapter 3
Atlanta, Georgia

Sean Wyatt was done, and he knew it.

He'd faced his fair share of adversity and been able to escape every single time. More than once, the margins of his getaway had been narrow at best.

There'd be no escaping this time. His government training and years as a special operative in the elite Axis agency couldn't save him.

He stared into the dark brown eyes of his opponent with his icy grays. The enemy's orbs gave away no secrets and allowed him no mercy.

"I don't suppose we could just forget this happened and walk away?" he asked.

Sean knew he sounded desperate. At this point he didn't care.

"No," the opponent said.

How could someone make one word sound both sinister and sexy at the same time?

He looked down, hoping there might be some solution he'd missed, a move he could make. There was nothing.

He sighed. "Well, I guess this is it. I had a good run."

"No you didn't. It took less than thirty minutes."

"It's a figure of speech."

Sean lifted his right hand and placed his fingers atop the king on his side of the chessboard. "Anywhere I go, you've got me. You win."

The stone cold face across from him broke into a grin. "You really aren't very good at this game," Adriana said.

"Why do you think I never want to play?" He mirrored her smile and then grabbed his coffee cup. "Want a refill?"

"Always."

Adriana leaned back in her chair and glanced out the huge window of Sean's kitchen. The rebuilding of his home in Buckhead, which had been leveled by a fire, had just been completed a month earlier. Sean had barely escaped the attempt on his life. His home hadn't been so lucky.

Fortunately, he had other places to stay during the reconstruction.

He walked over to the coffee machine and poured two fresh cups. As the rich brown liquid filled each one, he savored the aroma for a moment before returning to the table.

He set Adriana's cup down in front of her and took his seat, still holding the cup. Her gaze fell on him, and the two simultaneously enjoyed a quiet sip in mid-stare.

"It's good to have you back," he said, breaking the silence. "I missed you."

The words must have been the right ones because they produced another smile. "I know you did," she said.

He guffawed at her reply and shook his head.

She laughed and eased his suffering. "I missed you, too."

"Thank you. And I know."

Her eyebrows went up a notch. "Oh do you?"

Sean shrugged. "Sure. What's not to miss? I'm cute, funny, dashing."

"You're not that dashing."

"Maybe not dashing. Charming?"

She pressed her lips together to keep from laughing again. "Yes. Charming, definitely. I wonder, are you so charming when I'm not around?" Adriana stared at him with a playful glimmer in her eyes.

"When you're not around, I'm usually running for my life. At least that's the way it seems."

"That's not entirely true. Your last two assignments with Tommy didn't involve anything out of the ordinary."

He nodded, thinking about the past month. "You're right about that."

Her expression changed to one of pity. "Aww. You almost sound sad about it."

"No," he dismissed the notion. "It was nice to not be chased. Don't get me wrong, there's something thrilling about the chase."

"Is that why you chased me?"

His lips creased. "As I recall, there was no chasing involved."

"You mean after I saved your life in the hotel in Vegas?"

"Right. You just kind of showed up."

"So you flying to Greece to save me from that maniac wasn't chasing?"

Sean blushed. "That was a guy just trying to save the woman he loves." He started to lean across the table to give her a kiss.

"And where are you off to next?"

The question caught him off guard, and he paused. "What do you mean? I have some time off. Tommy hasn't lined up anything until later next month."

Her eyes flickered. "Then why is he here to see you?"

"What?"

Sean turned his head and looked out the window. He hadn't seen his friend pull into the driveway. Tommy was already getting out of his new BMW.

"Not expecting him?" Adriana asked.

Sean sighed. "No. He's probably just popping by on his way into the office. You know how he is about his coffee."

"I'll get the milk out," she said and got up from her chair.

"No, don't worry about it," Sean insisted. "Relax. I'll get him set up."

She eased back into the seat but wore a suspicious look on her face.

Sean backed over to the refrigerator, keeping an eye on her. He almost ran into the kitchen island but deftly swiveled his hips to avoid it. As the front door opened, he placed the milk on the island's granite surface next to a clean coffee cup.

"Hello?" Tommy's voice echoed from the foyer. "You guys in the kitchen?"

"Yeah, Tommy. We're in here."

A few seconds later, Tommy stepped into the room. His laptop bag hung from his shoulder across a crooked tie and an untucked button-up shirt.

"I thought I smelled coffee." He noticed the cup and milk on the island. "Oh, is that for me?"

Sean slipped back into his seat at the table and nodded while taking another sip.

"Sweet." He moved like a wild animal taunted by the smell of fresh meat, making quick work of the milk and coffee pot until his cup was nearly brimming. He started to raise the mug to his lips and then realized he'd not greeted his hosts.

"Where are my manners? I'm so sorry, Adriana. How are you?"

She laughed. "I'm fine, Tommy. Drink your coffee."

"Thanks," he said and took a long sip. Afterward he let out a long, satisfied "Ahh."

"So what brings you over at this hour of the morning? On your way to a meeting, perhaps?" Sean raised an eyebrow. He knew better. Tommy was up to something.

Whenever his friend popped by on the way to the office it was because he either wanted something or had a new gig for them. Sean had quit working for the International Archaeology Agency a few years back. As fate would have it, he hadn't remained retired for long. His attempt at running a business in Destin failed miserably, in large part due to the fact that he had to leave it more than once to fly across the world.

Tommy put both hands out wide in a display of innocence. The coffee in his right hand sloshed to the point it nearly spilled over the edge. Somehow he managed to keep that from happening.

"What are you talking about? I don't need a reason to come visit my best friend in the entire world." His eyes shot from one side of the room to the other. "House looks great by the way."

"So what's going on now, Tommy? A new assignment pop up out of the blue?"

Tommy slid into one of the open chairs at the table and stared at the chessboard. He ignored the question at first. "She beat you again?" he asked, motioning to the board. He passed a playful glance at Adriana. "He's never been very good at chess."

"You're not here to talk about my chess career, buddy, so just spit it out." Sean sounded irritated, but he was partially amused.

Tommy's nose crinkled as he nodded at Adriana. "You beat him again."

"Of course I did. He's terrible."

The two turned their judgmental gaze at Sean, who just rolled his eyes. "Fine. Yes, I suck at chess. I don't care. Just tell us what it is you want so we can get back to our vacation."

Tommy leaned his head back a bit as if he were being blown by a bitter wind. "Whoa, someone is a little defensive."

Sean started to say something again, but Tommy cut him off. He put a hand out to keep his friend from standing up. "Okay, I kid. Seriously. I won't bother you about your chess skills—or lack thereof—anymore. You're right. I'm here to ask you a question."

"And by question you mean you want to see if I'll go with you somewhere on the other side of the planet."

Tommy bit his top lip and pointed his finger at Sean. "Funny you should say it that way."

"What?"

"As it turns out, that's exactly where I'm going. The other side of the world, I mean."

"Look, Tommy, I've been looking forward to spending some time here with Adriana. We're going out to Las Vegas next week, and I'd really like to play some golf."

Tommy raised both eyebrows and pushed his glasses up the bridge of his nose. Sean had noticed them when his friend came in. Tommy typically had to wear his glasses when he'd forgotten to get more disposable contacts.

"I'm not here to ask you to go somewhere with me."

Sean and Adriana exchanged a curious glance and then looked back at their guest.

"You're not?" they almost said simultaneously.

"No, I'm not." Tommy pretended like he was hurt by the insinuation.

"Oh," Sean said. "Okay. So you really did just stop by to say hello?"

Tommy winced. "Not exactly. There is something I need you to do."

"But it doesn't involve flying across the globe?"

"No, nothing like that. I was just gonna see if you would take care of HQ for me."

Sean wanted to make sure he understood correctly. "You mean you want me to take care of the lab and offices?"

"Yeah, but it's not that involved. No one will be there. I gave the kids next week off. They protested since they're pretty much there all the time by choice. But I basically made them an offer they couldn't refuse."

"Wow. I'm impressed."

Alex Simms and Tara Watson, affectionately known as "the kids," were Tommy's laboratory assistants. They were two of the most brilliant researchers he'd ever met and had an incredible knack with technology. It was Tara and Alex who'd brought in the new quantum computer units and elevated IAA capabilities years beyond any competitor. If they had a weakness, it was that they enjoyed their toys a little too much.

"Tara was starting to get a little pale. So I booked them a vacation to the Caribbean."

"Sounds romantic," Adriana said.

Tommy rolled his shoulders. "Maybe. I don't know about those two. You'd think working together all the time there'd be some kind of feelings, but I've never sensed it."

"And those senses of yours are so astute."

Tommy cocked his head to the side. "You mean like yours were about the girl in Japan?"

Sean snorted a laugh. "Fair enough."

"So anyway, I need you to come in with me so I can just show you a few things. All you'll have to do is check the systems to make sure they're all online in case I need to access anything remotely. While you're there, you can just make sure everything is okay."

"Sounds like I'm taking care of your cat."

"If I had a cat, yes. That's probably accurate. If you're not doing anything, I figured you could come in with me this morning, and we could knock it out. I'm flying to Australia in a few hours."

"I love it when you assume I've got nothing else going on in my life."

Tommy's lips creased and displayed a toothy grin. "What are friends for?"

Twenty minutes later, the three were headed into Downtown Atlanta. The IAA building was located near Centennial Olympic Park. When Tommy's parents died in a plane crash, he'd used the money to found the agency and carry on their legacy in history and archaeology. The area around the building had been fairly trashy at first, but in the years since he created the IAA, things had changed dramatically.

Entire blocks had been torn down and replaced by the massive Georgia Aquarium, museums, conference centers, and expensive hotels.

Tommy brought the car to a stop at a red light and tapped his fingers on the wheel.

"So, Australia?" Sean asked from the back seat.

"Yeah. You remember our old friend, Reece Skelton?"

"Yep. How's he doing?"

"Okay, I guess. Got an email from him out of the blue yesterday. Said a friend of his found this old paper in an antique desk. Turns out it was from a guy named R.H. Mathews."

"Never heard of him."

The light turned green, and Tommy accelerated through the intersection. "I hadn't either until I did a little research on him. He was an amateur anthropologist."

"Like you?"

"Hilarious." Tommy shook his head at the joke.

Adriana laughed.

"Don't encourage him," Tommy said to her. "Anyway, it was a journal entry from him. Seems he found something pretty important in a cave in New South Wales. Reece invited me down there to check it out. I figured I had some time—"

"So you'd just fly, like, fourteen hours across the world to have a look?"

"First of all, it's more like sixteen hours. And secondly, maybe I'll take a little time off when I get there. Things have been so crazy lately. I figured an Australian beach might be nice right about now."

"It is chilly here," Sean said. "Speaking of, I hope the weather stays nice for our trip to Vegas."

Tommy ignored him. "Anyway, I've tried reaching out to Reece since then but haven't been able to get ahold of him."

"Wait. So you're still going to fly down there even though the guy you're going to see hasn't responded to your calls."

"Or emails or texts. Yep. I'm a grown adult, Sean. And it's not like money is a problem. I can find a place to stay."

His point was true enough. Tommy was worth upward of a hundred million now. It seemed his investments could do no wrong.

"Well," Adriana interrupted, "I think it's great, Tommy. You deserve to take a trip like that. You work very hard."

"Thank you," Tommy said.

He turned a corner and came to the last light before they reached IAA headquarters about five hundred feet away. The steel side of the building shimmered in the morning sunlight.

"The kids still here?" Sean asked as he looked out the window to his right.

"Yeah. They don't head out until tomorrow."

Their conversation was stopped by a sudden boom.

In an instant, the external walls of the IAA building shuddered. Fire erupted out of the windows, sending shards of glass across the street and into the park. Smoke blasted out of every opening. Another blast sounded from inside the structure. One second, the IAA building was there. The next, it was consumed by a flash of fire and debris.

Tommy instinctively jammed the car into reverse and backed up. Luckily there was no one behind him.

His reaction hadn't been a moment too soon. A huge chunk of concrete struck the asphalt where the car had just been sitting.

The ground rumbled, shaking windows and signs in the buildings next to them. Meanwhile, the three in the car watched helplessly as the IAA headquarters collapsed in on itself.

White and black clouds rolled out a hundred feet in every direction.

The car's three occupants were speechless.

Sean's instincts were to run to the building to see if anyone needed help. He opened the car door and got out. The other two did as well. All three of them knew there was nothing they could do. The facility was completely destroyed.

Worse, anyone inside would be dead.

Chapter 4
Sydney

"It's done."

Bernard Holmes allowed a weak smile to escape his lips as he held the phone to his ear. "You're certain?"

"Turn on the news, and see for yourself. It's all over every station. The media is calling it a terrorist attack."

The media, so predictable. Of course they would call it that. He'd counted on it. Americans were so on edge about terrorism that the moment anything smelled remotely like an attack, they were ready to label it. Next, people would demand justice; the authorities would claim they had leads. Eventually someone would get pinned for the atrocity. Public outcry would accept nothing less.

"I'll have a look later. I'm indisposed at the moment." He surveyed the room warily to make sure no one was listening. Then he lowered his voice. "You're sure they're all dead?"

"That's what our man told me."

"And what of the email to Schultz?"

"He didn't send it to anyone else. If he spoke to someone about it, doesn't matter now. The evidence is gone. Without Mathews's clue, it's just another myth that will vanish into thin air."

Violins played in the background. The chatter of wealthy socialites mingled with the music. Holmes was a tad surprised so many had stayed into the late hours of the evening. Expensive wine and champagne tended to have that effect on people.

Holmes was the chairman of Enertech, one of the major players in the booming Australian oil industry. His was the third most profitable in the country, pulling in billions in profit thanks to the discovery of a new shale deposit.

But third place wasn't good enough. His ego demanded more, as did his shareholders. Sure, he had a personal net worth of over a billion, but that could disappear in an instant. He'd had it all and lost it all before. Holmes wasn't about to let that happen again. Once he had control of the majority of Australia's oil, he'd be unstoppable.

"It sounds like you're at a party." The man on the other end of the line interrupted his thoughts. "I'll leave you alone, sir."

"It's a fundraiser. I have to keep up appearances."

"Sounds awful."

"It's not so bad. The food and alcohol more than make up for the tedious company."

"No offense, but I'll take a cold Toohey over champagne any day."

Holmes smiled and nodded at a silver-haired man that walked by wearing a tightly pressed tuxedo. It was the mayor of the city. As soon as he was gone, Holmes allowed his fake smile to disappear.

"None taken. What about your man in the States? I trust you're going to tie up that loose end."

"He'll be getting on a plane to come back right about now. That flight won't make it very far. I went ahead and put out a few footprints for the American authorities to find that will lead them straight back to him. He'll be blamed for the terror attacks, and the story will be a distant memory within a month."

"Perfect." Holmes showed off another toothy grin, this time to an older woman.

Holmes was in his late fifties and had attended these sorts of functions more times than he cared to remember. It wasn't that he hated parties. He loved them. His life of opulence allowed for entertainment mere mortals couldn't afford. The fundraisers, on the other hand, were an irritation.

He likened them to a glorified beggars convention—full of people walking around with their palms out, hoping to get a scrap for their pet project or charity. Holmes donated, of course. He had to. Nothing better to fend off critics than to donate a million to some pathetic cause.

Another man of similar age locked eyes with Holmes from across the room. It was another one of the nonprofit guys. His last name was Stewart. That's all Holmes could remember. Stewart took the momentary exchange of glances as an invitation to come over. Holmes cursed himself in his mind for letting his eyes hold the gaze for a fraction of a second.

"What about the woman?" The voice on the phone asked. "You want me to get rid of her too?"

Holmes had already decided her fate before the question was voiced. "No. Not yet. She may still be of use to us, at the very least as leverage if things get tight. You can never have too many chips on your side of the table."

"Sounds good to me. I'll have my men keep an eye on her. I doubt she's going to try anything stupid."

"I'm going to have to go. I'll see you at the office in the morning. Find out what you can about that paper. The woman may not know anything, but keep pressing her. I want that relic."

"Understood. I'm on it."

"Oh. One more thing. Once we have the artifact, there's no reason to keep her around anymore." Holmes ended the call and plastered his faux smile across his face again just as Stewart came near.

"Ah, Mr. Stewart. So good to see you. How are things going?"

"Things are fine, Mr. Holmes, thanks in no small part to your contribution last year."

"Well, I'm just happy to help." Holmes passed a fake smile and put his hands behind his back, tipping up onto his toes and back down again. He had no idea what charity the man was running. Apparently, Holmes had written a check he didn't remember.

"That's good to hear. I have to ask, have you considered making another contribution this year? Or are all your allotments otherwise spoken for?"

Holmes eyed him suspiciously, allowing the other man to feel awkward for several seconds. Right at the point Stewart felt he'd overstepped his bounds, Holmes slapped him on the shoulder and started laughing.

"Of course I'll make another donation. Get in touch with my secretary, and we'll set it up."

Stewart sighed, clearly relieved on multiple levels. "Wonderful. Thank you again, so much, Mr. Holmes. I truly appreciate it. And you won't regret it."

I already do.

Chapter 5
Atlanta

Fire trucks, police cars, and ambulances packed the streets around the rubble that had been the IAA headquarters. Cops stood around the perimeter, making sure none of the onlookers got too close. Firefighters and rescue workers dug cautiously through the building's remains.

Sean, Adriana, and Tommy stood huddled together as close to the destruction as the police would allow. Even though Tommy was the owner of the property, it was now a crime scene.

The three stared in mortified disbelief at the carnage. A million questions raced through their heads, but no one said a thing. What could they say? In the hour since the explosion, the only words spoken had been to various authorities who were trying to piece together what might have happened and who was inside.

Sean did most of the talking. Tommy was in shock. All Adriana could do was console him and keep her arm around him.

As they looked on at the flurry of activity in and around the destruction, a young man's voice interrupted the group's silence.

"What did you do?"

Tommy blinked for a second and then spun around.

Alex and Tara were standing behind them with beleaguered looks on their faces and cups of coffee in their hands.

"You're alive!" Tommy shouted and wrapped his arms around both of them. He squeezed them tight, nearly causing Tara to drop her cup.

"Yeah," she said. "We figured we'd go get a cup of coffee."

"Looks like coffee was a good call," Alex said. "Otherwise we'd be at the bottom of all that." He took a sip from the cup, almost as if he was unfazed.

"Right," Tara agreed. "And it was also a good thing we ran out at the office."

Sean let out a long sigh of relief. "Boy, are we glad to see you two. We thought we'd lost you."

Tommy finally let go of the big bear hug he was giving them. A tear streaked down the side of his face. "Sorry. But you guys are like family to me."

Tara couldn't speak for a second, catching her breath from the hug and still shocked as she stared at the destruction. "Do you guys have any idea what happened? Who did this?" she asked after collecting her thoughts.

"I don't know." Tommy shook his head. "Was there anyone else inside?"

"No, I don't think so," Alex answered. "The maintenance workers don't come 'til the afternoon. As far as I know, we were the only ones there this morning."

"That's a relief," Adriana said.

"Yeah, but your building," Tara pressed the point. "All the equipment, the research—it's all gone."

"Don't worry about all that," Tommy said. "Everything was backed up in the cloud. And any artifacts we had in stock were down in the vault. They'll dig that out eventually. But it would have taken a ton of explosives to break through that steel and concrete."

"Kind of makes you wonder why the whole building wasn't just built that tough." Sean's comment drew an annoyed glance from Tommy. "Too soon?"

Tommy turned back to the kids. "You didn't happen to see anything unusual this morning? A stranger lurking around the area, maybe walking by the building a few times? Someone hanging out in the lobby, perhaps?"

The two thought for a moment. Tara stared up into the sky as if the passing clouds would jar her memory. She came up with nothing. "No, I can't think of anyone."

"Now that you mention it," Alex said, "there was a guy I saw jogging by."

"So?" Tara asked. "We see joggers down here all the time. It's a popular place for people to get in a walk or a run."

Alex's head turned back and forth. "No, this was different. I saw him twice, running in the same direction."

"The same direction?" Sean asked.

"Yeah. I didn't think much of it at the time, like maybe he was just doing laps around the block. Now that I think of it, though, the time span between the sightings was too close for him to have done a full loop."

Tommy pressed the issue. "What did this man look like?"

"Hard to say. He had black running gear on, long leggings, a jacket, and a matching cap. Oh, and he was wearing sunglasses. He did sort of have big ears, but the rest of his features weren't really discernible."

"That's all you can remember—his clothes?"

"Yes. I realize that if I was the person who had to give the police artist a description of a criminal that they'd never find the guy because I suck at giving descriptions of people. Even people I've known for long time. I'm sorry."

"It's okay," Sean said. "You've given us something to go on. I'll let the authorities know what to look out for."

"He would have changed clothes by now," Tommy said.

"Still, won't hurt to pass along the information. They could always get lucky."

Tara stared at the destruction. "I guess it looks like we may be on vacation for an extended period of time." There was a twinge of sadness in her voice.

"Don't worry," Tommy said. "We'll get you two set up with a temporary space by the time you get back. Enjoy the vacation time. You two both need it."

"I feel bad," Alex said. "I don't think we should be leaving with all this going on. I mean, shouldn't we stick around and help you go through the wreckage, figure out what can be salvaged."

"There won't be much to save," Sean said. "Whoever rigged that thing to blow knew exactly what they were doing. If that jogger you saw was the bomber, he's either a demolitions expert, some kind of special ops, or both. The point is, he knew what he was doing."

"Yeah," Adriana agreed. "That opens up a whole new problem, though." She voiced what she knew everyone had to be thinking. "Someone was trying to kill you."

"We've had our fair share of enemies," Tommy reflected.

"None of them have ever taken it this far, though," Sean said.

"Stab anyone in the back lately?" Tommy asked.

Sean's right eyebrow rose slightly. "Literally or figuratively?"

"Funny."

Tara chimed in. "Actually, I don't think he's kidding."

Sean winked at her. "Besides, as far as the bomber knew, I wasn't going to be there today. That means he was coming after one of you three, not me."

Alex turned his head and looked at Tara.

"Don't look at me," she said. "I don't have any enemies."

"That you know of," Alex said.

"Maybe it wasn't someone you wronged," Adriana interrupted. She swiveled and faced Tommy. "You said you were going to Australia, that you got an email about a letter or something?"

Tommy nodded. "Yeah. It was a journal entry by a long-dead amateur archaeologist."

"What was in that journal entry?"

He shrugged. "I didn't really understand all of it. He talked about something out of the ordinary he found at a cave north of Sydney. Then he mentioned a treasure he and his sick friend were looking for."

"Treasure?" Alex asked.

"Mmm hmm. He didn't say what it was but claimed they were close to finding it."

"Why didn't they?"

"Mathews said his friend was too ill to continue and it wouldn't be right to go on without him. Something about the friend being Aborigine and the treasure belonged to him."

Sean connected the dots. "He left a clue in his message. Didn't he?"

Tommy squirmed. "I mean, yeah. I don't remember all the details about the clue. But yes, there was a clue. I wasn't going to keep the treasure if I found it." He started sounding defensive. "I didn't know for sure if there was anything to it or not."

"It's okay," Sean said. "I'm positive Tara and Alex believe you." He waited for an uncomfortable moment until the others broke out in laughter. Then he slapped Tommy on the back and shook him. "Buddy, relax. You want to run off to Australia to hunt for some ancient Aboriginal treasure on your off time, be my guest. I don't care. It's your time to do with whatever you want."

"Yeah," Adriana said. "And now that this has happened," she motioned to the rubble, "We hope you understand that Sean and I will be coming with you."

Sean slid to the side and put his arm around her with a proud grin on his face. "You know there's no arguing with her, right?"

Tommy sighed. "Fine. How long will it take you to pack?"

Chapter 6
Adelaide

Adriana stared out the window at the passing countryside. "This friend of yours really lives out in the country, doesn't he?"

"Yeah," Tommy said. "Let's just say that Reece is more of the outdoorsy type." He and Sean exchanged a knowing glance.

"That's an understatement," Sean muttered.

Their journey to Australia had taken just under sixteen hours. Talking to the investigators, a few members of the press, and then more investigators put off their departure by nearly six hours. The FBI had been reluctant to let Tommy leave the country, but after a call to Emily Starks, the FBI suddenly backed down. Sean figured there was probably an executive order in the mix somewhere.

Once they arrived in Sydney, the plane refueled and took them south to Adelaide. After so many hours of exhausting travel, the three really just wanted to find a place to bed down for a few hours and get some rest. The flight had afforded them some sleep time, but sleeping on a plane was never restful.

Adriana continued to look out at the scenery. The rolling foothills were dotted with trees and green grass. White clouds with silver bottoms littered the bright blue sky. The three

Americans had immediately noted the temperature change when they got off the plane. Australia was entering the summer months and it was, apparently, warmer than usual.

"You're sure he's got room for us to get some sleep?" Adriana asked.

"Oh yeah. He's got a ton of space. Lives on a ranch not too far from here," Tommy reassured her.

"Ranch?"

"Reece doesn't do any farming or anything like that. Just has a bunch of property. Not sure why. Seems like an awful lot of upkeep."

"Maybe he's into the whole self-sustained living thing," Sean commented.

"Oh, Reece can survive on his own. That much is certain. He just chooses not to. Speaking of Reece, I haven't heard from him in nearly two days. He won't return my calls and hasn't replied to the three emails I sent."

Adriana turned away from the window and stared across the car at Tommy. "Wait a minute. So this guy doesn't even know that we're coming?"

Tommy's silence didn't exactly instill a ton of confidence in her. "Tommy! We can't just barge in on someone's home like that."

"Relax," he said. "Reece goes way back with Sean and me. He'll be happy to see us. Besides, he invited me. Remember? I'm more concerned about why I haven't heard from him in the last two days than I am about him telling us we're not welcome."

His argument didn't convince her, but there was nothing she could do about it. He turned on the blinker and veered off the main road onto a stretch of gravel that meandered up a gently sloping hill and disappeared over the other side.

"This is his place, so it's probably too late to turn back now anyway."

She shook her head and put her elbow on the door rim as she resumed staring out the window.

"Not that I disagree with you, Tommy," Sean reentered the conversation, "but it is strange for us to fly all the way across the world like this to see someone we don't even know is home or not."

"Well, we'll know here in a minute whether or not he's in town."

"Doesn't he run an adventure tour company? I'd imagine this part of year would be fairly busy."

Tommy shook his head. "Not lately. He's been struggling. Last I talked with him, he was considering taking some work with one of the other companies."

"Might not be a horrible idea."

"What makes you say that?"

"Reece has never been one to play by the rules. Might do him some good to get a little structure in his life. That's all."

Tommy could see his point. He steered the car over the last rise and began the descent down the hill toward the ranch house.

The home was a modest two-story building with a corrugated tin roof and wooden siding painted an ordinary brown. A wraparound porch provided a 360-degree view of the country.

As the car drew closer, Tommy tapped on the brakes. "What in the world?"

The other two noticed it as well.

"That can't be good," Sean said.

Reece's home looked like a war zone. The shattered windows and splintered siding gave testament to what happened. It was clear to the Americans. Someone had shot up the place.

"Who did this?" Adriana said in an absent tone.

Tommy stopped the car near the end of the driveway and put it in park.

Sean's eyes darted around the property in case the shooter, or shooters, was still around. He reached into his gear bag and pulled out the Springfield XD 40 nestled in the bottom. A second later he was on the ground, staring at the demolished front door.

Tommy and Adriana found their weapons and stepped out as well. They joined Sean at the front of the car where he was evaluating the best way to go in.

"You think they're still here?" Tommy asked.

"Doesn't look like it," Sean said. He took a fast look at a machine shed off to the left. It was still completely intact. "Follow me. Stay close."

He moved quickly across the gravel drive, staying on his tiptoes to make as little noise as possible. Adriana kept close behind, followed by Tommy. The latter accidentally tripped and kicked a short pile of rocks, making way more noise than he would have liked.

Sean froze at the base of the steps and fired a chastising glare at his friend.

"Sorry," Tommy mouthed.

Sean twisted his head back and forth with derision.

Tommy urged him on with a wave of the hand.

Sean turned his attention back to the front door. He cautiously moved up the steps until he reached the doorway. The ravaged wooden door and its frame were full of holes. Splinters of varying sizes littered the threshold.

Sean reached out his free hand and twisted the doorknob. It turned easily. "Still open," he whispered.

He pushed the door open gently and took a wary step back, using the doorframe for cover. Nothing moved inside the house. Three thoughts immediately went through his mind: there might be a body inside, the killer might be inside, or if Reece was still alive and in the house he might start shooting.

Sean needed to make a split-second decision. Based on the fact there were no other cars around and no one had started shooting at them, he went the safe route.

"Reece?" he called through the crack in the door. "It's Sean and Tommy. You in here?"

No response. *Given the circumstances, not good.*

Sean pushed through the doorway and into the first room. Shattered glass littered the floor. Bullet holes dotted a nearby sofa. The interior walls wore a smattered array of more tiny craters. In the kitchen beyond the living room, drinking glasses and plates had exploded all over the counter and floor—more collateral damage from the shooting.

"Reece," Sean said again. "Anyone in here?"

Tommy moved around to the left and checked a narrow hallway. Adriana stayed near Sean as he continued forward through the kitchen to a laundry room and small guest bathroom.

"Find anything?" Tommy asked.

"No. All clear," Sean said.

"At least we didn't find a body," Adriana added.

"True. But that could mean they took him."

The words barely escaped his mouth when the house was rocked by a thunderous boom.

The few pieces of mirror that remained on a wall just beyond Sean's position shattered as a bullet ripped through the wall and smashed into it.

The three instantly hit the deck, diving for cover behind whatever they could find. Sean instinctively stuck out a hand to shove Adriana to the floor, but her reaction was just as fast as his.

They curled up behind the dishwasher while Tommy took up a position behind the tattered sofa near the big front window.

Sean's immediate thought was that whoever came to kill Reece must have come back for them. But how would they know the Americans were coming unless they'd been monitoring them somehow? Sean scratched that thought out of his head. The killers had to be working in tandem with the bombing suspect in Atlanta. If that was the case, they'd most likely be operating under the notion that Tommy was already dead. It was unlikely they knew anything about Sean.

Then there was the fact that no car had pulled up. With the noisy gravel driveway outside, even an electric car would have made at least *some* noise as it pulled in. That meant the shooter was on the premises when the Americans arrived, which narrowed the possibilities considerably.

Either the killer decided to hang around on the property to make sure no one came looking for Reece—or Reece was the one who'd just fired.

Another shot rang out, and a piece of drywall exploded five feet above Tommy's head. It was followed by another five shots, each tearing through random points on the wall. The rounds zipped through the air and harmlessly out the other side of the house.

Sean listened closely. As the echo of the gunfire dissipated, he could hear movement just beyond the front of the house. The shooter was moving around to enter the building.

He had to act fast, and it was going to require a gamble.

"Reece!" he yelled out. "It's Sean and Tommy! If that's you out there, you better stop shooting at us! Not cool, man! Not cool at all!"

Tommy looked back at his friend, who was peeking around the edge of the kitchen cabinets. "What are you doing?" he mouthed.

Sean held up a finger and pointed at the front door.

Tommy crouched next to the sofa and took aim at the door in case the shooter decided to come through. Tommy had always been a decent shot with guns of all kinds. At this range, he'd never miss.

Footsteps tapped on the stairs leading up to the front porch. Tommy gripped his weapon a little tighter. Sean and Adriana stayed in their position, ready to fire if the person on the outside was an enemy.

The sound of footsteps stopped just short of the threshold, and the companions froze, waiting to see what would happen.

"It's about time you guys showed up!" Reece yelled through the crack in the front door.

Tommy visibly relaxed, the gun drooping slightly in his hand. "Reece? You okay?"

The door swung open, and the big Australian stood in the opening, silhouetted by the blazing light of the sun.

"Look at my house, Tommy. Does it look like I'm all right?"

Sean let out a short laugh and stood up from his hiding place. Adriana rose right behind him.

"Boy, are we glad to see you," Sean said.

"Yeah," Tommy agreed as he straightened up. "Although I don't appreciate you shooting at us just now."

Reece grinned with pride. He shoved his .45-caliber SIG Sauer back in its holster. "Maybe next time you'll let a bloke know when you're comin' to visit."

Tommy was incensed. "I tried calling, emailing, and texting you."

"Did you try my beeper?"

Reece flashed a quick glance over at Sean and then winked.

"What?"

"I'm just havin' a bit of fun with you, mate. How are ya, Tom?"

Tommy shook his head and put his weapon away. The others did the same, tucking their pistols in their holsters.

"I'm fine now that I know you're okay. When I hadn't heard from you for a few days..."

"You thought I was dead? Me? Aww, that's sweet, old Tom. But you should know me better than that."

"Actually," Sean cut in, "his first thought was that you were doing a tour."

Reece rolled his shoulders. "I wish that was the case, mate. But things haven't been so good on that front lately. It'll turn around sooner or later." His head circled from one side of the room to the other as he surveyed the damage. "My house, on the other hand— pretty sure she's a goner."

Sean stepped closer with Adriana in tow.

"Any idea who did this? Did they say what they wanted?"

Reece noticed Adriana and took his trucker hat off for a moment. "Brought a sheila with you, Sean?"

"Oh sorry. Where are my manners. This is Adriana. Adriana, Reece Skelton."

The Aussie gave a curt nod and put his hat back on his sweaty head.

"Pleasure."

"Wait a minute," Tommy said. "How come you automatically assumed she's with Sean?"

Reece raised an eyebrow, shared a short knowing glance with Sean, and then looked back at Tommy. "Come on, Tom."

Before Tommy could protest, Reece went on while Sean fought back the laughter. "To answer your question, no. I have no idea who they were or what they wanted. All I know is I was sitting here watching rugby and having a beer when I heard the SUV drive up."

"So you got a look at the vehicle?" Sean asked. "You didn't happen to see the shooter?"

"Nah," Reece said. "Didn't see them. Their SUV, yeah. But I doubt that'll be much help now. I heard 'em rollin' up, went to see who it was, and by the time I looked out the window, they started shooting. Nothing I could do but duck for cover and slither out the back like a snake. Been hiding in the machine shed for the last two days."

"You've been sleeping out there?" Adriana asked, entering the conversation.

"It's not that bad. Got a cot out there and an old Land Cruiser. If it gets too cold, I can just climb in that thing. You might have noticed cold isn't really a problem here right now."

"Definitely not," Sean agreed. "You've gotta be hungry. We need to get you something to eat."

Reece waved a dismissive hand. "I'm fine. Got plenty of stuff out there in the freezer and a camping stove with plenty of fuel."

"So have you been staying out there because you're worried the shooters will come back?" Tommy asked.

"It's not that I'm scared. It's that I want to get the drop on those nasty buggers. If they were to come back, I'd have the perfect angle to take them out. They never did come back, though. Figured I'd give it a few days before I migrated back to the house to start fixing things."

Adriana assessed the damage. "Looks like that might take a while."

Reece nodded. "Yeah, well, since I don't have any tours lined up in the next few weeks, I've got the time."

Tommy tried to redirect the conversation back on track. "So someone tried to kill you and you don't know why?"

Sean interrupted. "Since you've been hiding out in the shed, I don't suppose you heard about the bombing in Atlanta."

Reece's face scrunched into a frown. "Bombing? What kind of bombing?"

"Someone blew up the IAA building," Tommy said.

"We figure they were trying to take him out," Sean added.

Reece's eyes went from one guy to the other. "That's pretty deep. Odd someone would try to kill you and me in the same week, eh, Tom?"

He slapped Tommy on the back and enjoyed a good chuckle. Reece stopped laughing when he realized no one was laughing with him.

"Reece, don't you see the connection?"

"Connection? Nah. You're all the way on the other side of the world. I doubt anyone here wanted anything to do with you. Or the other way around."

"Except there *is* a connection," Adriana said. "You both received messages about the Baiame Cave."

The Americans stared at Reece until they saw the light go on in his head. His eyes grew wide with the realization. "Wait a minute. You're tellin' me that those guys who came by and shot up my house did it because I read a bloomin' email?"

"I got your message, and a day later someone blew up IAA headquarters. We were lucky the building was empty."

"Reece," Sean said, "what can you tell us about the message in the email Annie sent?"

The Aussie shrugged. "Sorry, mate. I don't know much about it. I read it a few times, but I'm not sure what it means. Sounds like that Mathews guy was on some kind of treasure hunt. From what the note said, he didn't finish the job."

"Do you know anything about Baiame Cave or what the treasure might be in relation to that deity?"

Reece thought for a moment before responding. He put his hands on his hips as if that would help him dig through his memory banks. "Sorry, Sean. I don't know what it could be. I could take you there if you like. Might not be a bad idea to get out of the area for a while." A mischievous grin crossed his lips. "It'll be just like the old days, right, Tom?"

Tommy appeared reluctant. "That's what I was hoping to avoid."

"Old days?" Adriana asked.

Sean glanced at her with a smirk and shook his head. "You don't want to know."

Reece's jovial expression faded, and he looked down at the floor for a moment. He slowly raised his head. "You got me thinking, Tom. If they came after me because of that message, and they came after you, I wonder what they did to poor Annie."

Tommy's face remained like stone. "If she's still alive, we need to get to her."

"Unless they got to her already."

"Right. And if that's the case, we need to get moving."

Chapter 7
Sydney

The door to the little room opened, and a hulking figure of a man stepped in. He moved off to the side and allowed another man to enter. The second man stood a few inches shorter than the first but had an imposing physique—muscular and toned. He clearly spent more time at the gym than the average person.

The first man left the room and closed the door behind, leaving the second man with his new companion. A dim light shone from the center of the room from a cheaply made dome fixture. She had several like it in her home.

Before the guy sat down across from her, Annie started begging. "I don't know what you want, but please, let me go. I haven't done anything to anyone."

Shadows seemed to follow the man's face until he reached the center of the room and a simple wooden chair. Annie sat in a similar one. A mattress in the corner was the only other thing in the room.

"I know you haven't, Annie. And believe me, we don't want to hurt you, either." He turned the chair around backward and eased into it, propping his muscled arms on the back's top.

"Then why am I here? I've already told the other men I don't know anything about the

Baiame treasure other than what I read in that journal entry. I have no idea where the treasure is. If I did, I would have already told you. I don't care about any treasure. I just want to get back to my life."

She started to sob.

The man stood up and walked over to the corner where a box of tissues sat next to the mattress. He picked up the box and handed it over to her.

Annie took it and pulled a tissue out. She wiped her eyes with it and then blew her nose.

When she'd collected herself, he returned to his chair.

"I mean, what are you guys, some part of the government or something?" she asked.

There was an angle he'd not considered. He'd only spent two minutes in here, and without saying more than a sentence, he'd gained a foothold. All it took was a little listening.

Paying attention like that was something at which Jack Robinson had become particularly adept through the years. It had served him well as he rose through the ranks of the Australian special forces. It still paid dividends for him in the private sector.

"Yes, Annie. We are part of the government. And we desperately need your help."

"If you're part of the government, you can't hold me against my will like this unless I'm being charged with a crime."

Jack raised an eyebrow. "Do you want me to charge you with a crime, Annie?" He called her bluff. "Because I can make that happen. We could start with a little tampering charge, throw in a little treason. Why, if I didn't know better, I'd say you were responsible for the destruction of government and historical property."

The last statement was too much. "I never," she protested.

"You know that, and I know that, Annie. And we don't want to charge you with anything. We just need your help with that journal you found."

Her eyes welled up again, and he held out a hand as if that could dam the river of tears. "I already told you—"

"And we believe you. We believe you don't know much about this journal." He paused a second until she looked into his eyes. "It's okay, Annie. I believe you. Promise. I just need to ask you a few more questions."

"Then you'll let me go?"

"I'll do the best I can."

The tension in her face eased a tad, and Jack could see his words had soothed her.

"Attagirl. Now. I need to know the names of every person you sent a copy of that journal."

"I already told your men. The only person I sent that to was my friend Reece Skelton. He's interested in Aboriginal culture, and I figured maybe he could figure out what it meant. Maybe even give it to the right authorities."

He smirked at the last statement. "That's good, Annie. Tell me something. Have you ever heard of Tommy Schultz?"

Her face twisted into an expression of genuine confusion. "Tommy Schultz?"

"I didn't think you had. Just to be sure, do you know anything about the International Archaeological Agency?"

The second question caused her to think a bit harder. She glanced down at the ground and then stared into his eyes. "I think I've heard of it before, but I'm not sure."

He decided to see if he could jar her memory. "They're based in the United States— Atlanta, specifically. They recover important artifacts for private organizations and governments all over the world. Does that ring a bell?"

She thought again for another few seconds and then shook her head. "No. No, I don't think I've ever heard of that before."

Before she could ask why, he continued. "Annie, we have to be very careful about this situation. There was some sensitive material in that journal you shared."

"Sensitive material?"

"Yes." He nodded. "Extremely sensitive."

"But it just looked like..."

"I know. It looked like a treasure hunter's journal. Innocent enough, right?"

It was her turn to nod, albeit filled with uncertainty.

"You see," Jack said, "within that journal, we discovered a code embedded in the words."

"A code?"

"That's right. A code. And this code reveals the location to some things that could be potentially dangerous for a large group of people. It turns out this treasure Mr. Mathews was referring to in his notes could actually be a threat to the security of our nation. So you see why we have to be so cautious."

She mulled it over but wasn't able to connect the dots. "I still don't understand. What could that man have found over a hundred years ago that could pose a threat today?"

Jack smiled without breaking character. "Again, Annie, I'm afraid I can't share that information with you. It's sensitive material."

"Oh, right."

She bought the story. Now he had to see what else she knew.

"Hopefully we will have this whole thing resolved soon enough, and you'll be back in your museum. I just have to ask one more question."

She gave a reluctant nod.

"What do you know about the Baiame Boomerang?"

Annie thought for a moment. "I only know a little bit about Baiame from books I've read on Aborigines. He was one of the creator gods in the many stories they have about Dreamtime. Other than that, I'm afraid I can't be much help. While I do love history, I'm afraid my job is more in tune with cataloguing things from the past instead of learning about them."

"So you don't know anything about this deity's boomerang or where it might be?"

She shook her head. "No. I sent that email to Reece because I wanted to see if he could figure out the riddle at the bottom of the journal entry. Like I said, he's better with that stuff than me. I figured if someone went to the trouble of hiding that document in a false drawer, it must be important."

Jack's demeanor turned in a second. "And yet you didn't feel like that was something you should report to your boss or perhaps the authorities?"

"What? No." Her head twitched back and forth again. The new aggression from her inquisitor was clearly throwing her off. "I... What are you suggesting? That I was trying to steal it?"

Jack rolled his shoulders. "No one is accusing you of that, Annie. But you have to admit, it does look a little suspicious. I mean, you find some old note hidden in an antique desk, and you didn't tell anyone about it except a friend who may or may not be able to help you figure out what it means?"

"No," she shook her head violently at the accusation. "I was never going to steal it."

"No. Maybe you were just going to use it to find whatever treasure it mentioned. I imagine you don't make a great deal of money working at the museum. And you're getting up there close to retirement age now. Maybe you figured it was time to give your retirement plan a little boost."

"I never—"

Jack stood up suddenly, cutting her off. "Where is the paper, Annie? What did you do with the original? We know who you sent a copy to. Now we need to know where you hid the journal entry." His voice thundered in the tiny room.

She winced with every emphatic syllable until she broke out in another fit of tears. "It's at the museum. I swear, I never meant to steal it. I never cared about any treasure." Her words were barely intelligible with the sobbing and moaning. "I just thought it might interest my friend. I swear that's all."

Jack decided to play another card to make sure she understood the stakes. "Well, you got your friend killed, Annie."

The crying stopped for a moment, and she stared at him with eyes full of shock, of horror, of disbelief. "What?"

Jack gave a slow nod. "That's right. Your friend Reece Skelton is dead. Someone murdered him in cold blood, and we think it has something to do with what was in the journal."

A new bout of tears was fought off by the shocking revelation. "I...I... Reece is dead?"

Jack stepped close and crouched down so their eyes were level. "Annie. We can't protect you if you don't tell us everything you know. I need you to start with exactly where you hid that piece of paper."

Chapter 8
Sydney

Reece let the phone ring one last time before ending the call. "Still no answer," he said.

He'd tried calling Annie at least a dozen times over the course of their drive to Sydney. Each one had the same result.

The visitors had been fighting fatigue for the last several hours. As the car passed beyond the borders of the Sydney city limits, they started losing the battle.

Adriana slept with her head on Sean's shoulder. He managed to stave off exhaustion by replacing it with paranoia. Keeping a watchful eye on the road behind them kept him awake. Still, he was ready for a bed.

Tommy sat in the front passenger seat with his arms crossed and head leaning against the headrest. He'd decided to let Reece drive because dying in a fiery car crash due to a sleeping driver wasn't in anyone's best interest. Sean couldn't tell if his friend was asleep or not under those sunglasses, but sudden snappy movements alluded to him dozing off or waking up intermittently.

Sean let his eyes wander out the window to the passing city. Night washed over the buildings, shops, apartments, and condos. Somewhere beyond the skyline, the famous

Sydney Opera House loomed over the water with its dramatic white roof.

Tommy had made a call and set everyone up with rooms at one of the upscale hotels in the downtown area. The group agreed they would check in after they paid a visit to Annie's museum. The chances that she'd somehow be there were slim, but they at least had to check.

Reece parked the car around the back of the old brick building. Getting access to the museum after normal business hours had required another Tommy Schultz phone call, this time to the director of antiquities. The man—a guy by the name of Wilbur Kurt—had been almost excited to have agents from IAA coming in for a visit, much less the one in charge of the entire operation.

Wilbur was waiting for them at the back entrance when the group exited the car. He was a portly man with a ruddy face, splotches of red on his nose and cheeks, and a receding gray hairline. He greeted the visitors with an exaggerated smile and waved them over.

"Welcome!" he said. He eagerly reached out a hand to Tommy first. "It's just such an honor to have you here with us. I've heard and read so much about your exploits. The historical world is lucky to have you."

Tommy blushed in the pale light of a metal halide bulb shining down from a lamp post near the street. "Why, thank you. I really appreciate you accommodating our unusual request at this hour of the day."

"Not at all. Anything for you, Mr. Schultz."

"Please. Call me Tommy."

Sean, Adriana, and Reece all exchanged befuddled expressions.

Wilbur bit his lower lip at the offer.

"Thank you...Tommy. I'm honored." He stepped to the side and held the door open with one hand while motioning with the other.

Tommy twisted around for a moment to see the looks on his friends' faces. "Thank you, Mr. Kurt."

"Wilbur," he corrected.

Tommy patted the guy on the shoulder and stepped into the building.

The others followed, and Wilbur closed the door behind, rushing past the other three to catch up to Tommy.

"Wilbur," Tommy said, "these are my friends Sean, Adriana, and Reece." He put the side of his hand to his cheek as if about to share a big secret and lowered his voice. "Reece is a local."

"Ah well. It's a pleasure to meet you all. Any friend of the great Tommy Schultz is a friend of mine."

Again, Sean turned his head to Reece. This time he mouthed, "Great Tommy Schultz?"

Reece twirled a finger around his ear to indicate what he thought about the guy.

Wilbur didn't notice the interaction because he was already walking down the long corridor.

"I'm sorry if our coming here on such short notice is an inconvenience, Wilbur," Tommy said.

Wilbur shook his head vigorously. "Not at all. I must apologize. One of our curators disappeared a few days ago, and we haven't heard from her. Very unlike her, actually. She's one of the most reliable employees I've ever worked with."

The four visitors raised an eyebrow.

Tommy played coy. "You don't know what happened to her?"

"No. She was here earlier in the week. I believe she worked late one night. Then she never came in the next day. Or the next. We've called several times, even had someone go to her house to check on her."

"And?"

"Never answered," Wilbur said. "And her house was empty. It's like she just up and vanished." A somber tone overshadowed his boyish joy. "The police said they don't think any sort of crime occurred. Maybe she'd just gotten tired of working in the vault and needed a mental health day or two. Can't say I blame her. Every year when we do inventory drives me a little bonkers too. She'll turn up soon."

Tommy decided to move the conversation to the reason they were there.

"So you said that she was working on something in the vault? Like a bank vault?"

Wilbur chuckled. "No, nothing like that. We just call our stockroom the vault because it's down in the basement. It feels like being stuck in a vault when we're down there. Plus the entire room is encased in concrete to keep it fireproof."

He turned a corner and led the way down a wooden staircase. At the bottom, a short corridor ended at a pair of metal doors. The one on the left was open.

Wilbur stepped inside and put both hands out wide. "This is our vault," he said. "I have to admit, I'm so excited to be a part of one of your pursuits, Tommy. All the wild adventures you've been on... It's all just so exciting."

Sean leaned over to Adriana and whispered in her ear. "Maybe Tommy should have booked a room for two tonight."

She playfully swatted his shoulder as if to chastise him, but couldn't fight off a tiny snort.

"Well, Wilbur, it's not all fun and games out there." Tommy's voice took on an overly masculine tone. "But it has its moments."

Sean had heard enough. "Yeah, so if I may cut in. We've had a long trip and really need to get some rest. So if it's not too much trouble, is it possible for us to have a look around and see if we can find anything that might help us...I don't know...find your missing curator?"

An uncomfortable pause took over the room for five seconds. Wilbur turned to Tommy. "Is he always this rude?" he asked in a theatrical whisper.

"You have no idea."

"Yes, Sean," Wilbur said. "Feel free to look around. All I ask is you don't break anything." He directed the last sentence at Sean and Reece.

"Of course, Wilbur."

"If I may, Tommy. What is it exactly that you're looking for?"

Tommy decided to let him in on a piece of the story. "There's a document that was here. It's from around the turn of the twentieth century."

"Document? Well, if it's something like that you're interested in finding, you'd best start with the files over there." He pointed at the big filing cabinets next to a wooden work table. "If we have anything like that in here, it would be in that cabinet. Do you happen to know who wrote this document?"

"Mathews. R.H. Mathews."

Wilbur put a finger to his lips as if it would help his concentration, but he couldn't come up with a connection. "I'm afraid I'm not familiar with that name. Was he a writer, a politician perhaps?"

"No. He was an anthropologist at the end of his career. He found something of interest and wrote it down in a message that we believe ended up here."

"Really?" Wilbur said, clearly surprised. "What makes you think it's here?"

Tommy had backed himself into a corner, and now he couldn't think fast enough to figure a way out.

"Well, you see..." he stammered.

"We searched sales records and other inventory documents that led us to believe it had been stored here, possibly hidden away in a piece of furniture. If one of the people who work here found that document, it could be in one of your files." Sean explained, bailing his friend out of a pickle.

"Right," Tommy agreed. "So if we can just get a look at what you've got, that would be a big help."

The director eyed the two for a moment. "How fascinating," he exclaimed. "All this time I've had a secret document right under my nose and had no idea. May I ask to what this paper pertains?"

Tommy went with full disclosure in his response. "We have reason to believe it contains the location to an ancient Aborigine treasure. If we were to find an artifact of that caliber, you can imagine what it would mean for the tribes...as well as this museum."

The visitors saw the man's eyes light up like a child on Christmas morning. "Incredible. Well, please, take a look around. Take all the time you need. And if you need my help, don't hesitate to say so." He pointed at the filing cabinets. "You'll find everything in alphabetical order. I'll just be over here working on the computer."

"Thank you."

Tommy had hoped the man would leave them alone to snoop around, but he wasn't going to push his luck. He had the museum director eating out of his palm. No reason to change that dynamic.

The four visitors walked over to the filing cabinets and began with the cabinet marked *M* on the outside. Tommy pulled it open and started sorting through the files. The others watched over his shoulder.

Reece stole a quick look over his shoulder at the director. "He's a bit strange, isn't he?" he whispered.

"What?" Sean asked, making sure Wilbur couldn't hear his response. "You mean the man crush he has on Tommy?"

Tommy didn't look up. He was busily thumbing through the dozens of files and documents in the cabinet. "Jealousy is an ugly color on anyone, gentlemen."

"Because everyone aspires to catch the admiration of a stout museum director someday?"

Reece chuckled at the comment.

Adriana shifted her feet. Sean could tell she was restless. She was a woman of action and detested sitting around waiting while someone else did the work.

She stepped away from the others and looked down a row of boxes, stacked almost all the way to the ceiling on shelves that ran the length of the room to the far wall. There were only two such rows—the rest of the vault containing items such as furniture, sculptures, artifacts, and paintings. Adriana had seen a room like this before on a few occasions. Her hobby required it.

She'd spent years tracking down priceless art that went missing after World War II. Her skills as a master thief contributed to her success in recovering several and returning them to the rightful owners or governments. It was her attention to detail and a passion for research that accounted for the other portion of her success.

Wandering down the row, she noted a few boxes that were marked with nothing more than a large black *X*. Curiosity begged her to ask Wilbur what they were, but she thought better of it, realizing it could lead to a long, boring conversation with the man. Better to leave him to his work.

"It's not in here," she heard Tommy say.

Adriana pivoted and walked back to the files.

"Maybe we should check some of the other ones," Sean suggested. "She could have stored it by first name."

Tommy raised his head and shot his friend a look of haughty derision. "Really, Sean? Alphabetical by first name? What is this, amateur hour?"

Sean let the insult roll off his shoulders, but he laughed on the inside. "You never know; that's all I'm saying."

"Fine. Go check the R file if you want. I'm going to look through this one again."

Sean wasn't used to seeing this side of Tommy. He preferred the mopey, subservient version. He decided not to fight the battle and moved over to where he found a file marked with the letter *R*.

He flicked the locking button to the side, pulled on the handle, and when the file was open began flipping through the contents. Sean didn't really believe that he'd find the Mathews paper in the cabinet. If it was anywhere, it would be where Tommy was looking. Now he had to go through the process just for the sake of appearances.

Tommy reached the end of the file and sighed. "I don't understand," he said, frustrated. "It should be in there."

"Maybe she took it with her," Reece offered.

Tommy considered the idea for a brief second and then shook it off. "No. According to what we know about Annie, she wouldn't dare take something out of the building, no matter how interesting or tempting it might have been. If she found the paper here, then it must still be here."

"Maybe there is another room," Adriana suggested as she approached.

"That's possible," Tommy said.

"Then perhaps I should ask your friend there if there is anywhere else we should check."

Sean gave up on his file and moved back over to Tommy's. "Mind if I go through this one, you know, just in case?"

"Be my guest," Tommy said. "Maybe you'll have better luck."

Sean didn't respond. He stepped between Tommy and the row of papers and folders. Then he wedged his hands between two random sections and pulled the two ends apart. There were good amount of files on either side, but Sean was able to get enough space between the two to see down to the bottom of the drawer.

Lying there—inconspicuous beneath the other folders and files—was a single sheet of drab paper encased in protective plastic. Sean's lips creased on the right side of his face. He turned his head to the museum director, who was busy pecking away at the keyboard. "Mr. Kurt?"

The man looked up from his computer.

"Do you happen to have a pair of handling gloves?" Sean asked. "It's wrapped in plastic, but better safe than sorry."

Tommy moved close and stood on his tiptoes to see over Sean's shoulder. He sighed. "Always gotta show me up, huh?"

Chapter 9
Sydney

"Mr. Wyatt, I really must insist..." Wilbur was beyond irritated at this point.

After the museum director brought Tommy a pair of white gloves, he stepped back and watched as his American hero pulled the plastic-covered paper out of the drawer and placed it on the work desk.

If that had been where the saga ended, he would have been okay. It was what happened next that drove him up a wall.

He stood by and watched as Sean and Tommy stretched out the paper and pressed it hard against the surface of the work table.

"Wilbur," Sean said, "I appreciate the concern...and the lack of trust, but I'd appreciate it if you'd not bother me while I'm working with a potentially priceless and most certainly delicate document."

The two friends finished pressing the paper out flat and then covered it with a thin plastic film Wilbur had provided.

"I just think perhaps maybe you should let Mr. Schultz...I mean, Tommy...handle this sort of thing. It isn't the kind of work..." He stopped himself.

Sean finished the thought for him. "The kind of work grunts like me should be doing?"

Wilbur twisted his head to the side and backed down. Before he could say he didn't mean to offend, Sean cut him off.

"None taken, Wilbur. You're right. This sort of thing isn't usually my bag, but I'm better than nothing."

"Plus he's done this with me dozens of times," Tommy added amid an extremely concentrated stare. He'd not taken his eyes off the document during the entire process of the transfer.

Tommy's comment eased Wilbur's mind somewhat. "Just be careful. I can't believe Annie didn't tell me about this."

Sean leaned over the table. "Well, I'm sure she had a good reason for what she did."

Before Wilbur could rebut, Tommy stood up straight. "All done. Now it's protected from the air. Hopefully it hasn't sustained much damage."

Wilbur couldn't remove his gaze from the old paper. "I apologize, gentlemen, but what exactly were you trying to understand about this document?"

Tommy kept up the charade to keep Annie out of any sort of implication. "You see here," he pointed at the paper. "It's talking about some Aborigine treasure. Apparently this treasure is not insignificant."

Wilbur's reaction was dubious. "I've never heard of any Aboriginal treasure. They typically aren't a people who care for such things."

"Right," Tommy said. "That's what we figured too. That's why it must not be just a financial sort of treasure. Whatever this is, it must have some kind of spiritual meaning to them."

"Of course, something like that would be worth a lot of money," Reece added. "It'd be like the King Tut's tomb of Australia."

Reece's comment lit up Wilbur's eyes again. The visitors could see his mind racing with the possibilities. They knew what he was thinking as soon as the words dripped out of Reece's mouth.

"Incredible," Wilbur whispered. "And...and you think if I help you with this...I mean if you find this thing...would you be willing to let me display it here for a short time?"

Tommy's eyes narrowed like he was about to share a personal secret. "Let me put it this way, Wilbur. I won't forget your help, and I'll make sure the guys at the national place get in line behind you."

Wilbur could barely contain his excitement. The visitors half expected him to squeal. "So what do you think it all means?" He looked back down at the Mathews paper.

The visitors huddled around and read through it again. None of them needed to. They'd pored over it a dozen times already before arriving. Their show was for Wilbur's benefit, and Annie's.

The Americans had another reason for wanting to see the original copy. They hoped there was something else the digital version wouldn't show. As they stood around—gazing at the document—they realized it had nothing left to offer.

"Well," Tommy finally answered, "we're not entirely sure. These directions are fairly vague. It sounds like we should visit this Baiame place."

"Baiame? Like the ancient Aboriginal god?" Wilbur asked. "There's a cave to the north of the city where some cave drawings feature that deity. Do you think maybe that's what the document is talking about?"

The visitors had already surmised that was the next place they needed to visit. No need to cut the act now.

"How far away is this place?" Sean asked.

Wilbur shrugged. "Depends on how fast you drive, traffic, that sort of thing. But not too far."

They'd seen and heard enough. Sean, Tommy, and Adriana badly needed some rest. Reece's eyes were starting to get droopy as well. Time to wind it up and head to the hotel.

"What about this mention of forty-five suns?" Wilbur said.

"It's the way they tracked time in the ancient world," Tommy answered. "Remember, everything was based on the movement of the sun, moon, and stars back then. These circles are suns, as best we can figure. And they stacked them this way to demonstrate multiple days."

"Of course." The museum director almost smacked his forehead with his hand for not thinking of it.

Tommy still wanted to know about one other possibility. They needed to search the desk where Annie found the document. It might still contain something useful. "Wilbur, you don't know where Annie found this thing?"

"No," Wilbur answered. "I haven't the foggiest." Then it hit him. "Wait, you said you'd obtained something about that information prior to coming here."

Tommy beamed as if he was about to reveal a big secret—a continuation of the act. "That's right, Wilbur. You want to know what's been right under your nose this whole time without you knowing?"

The museum director nodded eagerly.

"Perhaps you could save us some time. Do you happen to have any antique desks sitting around in here?"

"As a matter of fact, we do have one. It's on the other side of the room. Follow me."

Wilbur led the way by the row of boxes and the other six rows filled with all sorts of trinkets and precious items from yesteryear. He turned the corner and pointed at a large wooden desk down toward the other end of the row.

Tommy beamed. "Outstanding, Wilbur." He picked up his pace and strode rapidly over to the desk. He turned back as the others joined him. "Okay for me to open these drawers?"

Wilbur nodded. There was no chance he was going to say no at this point. The hook tugged on his adrenal gland.

Tommy carefully pulled out the first. Seeing it was empty, he moved to the second. It, too, proved vacant. The last drawer on the right stuck stubbornly on its rails but after a hard pull came loose. Still empty.

Tommy moved to the other side and investigated the final two drawers as he'd done on the right-hand side, but the desk contained nothing of interest. "I guess if there was anything else in here it's long gone by now," he said.

Sean looked underneath the desk's seating position and noticed the little flap dangling from the main panel. "And now it appears we know where the document was found."

He stepped back and let the others crowd around—each peering under the desk to see the hidden storage place.

"Classic," Adriana said.

"You've seen this sort of thing before?" Wilbur asked.

She shrugged. "You break into enough places, you'll see lots of things."

Her comment unsettled the museum director, but Tommy quickly intervened. "What she means is, it's not that uncommon. There must be a mechanism of some sort that got knocked loose to open the hidden door." He flipped over on his back and squirmed under the desk to get a closer look.

He turned on his phone's LED light and held it up to the rectangular hole in the wood. "It's pretty amazing craftsmanship," he said. "The hinges are invisible from the outside. And the seam is cut along the grain in the wood so it appears natural." He flipped the door up until it was almost flush. Tommy didn't close it all the way because he wasn't sure how to get it open again. From what he could tell, that could prove to be a tricky proposition.

"Whoever designed this definitely wanted to keep something hidden."

"Do you see anything else in there?" Reece asked, hunching over to catch a glimpse.

"No. Just the shelf where the document was probably stored. Nothing helpful... Wait a second." He leaned closer to the desk bottom and peered into the hole.

"What is it?" Wilbur asked. His impatient excitement had reached full climax.

"Not sure," Tommy said. "It's small. I mean tiny. I can barely see it. Looks like it was burned into the top of the wood." He craned his neck to the side. "It's a sequence of symbols."

"Symbols?"

"Yeah." Tommy's voice strained slightly. "They're not letters. Just a bunch of random signs."

"Take a picture with your phone," Sean said.

"Really? Thanks, Captain Obvious. I was just about to do that."

Sean chuckled at his friend's comeback. "Just saying; you're taking your sweet time."

"Is he always this impatient?" Tommy asked Adriana.

"I wouldn't know," she answered. "He spends more time with you than he does with me."

Tommy pointed his phone's camera into the recession. "Fair enough." He snapped a few images with the flash and then two more without. A second later he pulled himself out from under the desk and set the device on the desk surface.

A quick tap of the first image brought it to full size on the screen. He pinched his fingers together and then spread them apart to zoom in on the blackened symbols.

"See?" he said.

"Looks like a cipher," Sean said.

"Half of a cipher," Adriana corrected.

"Right."

"Where's the other half?" Reece asked.

"That's the thing about a cipher. The key is always kept somewhere else."

Tommy listened as he continued inspecting the symbols. "He's right. It's the best way to keep a code like this safe. People would give the key to someone they trusted or hide it in a place no one else could find it. Well, other than a person they intended to receive the message."

Wilbur hovered over the group. His fascination reached a fever pitch. "How do you find the key?" His eager voice nearly trembled in the excitement.

"Well, that's the hard part. You never really know. It could be anywhere. Chances are the key is somewhere far from here. Might be in some of his personal property or something like that. Difficult to tell."

"Sometimes," Adriana said, "the things that seem hardest to find are right under your nose." She turned her head back toward the work table where the Mathews document was encased in protective plastic.

The others followed her gaze and realized exactly what she was saying. Well, everyone but Wilbur.

"What?" he asked. "The paper?"

"Sometimes there are codes put into things like that," Sean answered.

"I didn't see anything unusual."

"You're not supposed to. It could be a sequence of words in a certain order that gives it away. Or maybe it isn't meant to be seen."

"What do you mean, isn't meant to be seen?"

"What he means is maybe it was written in invisible ink," Tommy answered.

Wilbur's eyes were already at the point of bursting from their sockets. Somehow they widened just a bit more. "Invisible ink?"

"Yeah. You've heard of it before, right?"

Wilbur nodded. "Yes, but I've never actually seen it. You think there might be a hidden message on the document?"

"It's worth a look. Tell me, for preserving larger items, you probably do some shrink wrapping, right?"

"From time to time."

"That means you probably have a heat gun lying around."

"Sure, but..." Wilbur saw where Tommy was going with the conversation. "That's pretty hot. Won't it damage the paper?"

"Not if we're careful," Sean reassured him. "It's protected by that plastic now. If we keep the tip of the gun far enough away, it should distribute the heat evenly."

Wilbur slowly nodded. "Ah yes. Of course. I'll be right back."

The visitors watched as the man scurried away like a chubby rat in a maze. When he disappeared through the door, they made their way over to the table and inspected the document again.

"You think something might be on this?" Reece asked.

"Only one way to find out," Tommy said.

To the naked eye, nothing stood out right away. While they waited, they pored over the document to see if there was anything out of the ordinary in the way it was worded. After a few minutes of reading and rereading, though, they didn't find anything that remotely looked like a cipher key.

Wilbur nearly burst through the door, proudly clutching a red-and-black heat gun. "Here it is," he announced. A minute later, he'd plugged it into a short extension cord close to the table and held it up for one of the Americans to take.

Tommy and Sean gave a questioning look at each other as if to ask who wanted to do it.

"It's your show," Sean said. "I'm just the co-star."

Tommy sighed and grabbed the gun. He flipped the button, and warm air began flowing through the nozzle. He kept the device several inches above the plastic so as not to overheat the protective layer and accidentally melt it. His hand passed the heat gun back and forth, spreading the warmth evenly across the surface.

"How long does it usually take for the ink to appear?" Wilbur asked in a hushed tone, as if speaking too loudly might mess up the process.

"Not long," Sean answered. "In fact, it should show up right about now."

Everyone leaned in closer, anticipating the moment of truth. The hidden message, however, never appeared.

Tommy gave it a few more passes with the gun and then switched it off. "I was afraid of that."

"What are you doing?" Wilbur asked with desperation in his voice.

"If there was anything written on this document in invisible ink, we would have seen it by now."

"Maybe you need to give it a little more time. Do you think the plastic is keeping the warm air from activating it?"

"Sorry, Wilbur. If there was something to see, we would have seen it. I don't think there's anything here."

"He's right," Sean said. "The key must be somewhere else."

"What if we took the plastic away, you know, just for a minute? Maybe you could get some hot air directly onto the paper."

Adriana put her hand on the man's shoulder. "It's not worth risking the document," she said. "Trust us. There's nothing here."

Wilbur's shoulders slumped. A crestfallen look washed over his face.

"I wish there was something here," Tommy said. "Would make things a lot easier."

Reece had been quiet for several minutes. "Do you suppose this Mathews bloke might have referenced the key in the journal entry itself? Seems pretty clear to me that we have to go to the Baiame Cave. Says that's where the journey began for him. Maybe we're supposed to walk in his footsteps, so to speak."

"Good point," Sean said. "Notice that last part about the foreign stone?"

The group reexamined the paper again.

"Yeah," Tommy said. "That has to be it. Good thinking, Reece. Let's get some sleep and head up there tomorrow."

"Are you sure there's nothing else on this document?" Wilbur asked. A twinge of tension trickled through the words.

"Let it go," Reece said.

"Don't worry, Wilbur," Tommy said. "If we find anything out there, you'll be one of the first to know."

Chapter 10
Sydney

Wilbur heard something click several feet behind him.

He'd just closed the back entrance to the museum and was about to head to his car. The visitors had only left ten minutes ago. For a second, he thought one of them might have come back.

"Going somewhere?" a familiar voice said from the shadows on the other side of the alley.

Wilbur spun around, startled and terrified. "I...I was just locking up."

"Looks like you're about to go home for the night."

"Yes...yes, I was."

"Seems like you're leaving something out, Wilbur. Like you did in our previous conversations."

"Leave something out?" Wilbur shook his head in little bursts. "No, I wouldn't do that. I'm helping you guys, remember?"

"You don't seem like you're being very helpful."

"What did you tell them?" Jack stood over Wilbur with a gun pointed at the man's forehead.

Wilbur's hands shook violently. His legs weakened, and he almost dropped to his knees. "Nothing. I swear. I didn't tell them anything."

"That's funny, because it seems like they found something in your museum that you didn't tell me you had."

"I...I can explain."

"You'd better."

"It was the Americans. They...they found the original document in one of the file drawers. I swear, I didn't know it was in there. Honest." Wilbur stuttered his way through his explanation.

Jack didn't believe him. "Now, Wilbur. How is it that the museum director doesn't know what his own building is storing?"

Wilbur's eyes welled up. He was on the verge of sobbing. "I'm telling you, I didn't know the original document was here. I swear. It was in some hidden door in an old desk. I don't know how Annie found it or what she was doing with it. I just saw the fake bottom of the desk for the first time tonight."

"The original, what else was on it that I need to know about?"

"Nothing," Wilbur's head twitched back and forth rapidly. "There was nothing different on it. It was the exact same as the email."

"Then why were the Americans so bent on seeing it?" Jack's patience began to wane. He felt the trigger tense against his index finger.

"I...I don't know," Wilbur stammered. "They thought there might be a code or something in invisible ink."

"A code? What code?"

The keys jingled in Wilbur's hands. "Here. Come inside. I'll show you. Just...please, put the gun down. Please."

Jack drew in a slow breath through his nostrils as he sized up the fat museum director. Wilbur's face was flushed red, and sweat poured down his temples and forehead. If Jack didn't know any better, he'd say the man was about to wet himself.

"Hot night out, isn't it?" Jack asked.

"What?" Wilbur was thrown off by the random question.

"You're sweating, Wilbur. Must be because it's warm out."

"Oh. Yes. Yes, that's it. Hot air. Please, come inside where it's cooler. I'll show you what they found."

Jack only took another second to consider the invitation. "All right, Willy. But if you try anything stupid, I'll splatter your brains all over this little museum. Understand?"

Wilbur's head ratcheted up and down.

"That's a good boy. Would be a shame to have to kill you after all the money our employer's invested in you."

"Right. Right...I'm an investment." He fumbled the keys and finally slid the correct one into the lock.

Inside the dark museum, Wilbur hurried over to the alarm panel and turned it off before the incessant screaming began. When he was done, he rushed back over to the vault door and unlocked it. He flipped a couple of light switches, and the two rooms lit up.

"This way," Wilbur said, motioning with his right hand.

He waddled into the next room and pointed at the work table to his left. "See? They didn't take it with them. Said there wasn't anything helpful on it."

Jack followed him and closed the door behind. He gazed at the paper for a moment, rereading the message he'd already seen via email.

Wilbur had been the one to let Jack know what Annie found. The email system was set up so that he'd be notified whenever a message went out. Initially, it had been a precaution to prevent people from goofing around on company time. On this particular occasion, it was a system that made Wilbur a good deal of money.

He knew Bernard Holmes was interested in Aboriginal artifacts, though he wasn't sure why. It didn't matter to Wilbur. All he knew was that the man had money and was willing to pay top dollar for any information that might lead to anything rare from the Aboriginal history.

Jack had been the one to come by and inquire about the email. He'd also warned Wilbur that others might come by to find out what it meant. He'd made a mistake in believing the Americans were dead. Apparently, his assassin who'd bombed the IAA building in Atlanta botched the detonation.

Jack diverted his eyes away from the Mathews document and took a look around. "You certainly have a lot of old stuff in here, Willy."

Wilbur ignored the goofy nickname Jack had decided to use. "Yes. Yes, we do."

"How long you been working here?"

Wilbur swallowed and attempted to keep his composure. "Too long, Jack. Far too long. That's why your...our employer's request was so fortuitous. Thanks to his investment, I'll be able to retire a bit sooner than expected."

"Ripper, Willy. Ripper." Jack slowly stepped around one of the aisles and stopped at a statue of a woman with one arm. Her flowing gown had been pulled down, exposing her breasts. He tapped the stone with the edge of his gun's muzzle. "I always wondered why these artists were allowed to get away with stuff like this."

"Wha...what?"

"I mean, back in the old days, nudity was everywhere. It was on paintings, sculptures like this one. I always wondered why the fascination."

"Well, the human body was considered a beautiful thing, Jack. Anyway, like I was saying, the Americans didn't find anything useful, so they went on their way."

Jack ran the tip of his gun along the sculpture's arm, all the way to the fingertips.

"You in a hurry to get me out of here, Willy?"

"No," Wilbur said. He forced a short laugh. "No. I'm just tired."

"Ah yes. You must be tired. Been here all day, no doubt."

Wilbur answered with a nod.

"You should probably get some rest."

"That would be good."

"I wonder why you call this room the vault."

Wilbur wasn't sure where the conversation was going, but it was all over the place. One thing was certain, he didn't like Jack's tone.

"It's surrounded by concrete. It's fireproof. This whole room is basically a bomb shelter."

Jack's head went up and down. "Pretty much soundproof then, too, eh?"

"Sure, but I don't see—"

Jack whipped his pistol around and fired. The round zipped across the room and tore through Wilbur's right shoulder.

For the first few seconds, he didn't know how to react. Then his nerves sent burning pain to his brain. Wilbur howled and clutched the wound with the opposite hand.

Jack rushed over to the museum director as he dropped to his knees. "I'm so sorry, Willy. It must have gone off by mistake. I'm so sorry."

He caressed the man's fleshy face with the smoking muzzle.

"You shot me," Wilbur whimpered.

"I know, Willy. I know. These things happen."

He pressed the muzzle against Wilbur's temple and stood back. "I'd hate for this gun to go off again, Willy. Now if you don't mind terribly, tell me what the Americans found."

The sobbing commenced. "I told you. They didn't find anything." Wilbur nearly choked on the words.

"Oh? Then why were they talking about a cipher and a key when they left here?"

Wilbur's eyes widened. "Yes. The cipher. They found a cipher in the desk back there." He pointed with his good arm at the antique desk near the back of the room.

"Forgot about that, did you?"

Wilbur couldn't shake his head fast enough. "No. I swear. I didn't think it was important. It's just a bunch of weird symbols. Without the key, it's useless. They don't even know where it is."

"Show me."

Jack dragged the heavier man up by his ear like he would a little child who'd misbehaved. He pulled him back to the desk and shoved him back down on the floor again. "This desk?" Jack asked.

"Yes. Yes, this is the desk." Wilbur clutched his shoulder wound in a vain effort to stem the bleeding.

"Where did they find these symbols?"

Wilbur winced and jerked his thumb at the underside. "Underneath. There's a false panel. Annie must have triggered it to open by mistake. The Americans didn't even know how it happened. They said the cipher was burned into the wood."

Jack flashed a warning glare at the injured man. "Don't go anywhere, okay?" He winked at his own joke. He knew Wilbur wouldn't try anything stupid. The man was a pushover.

Jack slid under the desk and stared up at the opening. He pulled his phone out of his pocket and turned on the light. "I don't see anything in here, Willy. Are you having a laugh with me? Because if you are, I think you know what will happen."

"No, please. It's there. They had to look closely. One of them stuck his phone up close to the hole and took several pictures. I never saw the actual symbols, only the images on his phone."

"Fair enough," Jack said. He raised his device close to the hole and shined the light inside. He twisted his neck a few inches and then realized what the fleshy man was talking about. "Oh yeah. There it is. Got it." He pressed the button on the screen several times to get as many pictures as possible. Then he slid out and stood up. "Come on, Willy. Lets have a look, shall we?" He grabbed the collar on Wilbur's shirt and yanked him up again.

Jack passed his phone to the uneasy museum director, who nearly dropped it on the floor. He managed to hold on and showed the image on the screen to Jack, who kept his weapon planted in Wilbur's lower back.

"What are we lookin' at, Willy?"

"I already told you. I don't know. It's just a bunch of symbols. See?" He pointed to the two lines of odd signs. "The Americans didn't know what they were."

"You're telling me that you've been working at this old museum for the better part of three decades and you have no idea what these mean?" Jack's volume increased with each word until he finished the sentence at full crescendo.

Wilbur winced at the booming voice echoing through the room. He managed to calm himself long enough to answer. "No. No one knows what these mean. They're not like hieroglyphs or petroglyphs. These are something altogether different. They were designed to be undecipherable."

"Then they're useless. And so are you." Jack stepped back and pointed the gun at the back of Wilbur's head.

"No! Please! Wait!"

Wilbur grimaced, expecting to hear the shot and his life to end. It didn't come.

"Why, Willy? Huh? Why shouldn't I just kill you right now?" Jack's voice roared.

"Because."

"Because why?"

"You need a key to unlock the meaning of these symbols."

"And where is this key?"

"I already told you, I don't know. The Americans don't know either."

Jack was tired of this blubbering fool. He'd seen men like this before. Cowards, all of them. They were unwilling to stare down the barrel of a gun, as if that would help their pitiful circumstances. The bullet would do its job whether they looked or not. This one, however, was particularly pathetic.

"You're not helping your case, Willy."

"Please, I know where they're going next."

Jack paused a moment and then lowered the weapon. "I'm listening."

Wilbur's heart pounded in his chest. Perspiration dripped off his nose to the concrete floor in huge drops. He hesitated before he felt it was safe enough to turn around and face Jack. "They...they're going to a cave north of the city. It's called Baiame Cave, close to Milbrodale. I got the impression they believe the key might be there somewhere. If you just get me to a doctor so I can have my shoulder patched up, maybe I could show you where it is. I might even be able to find the key for you and decipher the code."

Jack listened to Wilbur's plea. Milbrodale? He'd never heard of it. Then again, he'd never heard of most of the backcountry towns in Australia. He'd grown up in the city. After his rugby career ended due to a catastrophic knee injury, no team would even take a look at him. So Jack did the only thing he ever knew how to do. He mugged people, beat people up, and he did it well. When Bernard Holmes offered him a job, he sharpened his skills further and eliminated anyone who stood in his way.

He considered Wilbur's offer. The portly man was injured. He'd slow things down. His request for a doctor was absurd. No way Jack was going to take the guy to a hospital. That meant he'd have to take him to Holmes's private physician, a man who only worked for cash.

There was another option that Jack kept coming back to. He didn't need Wilbur anymore.

"I have to say, Willy, you do a good job of begging. I mean, you really go for it with the tears and the choking voice thing. I've seen my fair share of it through the years, and you're probably one of the best."

Wilbur's eyes filled with hope. "Does that mean you're going to take me with you? You won't regret it. I promise."

"Actually, no. You see, they invented this new thing called the internet where I can find information on pretty much everything I need—say, a map for example. So I can find this cave and Milbrodale on my own. Seeing how you probably wouldn't know what to look for or where to look for it when we got there, there's really no point in me bringing you along. And then there's the problem of your bleeding shoulder. I can't have you getting blood all over the interior of my car. I just had it cleaned two days ago. I'm sure you can appreciate my predicament."

Fear crept back onto Wilbur's face. "Okay, sure. You don't have to take me along. I can take myself to the hospital. No worries."

Jack wagged the gun around carelessly. "Now you see, I can't have that either."

"Why not? I won't tell anyone what happened. I'll tell them it was an accident. They'll never know."

"Ah yeah, but there will be an inquisition, Willy. Those docs are nosy types. Always trying to get to the bottom of things with their reports and such. Sooner or later they'll come around. And you don't exactly strike me as the strong type who can keep his yap shut."

Wilbur's desperation reached its height. "I'm an investment, Jack. Mr. Holmes has spent a good deal of money for my help. He won't be happy if you do this."

A thin, sickly smile crossed Jack's lips. "Do you really think Mr. Holmes cares about that paltry sum he gave you? He writes off ten times that every year. He won't have a problem with me writing you off as well."

"No. Please. I can. I won't say anything."

"I know you won't, Willy. I know you won't."

The muzzle flashed suddenly. For a moment, Wilbur's body wavered, leaning one direction and then the other. The bullet hole in his forehead made sure he was dead before he hit the floor.

"There you go, Willy," Jack said, taunting the dead man. "Have a rest. You've had a tough day."

Jack stepped over the body and made his way to the front of the room. He stopped next to the document and leaned over. For a brief moment, he considered stealing it, but it was the same as the one he had in his email. Email could be accessed through his phone. Carrying that paper around was a pointless hassle.

He strode out the door and closed it behind him. A quick search on his phone yielded the results he wanted. It was getting late, so he'd wait until morning to head to Milbrodale. No way his quarry was going there tonight. They'd be exhausted from their journey. He might as well catch a little sleep too.

Tomorrow, he'd get the key to the cipher and take out the Americans.

Chapter 11
Milbrodale

Sean got out of the car and stretched his legs. Then he put his arms over his head and stretched them as well.

The drive from Sydney to Milbrodale took right at two and a half hours, although Reece claimed he could make it in two flat. The cave was only a few minutes away from the little town. Its location was on private property, but the owners allowed visitors due to the historic nature of the cave.

The others got out of the car and looked around.

Reece was the first to speak up. "Awfully quiet around here."

They got an early start in an effort to beat any tourists to the site. Tommy and Sean had long ago found it best if they could work without prying eyes on them at all times. Their plan had worked for now. They were the only people around.

"Let's take a look at this thing," Sean said.

He led the other three up the steps of a narrow trail until they reached the huge overhang known as Baiame Cave.

"Looks just like in the pictures I saw online," Tommy said.

"Yeah, but it's much bigger than I expected," Adriana added.

The cave drawing of the Aborigine god Baiame stood out against the backdrop of sandstone. The body of the deity was thin with a bald head, painted a dark reddish brown. Two bright white orbs occupied where the eyes would be. While the legs were fairly long, the arms were what most people noticed first. The long appendages stretched more than a dozen feet across the cave ceiling. Under the arm to the right, two illuminated boomerangs were depicted hanging in midair. To the left, tracings of hands and tools were surrounded by a chalky white substance.

"How old is this thing, again?" Sean asked.

"Some have suggested thirteen thousand years," Tommy answered.

Sean raised an eyebrow. "Give or take a few thousand, right?"

"Almost always."

Adriana stared up at the cave art, mesmerized. "This is incredible. It's just stunning to look at."

"Indeed," Sean said.

The four stood silent for a minute before Reece spoke up again. "So what is it exactly that we're looking for?"

"A foreign stone," Sean answered. "Turned and unturned."

"That second part is a little odd. What do you think it means?"

"No idea."

Tommy stepped closer to the ceiling, keeping to the path so as not to disturb the integrity of the site. He tilted his head one way and then the other. "Maybe there's something in the drawing we're supposed to figure out. Look at these hands." He pointed to the left side of the figure. "They appear to be in sort of random positions. But if you look closely, you'll see it looks like they're turning from one spot to another."

"Maybe," Adriana said. "But is this whole thing a foreign stone?" She put her hands out wide. "This cave rock looks just like the other rocks from around here."

"She has a point," Sean said.

Tommy put his hands on his hips. "So what is it then?"

No one had an answer.

"Maybe we should have figured that out before driving two-plus hours to get here," Reece joked. He chuckled and then noticed Tommy's ill expression. "Hey, I'm only kidding with you. We'll figure it out."

Sean stepped back away from the viewing area and gazed at the cave art. *A foreign stone, turned and unturned.* He ran the words from Mathews's document through his mind. *This stone couldn't be turned, not by anything they had back then. It's too big. He had to be referring to a different rock, something smaller that he could have turned around or moved.*

Sean twisted his torso and looked back down the hill. The slope was covered in tall grass that waved in the morning breeze. Something caught his eye. It was dark, unmoving. Was it an animal?

He walked away from the cave entrance and down the slope, wading through the grass and ignoring the signs that requested visitors stay on the path.

"Sean, where you going?" Tommy asked.

"Just looking at something."

He didn't turn around until he reached the strange piece of rock sticking out of the ground. It came up just past his waist. The stone probably went unnoticed by most visitors to the area, especially since it appeared that the grass was never trimmed. He put his hand on the rock's rough surface and bent down to get a better look at it. Sean wasn't sure what he was seeing, but one thing was certain: this stone wasn't from around here.

He got down on his knees and studied the earth around the anomaly. At first, he didn't notice any clear evidence of tampering. As he looked closer, however, Sean noticed a slight indention in the surface close to the downhill side of the rock's base. After a second inspection, he realized the groove matched the width of the rock almost perfectly.

"Hey, guys!" he shouted.

"We're right here," Tommy said.

The other three walked up to the rock as Sean whipped his head around, surprised to see they'd followed him. "Oh, good. You're here. Take a look at this."

Sean pointed at the indention in the ground. "It's hard to tell at first, but this thing was definitely moved at some point."

"You're right," Reece said. "You can see where the ground is a quarter inch lower there."

"Did you see anything that would pass for a cipher key?" Tommy asked.

Sean's head swiveled back and forth. "Nope. Just the rock."

Adriana stepped closer and examined the earth. "Whoever moved this did it for a reason. And they would have put it back to hide whatever it was they found. Maybe we should turn it over."

The three men balked.

"We're on private property," Tommy said. "Not to mention, tampering with a historical artifact is a big no-no."

Sean twisted his head around in both directions. "I don't see anyone. If we work fast, who will know?"

"Are you serious?"

"Look, all I'm saying is we see if this thing turns over or not. If we give it a little shove and it topples, we take a look at the bottom. If it doesn't move, no harm no foul."

"I'm game," Reece said. "Why not?"

"What? Really?" Tommy didn't stop his protest. "I just told you why not."

"Come on, Tommy," Adriana prodded. "Live a little."

Tommy sighed. His eyes flashed around the property to make sure no one was, in fact, around. "Fine. But let's make this quick."

The other three grinned at his reluctant concession.

"It's gonna be hard for us to move that thing with our hands," Reece said. "It would help if we had some rope."

"Huh," Tommy said. He fired an "I told you so" glance at Sean. "I'll be right back."

Sean put his hands on his hips, incredulous. "I can't believe you brought the rope again."

Tommy trotted down the slope toward the car and didn't look back as he responded. "You're welcome!"

A moment later he was back at the rock and looping it around the top. He secured it with a tight knot and then gave it a firm tug to make sure it was secure. Then he whipped out the rest of the slack down the hill from the stone.

The others had been watching him with curious interest as Tommy worked.

"So, we gonna do this like a tug of war?" Sean asked.

"Yep."

"Okay. Sounds like a plan. Reece, take the anchor spot."

The big Aussie nodded and grabbed the end of the black rope, looping it around his waist. He held it firmly in both hands. His forearms flexed as he readied himself for the pull. Sean took position in front of him, then Adriana, and then finally Tommy closest to the rock.

"On your mark, Tom," Reece said.

The four gripped the rope tight and waited for Tommy's signal.

"Ready?"

Everyone else echoed the word. "Ready."

"Pull!"

The group tugged hard, too hard. They weren't ready for the rock to budge so easily. The big stone toppled over on the first pull, and the four visitors lost their balance.

Reece fell straight on his back. Sean tripped over him and landed on top. Adriana felt the slack and deftly dove to the left of the two men. Meanwhile in the front, Tommy staggered backward several steps, waving his arms wildly until he lost his balance and collapsed onto the other two men.

Adriana put her hands on her hips and stared down at the goofy pile of guys near her feet. The men scrambled to get off of each other, but not before she started laughing.

"Okay, fellas. Break's over."

She stalked back up the hill to the rock and crouched down to have a closer look. Once the guys were back on their feet, they joined her—huddling around to see if there was anything under the stone's base.

Adriana wiped away some of the dirt sticking to the bottom. A small colony of insects scattered on the ground—probably seeing the light of day for the first time in their lives.

"Rows of circles within circles," she said.

"That's how the Aborigines kept time," Reece said. "They based everything on the rising and setting of the sun."

"Lots of ancient cultures did," Tommy added.

"Right. Looks like there are forty-five circles in all."

"Must be the forty-five suns Mathews's paper mentioned," Sean said.

"Yeah," Tommy agreed. "But look at what's etched below them."

Four sets of eyes gazed at the two rows of letters. Underneath each letter, a symbol was carved into the rock.

"Get a few pictures, Tommy," Sean said.

His friend snapped out of a mesmerized haze and gave a slow nod. "Yeah. Yeah.

Picture." He took a couple of pictures with his phone and then put it back in his pocket. "Turned and unturned," he whispered the words from the Mathews document. "Mathews must have found these circles and then put the rock back after he carved these symbols and letters into the base."

"Sounds like an awful lot of trouble," Reece said. "I'd have just left it there."

"Then anyone could find the key," Sean said. "He had to keep it hidden. Whatever Mathews and his friend were looking for must be pretty important."

"Or valuable," Adriana added.

"We need to get this rock back up where it belongs before someone comes around and notices," Tommy said, already starting to worry.

"Good idea."

The group flipped the rope around and carried it uphill.

"This is gonna be a lot tougher than knocking it over," Reece commented. "Better put your backs into it."

When Tommy gave the signal, the four pulled on the rope. This time, it didn't move easily like before. They grunted, dug their heels into the ground, and leaned back with every ounce of strength they could muster.

The top of the rock began to rise.

"It's moving," Tommy grunted. "Keep going."

Their arms flexed. Leg muscles burned. The rock rose slowly from its temporary resting place. As it reached the apex, the burden suddenly shifted.

"Whoa," Tommy nearly shouted. "Easy now."

The four eased up on their efforts and pulled less to make sure the thing didn't topple over the other way.

The rock's base hit the ground with a thud and came to rest exactly where it had been for so many years before. Beads of sweat collected on the foreheads of the visitors. The sun loomed higher in the sky now, beating down on them with an ever increasing heat.

"Let's get back to the air conditioning of the car and grab a bite to eat in town," Sean suggested. "Looked like there were some good places we passed on the way in."

The others agreed and started down the hill toward the car. Sean stayed by the rock for a moment, looking across the hills and meadows. The little alarm in his head was ringing. He didn't know why, but something was off.

It was a sense that he'd had since the days of working for Axis. Tommy called it paranoia. Sean called it survival instincts. He didn't feel it all the time—only when trouble was near.

The drive up from Sydney, he'd not felt it in spite of keeping an eye on the rearview mirrors to make sure they weren't being followed. That, too, was an old habit.

This was something different, though. It was the overwhelming sense that they were being watched.

Chapter 12
Milbrodale

"What do you usually eat for breakfast around here, Reece?" Tommy asked as the group got back in the car to leave. Sean brought up the rear, getting in the back seat with Adriana.

"Fried kangaroo."

Tommy had started to turn the key in the ignition but stopped and looked across at his friend with an appalled expression. "No. Seriously, that's gross."

Reece burst out laughing and glanced at the two in the back. Sean and Adriana snickered at the joke.

"Nah, Tom. Come on, man. We eat the same sort of stuff as you: bacon, eggs, toast, you know."

Tommy eyed the Aussie for another second before he was satisfied the man was telling the truth. He started the car and drove it back out onto the country road leading into town.

"There were a few promising spots we passed on the way in," Reece said. "Even though it's a bit late for breakfast, I bet they're still serving it."

"Doesn't matter to me," Tommy said. "Now that you mention it, lunch would be fine too." He didn't tell Reece that he was still thinking about the fried kangaroo comment.

Adriana turned to Sean. "We need to get Tommy a girl," she said quietly.

Tommy looked back at them in the rearview mirror, certain he'd heard his name. He missed the comment, though.

Before he could say anything, Reece interrupted. "What's this guy doing?"

He pointed at an old truck sitting sideways in the middle of the road. The vehicle looked like many Reece had seen in the outback on his adventure tours—used mostly by locals to haul stuff around on their property.

Tommy tapped the brakes. "I don't know, but we can't get around him."

The man next to the pickup truck was wearing a white T-shirt and gray pants. From a distance he appeared to be tall and muscular. His face seemed friendly enough. Maybe he was just happy to finally see another driver approaching. After leaving the Milbrodale city limits, the visitors hadn't seen another car coming or going.

The stranger waved eagerly to the oncoming car, and Tommy stopped only twenty feet away. He shifted the car into park and started to get out.

"Wait," Sean said. He peered through the windshield.

"What? I'm gonna ask this guy if he needs our help. It's not like we can get by him anyway."

"No. Don't open the door. It's an ambush."

The stranger tossed a rag into the bed of his truck and put his hands on his hips, waiting for someone to get out.

"What?" Tommy asked. He turned around and faced his friend. "An ambush? Who would ambush us out here? No one even knows we're in the area."

Sean's eyes never wavered. They remained locked on the man by the truck. "What's wrong with his pickup?"

Tommy eased back into his seat and faced forward. "Looks like he must have had some engine trouble. The hood's up. See, there's smoke coming out of the radiator." A faint waft of steam flowed out of the open pickup's hood.

"I don't like it," Sean said. "Why did he have to block the road like that?"

"I agree with Sean on this one, Tom," Reece said. "It is a bit unusual."

The stranger by the truck had a quizzical expression on his face, wondering what the delay might be.

"Put the car in reverse, Tommy, and slowly back away." Sean's even tone was full of warning.

"Are you serious? We're not gonna help this poor guy? It's burning up out there."

"Do it, Tommy."

Tommy hesitated for a second. Sean's instincts were rarely wrong about things like this, no matter how much Tommy detested admitting it. If Sean sensed something was amiss, it paid to listen.

"Okay, fine. But it's rude. I mean really rude. Imagine if you were that poor sap out in this heat with a broken down piece of crap truck like that and someone who could help rolled up and then backed away. I guess you never heard the story about the good Samaritan."

Tommy shifted the car into reverse and took his foot off the brake, letting the car ease back just faster than at an idle.

The stranger put out both hands as if to ask what they were doing.

Tommy's initial reaction was to look through the windshield. The stranded man no longer appeared desperate. He wore a menacing expression and held a black pistol out at arm's length. The muzzle flashed, accompanied by a loud pop. The bullet scraped the top of the car. He fired again, over and over.

It only took one shot for Tommy's instincts to kick in. He jammed his foot on the gas, and the car lurched backward. The engine whined, straining at the irregular speed in reverse. Steering proved to be problematic, but

Tommy jerked the wheel right and left, at least keeping the vehicle on the road.

The stranger took off on foot, chasing after them and still firing. One round found the left headlight. Another one nicked the windshield frame.

Tommy was about to whip the car around and shift into drive when he saw something coming in the rearview mirror.

Two black SUVs stormed toward them from a few thousand feet away—and were closing fast. The SUVs were taking up both lanes, giving Tommy and his passengers no way to escape.

"You know," he said to Sean, "now would be a good time to do some of that secret agent stuff you do so well. No pressure. Just a thought."

"Way ahead of you. Just slow down a little, but keep your foot on the gas."

Sean rolled down his window, but it stopped just above halfway down. "Oh, you gotta be kidding me."

"Child proofed?"

"Yeah."

Taking a cue from Sean, Adriana had retrieved her gun and rolled her window to the same stopping point. "I'll have to kick this out."

Adriana lay across the back seat, holding Sean in a tight hug to keep her balance.

"Ready?" Sean asked.

She winked at him. "Always."

"You are so beautiful."

"Anytime, guys!" Tommy shouted. "They're gonna ram us!"

Sean gave a nod. Adriana kicked, driving her heels through the glass and shattering the window to hundreds of pieces. They rolled up and poked their weapons out of each back window at the oncoming SUVs—now only a few hundred feet away.

"Wait for it!" Sean shouted at Adriana over the howling wind. "One more second!"

The trucks were within a hundred feet.

"Light 'em up, babe!"

Their pistols popped repeatedly. Tommy had slowed their car to keep it as steady as possible. Even at the slower speed, shooting from a moving vehicle presented a challenge. Fortunately, this wasn't their first time.

Sparks erupted from the asphalt near the SUVs' tires. One headlight exploded on the one to the right. Another round zipped through the windshield on the left, sending a cracked web across the glass.

The two SUV drivers panicked. The one on the right swerved toward the road's shoulder. The one on the left did the same at first, but seeing he couldn't escape the hail fire of bullets, jerked the wheel too far back the other direction. The vehicle veered right into the front quarter panel of the other in a violent thud and scream of metal. It plowed ahead and off the road, skipped the ditch, and smashed into a big tree. The SUV it struck twisted for a second and then flipped onto its top, rolled another forty feet, and then came to a rest on its side.

Sean sat back in the car while Adriana squeezed off the rest of her rounds at the closer of the two wrecked SUVs.

Another pop echoed from the road ahead. A round tore through the windshield and thumped into the leather of the back seat, just inches from Sean's head.

The stranger was still running after them, though he was losing ground with every step. The shot he'd fired was a lucky one from that distance. Even Sean wasn't accurate from that far away.

"Tommy?" he said.

"On it."

Tommy whipped the steering wheel to the right, and the car swung around hard, squealing rubber on asphalt. In the same motion, he flipped the gear shift into drive and stepped on the gas. Once more, the tires screeched. The car fishtailed for a second until Tommy corrected it and sped away.

In the rearview mirror, he saw the stranger jog to a stop and hold his weapon out for one last shot. The muzzle flashed, but the round sailed off to the right and plunged into the dirt.

Five seconds later, Tommy steered the car around a curve and out of harm's way.

He took a look back in the mirror at his passengers. "You guys okay?"

Sean checked Adriana and then nodded. "Yeah, we're good."

"Light 'em up, babe?" Tommy said. "Really? Since when do you say stuff like that?"

Sean smirked. "Got the job done, didn't it?"

"You guys are crazy!" Reece shouted. "Woohoo! Man, I miss you two!"

Tommy didn't share the Aussie's enthusiasm. "Reece, we were almost killed."

"Sure beats being bored to death. I mean, that's what was happening."

Tommy let out a sigh of relief. "Who were those guys, anyway?"

Sean slid a fresh magazine into his weapon. When it clicked, he pulled the slide back—just in case. "If I had to guess, I'd say it was the people responsible for bombing your building."

"No kidding. But that doesn't answer the question."

"I can't put my finger on it," Reece spoke up again, "but that guy on the road looked familiar. I've seen him somewhere before."

"Everybody looks that way from a distance, Reece."

"No, I mean he has a look to him. Like he played rugby."

Sean agreed. "He did have that body type. Big traps. Muscular frame. Wouldn't want to get tackled by that guy."

"That still doesn't answer the question," Adriana said. "If they're connected to the people who bombed IAA, then that means they tracked us here. If they could do that, they won't be done yet."

"Ticked off anyone lately, Tom?" Reece asked. He nudged Tommy in the shoulder with his fist.

"No more than usual. I don't think that's it. Whoever they are, it has to do with that email."

He steered the car around an S curve. The road straightened out for a stretch, heading up a mountain. The dense forest kept them in the shade of the canopy. The windshield had a slew of cracks running through it in random directions, but there was enough clear glass for Tommy to see out.

"We need to ditch this car," Sean said, thinking about the damage. "Rental company isn't going to be happy."

Reece chuckled.

Sean faced Adriana. "Would you call Wilbur and double check to see if that email was seen by anyone else? Maybe he found something he missed before."

"Sure," she said and started looking for the number to the museum.

"There's something else we need to consider, too," Sean continued.

"What's that?" Tommy asked.

"Up until last night, we didn't have a clue where we were going next. Coming here wasn't part of our plan. We hadn't told anyone about it."

"But we did tell Wilbur." Tommy's epiphany sent a cold silence through the car. The only sounds were the steady moan of the engine, the rumble of the tires, and the whistling wind through the bullet hole in the glass.

Sean reached over and touched Adriana's hand. "Hold off on making that call."

Tommy flashed a questioning glance in the rearview mirror. "You think Wilbur told them?"

Sean stared at the road ahead as he answered. "Right now, I think he's the only suspect, which means we don't know who we can trust."

"Just business as usual for us, then."

"We wouldn't have it any other way, would we?"

Tommy snorted. "I guess not."

Chapter 13
Milbrodale

Jack stood in the middle of the road, staring at the empty lanes that curved behind the forest. His breathing hadn't increased much. The sprint after the Americans had been a short one. He was accustomed to far more grueling exercise.

He turned his head and evaluated the damage. The SUV that struck a tree billowed smoke out of the crumpled hood. No one moved inside, at least not that he could tell from his vantage point. The vehicle on its side also showed sparse signs of life, though he couldn't see into the SUV because he was facing the undercarriage.

Jack walked off the road, down a short slope to the smoking vehicle. He opened the driver side door and jumped back as the driver slumped over and fell onto the ground. His neck was twisted at a grotesque angle, broken on impact. Jack leaned over the body and checked the passenger side. The second guy was dead too, caught at the base of his neck by a bullet. His hands were covered in sticky red ooze from futilely trying to stop the bleeding.

Before he walked away, Jack rubbed his shirt on the door handle to take away the fingerprints. Then he stalked over to the SUV lying on its side. From this angle, he saw inside through the cracked windshield. The driver wasn't moving, but it looked like his passenger might still be alive.

When Jack reached the vehicle, he could see the passenger wriggling around, trying to free himself from the seatbelt. Jack walked casually around to the roof. The glass moonroof had ripped free during the SUV's series of acrobatic flips. Jack could see right through to the struggling man.

The guy had a three-inch gash on his head that streamed three trickles of blood down his face. Not a life-threatening injury, but certainly one that would require medical attention.

"You okay in there?" Jack asked. He leaned against the roof with his forearm like he had nothing better to do.

"Hey, help me out of here. I can't get to the seatbelt release button. It's jammed."

Jack had already noticed the problem. Now he saw another one. The man's leg was broken, twisted to the right from just below the knee. The guy had to be in shock to be so focused on getting out of the vehicle and not screaming in agony.

"He dead?" Jack motioned with one finger at the driver.

The passenger gave a reluctant nod. "Yeah, man. He's dead. Please, you gotta help me out of here." The desperation in the man's voice sounded pathetic to Jack. Two times in twenty-four hours he'd had to listen to the sounds of weak men begging to be spared.

"I can help you," Jack said.

"Thank you. Please, hurry. My leg's broken. I need to get to a hospital."

"Yeah, before I help you, though, I have to ask you a quick question."

"What? Just get me out of here, man!"

Jack cocked his head to the side. "Now, now. Patience. Being rude isn't going to make me help you any faster."

The passenger grunted, still reaching for the seatbelt release button. It was blocked by a twisted piece of metal jammed into the dash and running into the back seat.

Jack continued. "I am just curious about something. When you and the other truck approached, why did neither of you gunmen open fire at the target?"

"What? What are you talking about, Jack?"

Jack drew his weapon and checked the chamber. One round left. He pointed the gun at the man and paused a second. "I asked a simple question. The answer is equally as simple. Why didn't you shoot at the target."

"Are you crazy?"

"Don't make me use this bullet on you. We hired you four because you were supposed to be good at this sort of thing. And you went and made a mess of it. I just want to know, why you didn't take even a single shot at the target?"

The passenger grimaced. Either the pain from his broken leg was beginning to set in, or he realized the threat he faced was very real. "I don't know," he said. "I thought we were supposed to just box them in."

"Which you did...initially. That leads me to my next question. Why did this idiot and the other one think you all would lose a game of chicken against a smaller car?"

"I...I don't know, Jack. I wasn't driving. I don't know what was going through those guys' heads." He swallowed hard, and his pleas descended into groveling. "Please, Jack. I've answered your questions. Help me out of this thing."

"It's just that...if I saw a smaller car coming my way and the people inside started shooting, my initial instinct would be to shoot back. You have a gun in there, right?"

"Yes. We have the guns you gave us."

"Then again, I wonder why on earth you decided not to use them."

The passenger used the only excuse he could think of that wouldn't further enrage his superior. "Look, Jack, I don't know about the other guy, but I know I didn't want to risk missing the target and hitting you instead. I mean...you were out there in the middle of the road. If I opened fire, you could have been killed." The man swallowed hard again after he finished. He was definitely in shock. Extreme thirst was one of the symptoms. "Please. Help me."

Jack gave an emphatic nod. "Okay. I believe you. That makes sense. After all, I can't be dead, now can I?"

"No. No, you can't." The passenger's voice filled with relief.

"Except," Jack said, tapping his right cheek with an index finger, "that does bring up another issue."

"What? What issue? Come on, Jack. Get me out of here."

"Well, you see it's very simple. Mr. Holmes hired you four because he believed you were capable of handling the job. I have to admit, in spite of his misplaced belief, I really thought there was no way to screw this up, but you did."

"Just shut up and get me out of here, mate!"

Jack shook his head. "No, that won't do. You see, if I get you out, you'll have to go to a hospital. Well, we can't have that, now can we? I mean, doctors ask so many questions." He remembered using a similar line on the museum director the night before. "No, I think the best way to help you is to keep you permanently quiet."

"No! Jack, please—"

The gun blast cut him off. Jack straightened his neck and looked around. A sudden silence settled over the road. He took a deep breath of the fresh forest air and then started back toward the pickup truck.

He picked up his phone and called Holmes.

"What's happening?" the older man said.

"We have a problem."

After three seconds of quiet, Holmes responded. "Problems are what I pay you to solve."

Jack wasn't one to dodge responsibility. It was why he called his employer immediately instead of stalling, putting it off as long as he could. He believed in taking his medicine quickly and moving on. Jack also wasn't afraid of anyone. Was Bernard Holmes a dangerous man? Sure, in that he had billions of dollars. But Jack was dangerous too, in many other ways. There was a mutual respect between the two. If Jack didn't know any better, he'd say Holmes even feared him a little.

"I have confirmation the Americans weren't killed."

"Which ones?"

"All of them. They must not have been in the building when it blew."

Holmes thought for a moment before continuing. "What are you going to do about it?"

"We suspected one of them survived. We knew where they'd go and what they'd be looking for."

"Let me guess: they got away."

Jack remained calm and drew in another deep breath of fresh air. "Yes, they got away. I'll have to replace the men."

"How many?"

"All of them."

"All of them?" Holmes was on the verge of outrage.

"Yes. And this time, I'll handpick them myself. None of these cookie cutter guns for hire. Don't worry, sir. I'll take care of it."

Something still troubled the billionaire. "Fine. Do whatever it takes, but how are you going to find them again?"

"I already have an idea of where they're headed right now. I'll throw out a net. Sooner or later, one of the fish will swim in."

Chapter 14
Richmond, New South Wales
Australia

Tommy didn't stop the car until they reached the town of Richmond—a quiet suburb to the northwest of Sydney. He pulled into the parking lot of the first cafe they spotted and stopped the car in a spot around back. No one had been following them for the last hour or so, but he'd rather be safe than sorry. *Never make it easy for the bad guys.*

The four left the car and went inside the little diner. Two men sat at a counter, eating sandwiches and potatoes. Sean led the way to a table in the back corner.

When they were seated, a friendly-looking waitress in a blue dress with white collar walked over and offered to take their order. She looked about fifty years old, with a few streaks of gray running through her reddish-brown hair.

After they gave their drink orders and asked for a few more minutes to decide on food, the waitress returned to the counter to start pouring the drinks.

Tommy leaned in close like he was about to share a big secret. "So let's take a look at this."

He set his phone down on the table and opened up the image of the key.

"It might be easier if you send me that picture and then pull up the one from the desk." Sean suggested. "That'll save us the trouble of having to write everything down."

"Good idea." Tommy hit the share button on the image, and a moment later Sean's phone vibrated.

Sean set his phone next to Tommy's and opened the picture so they could compare them side by side.

"Okay," Tommy continued, "we have a message and a key. This might take a minute to figure out since the cipher is stacked."

"You figure out what you'd like to eat, yet?" the waitress interrupted.

Tommy nearly jumped out of his skin. He yanked his phone back like he was looking at something he shouldn't have.

"We'll just need another minute," Adriana said in a polite tone.

"Not me," Reece said. "I'll have a burger, cooked medium."

"You know what?" Sean said, "Four burgers. Although I'll take mine medium-well if that's okay."

"Same here," Adriana added.

"What if I don't want the burger?" Tommy asked, looking like he'd just lost his favorite puppy.

"Then look at the menu and decide on something else," Sean said. "I'd really just like to stop wasting this nice woman's time."

"It's no trouble, mate," she said. "You two Americans?"

Sean nodded while Tommy kept poring through the two-sided menu. "Just flew in from Atlanta last night."

"Oh, I've never met anyone from there. How's the weather right now?"

"Cold," Sean said. "Winters there are hit or miss. This year, it's hit."

"I know what you mean." She turned to Reece. "Now you're a local, for sure. But you," she pointed at Adriana, "I have no idea where you're from."

Adriana kept her tone as cool as her expression. "I'm from all over."

"Fair enough," the waitress said in a cheerful tone. She looked back to Tommy. "You decide on what you want to eat yet?"

He gave a defeated nod. "I'll have the burger. Well-done, please."

"All right, then. I'll have your food out in a few minutes."

She bounced away, and when she was out of earshot, Tommy slid his phone next to Sean's again.

"All that fuss, and you ended up getting the burger anyway," Sean said. His eyes dripped with derision.

"Yes, fine. I got the burger. Mind if we continue?"

"By all means."

Reece and Adriana shared a chuckle at the interaction.

"Okay," Tommy began, "let's take the first symbol here."

They worked for the next ten minutes, matching every sign to a letter on the key until they'd figured out the first five letters of the code from the desk.

As soon as Reece saw the fifth one, he stopped them. "Walkabout," he said.

The Americans looked over at him, expecting further explanation. Instead, he simply took another sip of his drink.

Tommy was hunched over the table with his elbows on the surface. He put his hands out, palms up. "You gonna elaborate on that?"

Reece leaned back and pointed at the phone. "The word you're trying to figure there is walkabout. It's a fairly unique term. Never heard it used outside Australia. Though, to be fair, I've not been in a lot of other places."

"You sure?" Tommy asked.

Reece shrugged. "You're welcome to go ahead and spend the next ten minutes trying to figure it out yourself, but you'll come to the same conclusion. It's walkabout, mate. And our food's here."

The other three turned just in time to see the waitress stop at their table with four plates of burgers and fries.

"Here's the well-done, for you," she set the plate down in front of Tommy and then passed around the rest. "Can I get anything else for you?"

"No, ma'am," Sean said. "This looks great."

"I'll be sure to let the cook know."

She walked away, and the group continued their conversation.

"Okay, I believe you," Tommy said. "It's walkabout. But what does that have to do with the Mathews paper? It doesn't make any sense." He picked up a knife and cut his burger in half.

Reece picked up his sandwich and took a big bite. He chewed for twenty seconds before he answered the question. "I have no idea, Tom. That's your department. I'm just the guide, remember?"

Adriana snickered. She held her burger in one hand while she stared at the phones. "Can you pull up the Mathews document again?"

"Sure," Tommy said.

He tapped the phone, scrolled to his email, and then opened the attachment. He slid the device closer to her and sat back to take a bite of his sandwich.

Adriana and Sean reread the document again. Sean spoke up first.

"This part about forty-five suns. That has to do with the passage of time. Essentially, it means forty-five days."

"Right," Tommy agreed through a mouthful of food.

"But we don't know how that applies to a distance."

Adriana's eyes widened. "Yes, we do." She set her burger down on the plate and scooted forward. "That's what walkabout means. The distance traveled is forty-five days on foot. Walkabout." She put her hands out like a blackjack dealer who'd just finished a shift.

The other three nodded slowly as they connected the dots.

"Right," Tommy said. "But that still doesn't give us the location. Everyone walks at a different speed."

"Yeah," Reece agreed. "Plus that direction is a little vague. Northwest?"

Sean pointed at the phone. "It says to begin with Baiame." He closed the picture on his phone and pulled up a map. A moment later, they were looking at the town of Milbrodale. "So we start there and have to figure out the distance."

"On average, I'd say people walk around three miles per hour, give or take," Adriana said. "If we figure that each of these circles represents a twelve-hour period of time for walking—"

"Why twelve?" Reece asked.

"Because that's the average length of a day over the course of a year."

"Oh right." The Aussie took another bite of his burger.

"So if we take twelve and multiply it by three, we get thirty-six. Then multiply that by forty-five, and we get 1,620." She glanced at Sean's phone and realized the task would be simpler with a real map.

"Babe, would you mind going over to that rack by the door and taking one of the maps?"

Sean grinned at her. "Sure." He got up and walked away.

Tommy's eyebrows furrowed. "Babe? What is it with you two?"

"What?" she said. "We haven't seen each other in a while." Adriana popped a fry in her mouth and grinned innocently.

Sean returned and plopped the map down on the table. While Tommy unfolded it, Sean finally had a chance to eat a little.

"Okay, we're here," Tommy pressed his finger to the map. "Milbrodale is up here." His finger traced up to the town they'd passed through earlier. He placed his phone on the chart near the bottom that showed two lines measuring scale to distance, and then pinched the edge of the device to mark it.

Sean realized what he was doing. "Very scientific," he said and took another bite of the burger.

"It doesn't have to be," Tommy defended. "Remember, we aren't sure 1,620 miles is the right distance. But it might be close."

"Fair enough."

"So, we take this and extend out until we get to sixteen hundred miles." Tommy moved his phone, held a point with his finger, moved it again, and repeated the process four times until he reached the point he believed represented the distance. "Any of you got a pen?" Tommy went from one blank face to another until another voice spoke up.

"You can use mine," the waitress said, hovering over Sean's shoulder.

Tommy looked up, momentarily surprised. She smiled down at him, holding a pen out.

"Thank you," Tommy said. "I appreciate it."

He took the pen and then drew a rough arc around the area to the northwest of his starting point.

"If you don't mind me asking, what are you doing with that map?" the waitress asked as she watched with keen interest.

"Looking for buried treasure," Sean said.

"Like a bunch of pirates?"

"Yeah, except without the boats," Reece added.

The woman seemed to accept the answer and walked away to tend to other customers.

Tommy was deep in thought, gazing at the map.

"You okay, buddy?" Sean asked.

Tommy's eyes blinked rapidly. "Yeah. Yeah, I'm good. It's just..." His voice trailed off.

"Just what?"

His finger was planted on a spot on the map just beyond the curved arc he'd drawn a moment before.

"It's Uluru," he said.

Adriana didn't understand. "What?" Adriana asked. "What's Uluru?"

"For a long time it was called Ayers Rock," Reece answered. "Though most of the locals knew it by its Aborigine name, Uluru. It and Kata Tjuta are major tourist attractions."

"Kata Tjuta?"

"Yeah. It's like the sister rock formation not far from Uluru. There are these three massive sandstone rocks the size of mountains. Each one's got a ravine separating it from the others."

"Wait," Sean stopped him. "What did you just say?"

"It's the sister rock formation?"

"No. No, the other thing—about the ravines."

"Oh. Yeah, there are three big rocks and a ravine between each one."

Sean pulled Tommy's phone close and went back to the email. He read through it again until he found what he was looking for. "The northern chasm of the three. That's what Mathews was talking about. The next place we have to go is in one of those ravines at Kata..." He struggled with the name.

"Tjuta," Reece finished the sentence for him.

"Thank you, Reece. Kata Tjuta."

"Okay," Tommy said. "I don't mean to be devil's advocate here, but let's break this down for a minute. Are we really sure that's the place to go? I mean, we're assuming someone was walking thirty-six miles a day for forty-five days. That's more than a marathon a day."

"They'd have to use horses or some other kind of pack animal," Adriana said. "Tommy's right. That kind of mileage would be nearly impossible under perfect conditions."

"And conditions are rarely perfect in the outback," Reece said.

"Hey, if you have any other ideas I'm listening." Sean finished the last few bites of his burger and took a sip from his beverage.

After a minute of consideration, Tommy put his phone away and looked hard at the map. "Right now it sounds like the only possibility. If you look around this whole area," he traced an imaginary line with his finger around a broad space, "there's nothing but wilderness and small outpost towns."

"Alice Springs isn't far from the park. Nice resort town," Reece said.

Sean dabbed his lips with a napkin and then set it on his lap. "So you're saying we're going to Uluru?"

"Yeah," Tommy said with a sigh. "We're going to Uluru."

"I knew you'd come around. I just wish there was a faster way to get there."

Chapter 15
Sydney

Annie stared at the floor. She'd not slept well since being thrown into this prison, or whatever it was. The mattress on the floor was soft enough. That wasn't the problem. Who could sleep when they were being held against their will?

She heard the floor creak just outside the door. It was a sound with which she'd become familiar. The noise came every time someone arrived to give her a plate of food or ask if she needed to use the bathroom. This visit wasn't one of the regularly scheduled times, so she wondered what was happening.

The door opened a moment later, and a man in a tight navy-blue suit with an emerald-green tie walked in. Based on the attire alone, she judged him to be wealthy. Who he was, however, remained a mystery. Something about his face was vaguely familiar, but she couldn't place it.

"Who are you?" Annie asked. Her defiant tone did little to keep the man away.

He pulled up a wooden stool and sat down, resting his arms on his knees. She remained on the bed, leaning her back against the wall.

"I'm the one who is deciding your fate, Annie."

Every ounce of her being wanted to jump out of the bed and strangle him. That would do no good. There was a guard at the door who would be on her in a heartbeat. All it would do is make things worse for her. Up to this point, she'd been imprisoned, but not tortured. That could change.

"I've already told your men everything I know. I don't know where any treasure is. I'm just a museum curator." Tears welled in her eyes, and she rubbed them back with her forefinger.

"Now, now, don't cry. There's no reason to cry. I'd prefer it if I didn't have to harm you, Annie. After all, I'm no monster."

"Then why are you keeping me here?" she pleaded. "I've given you everything I know. Just let me leave, and you'll never see me again."

"Soon, Annie. I promise." He looked around the sparse room. A few clothes were strewn about. The television remote was sitting on the floor next to her. "I'm just wondering, Annie, have you watched the news today?"

She eyed him with suspicion. "No," she muttered. "I haven't watched much television since your men brought me here."

He pouted his lips and gave an understanding nod. "Well, I recommend you watch the news today. Very interesting developments going on in the city."

The visitor reached down and grabbed the television remote and hit the power button. The flatscreen hanging in the far corner flicked to life. He changed the channel to one of the local news outlets and turned up the volume.

The sports anchor was showing Australian football highlights. When he finished, the screen displayed the score for a moment and then switched to one of the main anchors. The white text in the top corner of the screen displayed the words *Murder at the Museum*.

"In our top local story, it has just been confirmed that Wilbur Kurt—director of Sydney's Metropolitan Museum of Art—was found dead this morning in the basement of the museum. Authorities have confirmed that this is a homicide investigation. It appears Kurt died from multiple gunshot wounds. Police believe it was an execution-style murder and could have been carried out by someone he trusted."

Annie covered her mouth with her fingers. Her wide eyes filled with horror. A low screech escaped her lips.

The news anchor continued. *"For most of the day, there were no suspects in the case, and security cameras seem to have failed. We now know, however, the authorities have a released the name of a suspect: Annie Guildford—longtime friend and colleague of*

Kurt—is being dubbed the prime murder suspect. Police have searched Guildford's home, but have not been able to locate her. No motive has been established at this time. If you see Guildford or know anything concerning her whereabouts, please contact the New South Wales Police. She is likely armed and extremely dangerous."

"What?" Annie said in disbelief. "I didn't...how did..."

"How did you kill your longtime friend and colleague?"

"No!" she shouted. "You're a monster!" Annie jumped out of the bed and rushed him.

He stood quickly and punched her in the gut before she could block it. She doubled over and fell to the floor in a sobbing heap.

"Why?" she moaned amid a flood of tears. "Why did you kill him?"

"I'd be more concerned with why the police think you did it, Annie. Wilbur wasn't a good person. I paid him. After all, he's the reason you're here right now."

She clutched her abdomen with both hands and remained in a fetal position for another minute before she rolled over onto her other side. It took one more minute before she sat up.

"What are you talking about?" she said through clenched teeth.

"Wilbur worked for me. I paid him to let me know if anyone ever found anything by Mathews."

Disbelief flowed from her eyes. It covered her entire face. How was that possible? She'd known Wilbur for decades. Now he was dead, and he'd taken money from this man to betray her?

"I know it's a lot to take in, Annie. I didn't want things to have to go this way, but you see, I always get what I want."

Annie grimaced as she pushed herself up from the floor. A fresh surge of pain ripped through her gut. "All this time I've been locked in this room, no one has told me what it is you want. Your men have come to see me over and over again, asking me questions, seeking answers I don't have. Not one time has anyone even mentioned to me what all this is about. So, whoever you are, would you please just do me the honor of telling me what is going on and exactly what it is you're looking for? I mean, who knows, maybe I can help you."

She sounded beyond desperate. Her hands hung loose at her sides. She spoke the truth. Annie just wanted some answers. If she couldn't escape or wasn't going to get out of this alive, the least she could do was learn what was going on.

The man considered her plea for a moment and then answered. "You may call me

Bernard. And I am looking for a treasure of incredible value."

"Yes, I know," she said. "I got that much out of your men. But what treasure? What could be so valuable to someone like you that you have to kidnap an innocent woman and murder an innocent man?"

He raised a finger. "Ah, but Wilbur was not innocent. Remember?"

Annie still wasn't sure she believed what Bernard said about Wilbur betraying her, but for the moment she went with it. "Fine."

"As to the treasure, it will be one of the greatest finds of all time."

She put her hands on her hips. "Is that what all this is about? Your ego? You want to strut around with some treasure you found so you can get attention from the world?"

"Hardly." He almost laughed at the notion.

"Then what is it?" she begged. "You obviously don't need the money."

Bernard thought for another minute before responding. What could it hurt? When Jack found the treasure, Annie would be taken into the outback where she'd be bitten by a venomous snake. The press would have a field day with it. He could see the headlines now. *Murder suspect killed by poisonous snake while trying to evade police.* Of course, they wouldn't find the body for weeks, not until an anonymous tip from a camper came along.

"Very well, Annie. If it will help you get some sleep—which you obviously need—I'll tell you what it is I'm looking for.

"In the many Aborigine creation myths, there is one that stands above all others: the story of Baiame."

She thought fast to keep up. *Baiame?* That was the name she'd seen on the Mathews document.

Bernard kept going. "Baiame was the greatest of the deities, the creator of all things."

"You don't strike me as the religious type."

He smirked. "Oh, I'm not. But in this case, I'm willing to go on a little faith. Anyway, this Baiame character was revered by the Aborigines. Some still worship him to this day."

She wanted to ask where this whole story was going, but she decided against it. She'd already felt his wrath once.

"One of the myths surrounding Baiame refers to his great boomerang, a powerful weapon, but also one of the tools he used for creation. It is said that all boomerangs were designed from the great boomerang of Baiame."

Bernard paused for a moment to let the climax of his story build. "This boomerang can be seen on a cave ceiling in Milbrodale. It's been a historical attraction for a great many years. I'd heard stories, of course, about the great boomerang—how it was made of gold and could create life or destroy entire civilizations. For a long time, I didn't give the legends much credence. That is, until you stumbled upon the Mathews document."

Annie slumped back onto the edge of her mattress. "Are you telling me that all of this is about a mythical golden boomerang? That's it?"

Bernard put his hands behind his back and raised up on his tiptoes. He lowered himself back down and then drew in a deep breath through his nostrils. "As you mentioned before, Annie, I don't need the money. Even at its most outrageous sum, the golden boomerang of Baiame would be a drop in the bucket for someone like me."

"Then why?"

"Some men in my position are passionate about attention. They would seek to find something like this for no other reason than to elevate their egos, as you also suggested. I, however, am not doing it for that reason, either."

She shook her head as she stared at the far wall. "For what, then? What could be worth murdering innocent people?"

"I suppose it takes a little imagination, Annie. I doubt your line of work lends itself much to that sort of thing. As far as my plans for the boomerang, I'll keep those to myself for now. When things begin to unfold, you'll be one of the first to know."

He turned his back to her and started walking out of the room.

"You can't get away with this!" she shouted.

"Get away with it?" The man cocked his head to the side and looked over his shoulder. He shot her an expression like she was crazy. "Annie, I most certainly will get away with it. Who will stop me?"

Chapter 16
Uluru-Kata Tjuta National Park, Northern Territory
Australia

"Well, that was awful," Sean said as he stepped out of the car. He stretched his arms up as far as he could to the night sky. "Next time, we definitely hire a plane."

"I'll second that," Reece said. "Was wondering why you didn't get us a plane. Don't you guys do that all the time?"

"With everything going on back home, I thought it might be best if we stayed on the ground while we're here," Tommy said.

The drive to Uluru-Kata Tjuta National Park took them close to thirty hours, and that was driving in shifts—almost nonstop.

En route, Tommy called a hotel in Alice Springs and arranged for rooms. They still had three or four hours of daylight when they arrived, but after a long trip—a quarter of which was at night—they'd need a soft bed and some good rest.

The sun beat down from the western sky. The hottest part of the day had passed, and things would start to cool significantly as dusk set in. Reece had warned the others they'd need to leave the park before it got dark because they were unprepared for the conditions, which could be chilly at times.

Uluru rose from the plains, challenging the sun as it dipped lower in the sky. Sean had always wanted to visit the famed Ayers Rock, but this was as close as he'd get on this trip. They had to figure out what Mathews had hidden at Kata Tjuta. After all, a woman's life possibly hung in the balance.

"The trail's over here," Reece said, pointing beyond a wooden fence and a sign that warned people not to take photos.

"What's with the no-camera rule?" Adriana asked.

"It's a sacred Aboriginal place, this. We're lucky to still be allowed to visit it. Aborigines believe that rock formations are ancestors or even deities."

A reverent silence overtook the group for a moment.

Reece looked around at everyone. "I didn't say we shouldn't go in. Come on. We're burning daylight here."

He traipsed ahead and onto the path. The Americans shared a short chuckle and then followed after.

The trail wound through the flats surrounding the massive rock formations, bending around brush and small boulders. After several minutes, it straightened out and grew wider the closer it got to Kata Tjuta.

"You have to be careful out here," Reece warned as the group neared the three big rocks. "Nasty snakes and spiders in this part of the country." His comment seemed directed at Adriana.

"You don't have to worry about me," she said. "It's these two you need to warn. They'll freak out at the first sight of anything slithery or creepy."

Reece boomed a laugh that echoed off the sandstone monoliths.

"Not true," Sean said. "So long as the spiders and snakes are a good distance away—"

"And dead," Tommy finished.

"Right. Then we're okay."

"I'd be more worried about Sean climbing that rock right there." Tommy pointed at the giant stone to the left.

Sean stopped in mid-stride. "Wait a minute," he said. "The riddle claimed the clue was at the bottom of the chasm. Not at the top. We won't be doing any climbing today...I hope." He muttered the last two words to himself.

Sean's fear of heights had been well documented over the years. He wasn't sure where it had started, but it was something that had dogged him his entire life. Whenever he found himself somewhere more than twenty or thirty feet up, his muscles froze, and he could barely find the courage to move.

"I doubt we'll have to climb," Adriana said, coming to his anxiety's rescue. "Like you said, the riddle is very clear about the location of whatever it is we're supposed to find."

"Maybe we should go ahead and hike to the top anyway," Tommy prodded. "You know, for the exercise? Or maybe the view is worth the climb. I bet you can see hundreds of miles up there."

"Okay, I get it, Tommy. Let's all poke fun at the guy who's afraid of heights. Be careful what you ask for. If we have to hike to the top of that thing, guess who's going to pass out on the way up."

"Here we go again. I'll have you know, I've been going to the gym a lot more lately."

"Taking a spin class?"

"Yes...no!" He tried to correct himself, but it was too late.

Reece stopped and looked back at Tommy. "A spin class? You take a spin class?"

Tommy sighed. "Yes, okay. It's good exercise, and I'm trying to get in shape."

"So you pay someone to tell you how to ride a bicycle that isn't going anywhere?"

"Yes, now can we please just keep going? We need to hurry if we're going to get back by nightfall."

"All right, Tom. Relax. We've got plenty of time."

Reece led the way through the last bend in the trail. At the base of the mountainous rocks, the visitors were able to truly appreciate just how overwhelmingly enormous the formations were.

"I can see why ancient people would have had such respect for these things," Adriana said. "They dominate the landscape."

"Yeah," Reece agreed. "They're big 'uns." He pointed to the left. "Let's keep moving."

They marched for another five minutes until they reached the wide gap between the center rock formation and the one farthest to the north. A dry wind rolled across the plains and kicked up spurts of dust.

"I have to ask," Reece said, "do you guys have any idea what we're looking for? I mean in general, not just here. It's just that, I see why we're here at this place. We're looking for a treasure map or something. But what's the treasure?"

Sean and Tommy exchanged glances. Sean answered first. "Honestly, we're not real sure about that. For that Mathews guy to go to so much trouble looking for it and set up this elaborate crumb trail, though, I'd say it's gotta be significant."

"Yup," Reece agreed. "I was thinking the same thing."

"Don't you think that's something we should start considering?" Adriana asked. "I've been wondering the same thing. What if we find it but don't know what it is we've found?"

"I suspect," Tommy said, "that when we discover whatever it is, we'll know it."

"I hope you're right," Reece huffed. He stopped at the opening. "This is where the clue said to go." He pointed into the chasm between the big rock formations. "So keep your eyes open."

Tommy pulled out his phone and looked at the riddle again. "It says something about rivers marking the way. Are there any rivers here?"

Reece's head slowly twisted back and forth. "Nope. Afraid not, mate."

Tommy jerked back. "Wait. Then how is this the right place?"

"Rock art, Tom. Be on the lookout for drawings on the stone. I suspect that's what the riddle means."

"Oh. Yeah. I knew that," he lied. "Rock art and snakes. Got it."

"Actually, even though Australia has some of the most venomous snakes in the world, it's pretty rare when they bite a human."

"Pretty rare?" Sean asked with a twinge of apprehension.

"Yeah. It doesn't happen often, but it does happen. Usually when someone is drunk and showing off for a friend. Or sometimes when people are somewhere they shouldn't be."

"Like a rock canyon in the middle of the Australian outback?"

"Don't worry," Reece said. "We won't see any snakes. And if you do, just shoot it." He flashed a wink and loosened the pistol in his holster. He trudged ahead without looking back.

"That doesn't exactly instill a bunch of confidence, does it?" Tommy asked.

"Nope," Sean said.

Adriana shook her head and walked by the two friends. "Catch up, you two. Want me to hold your hand?"

"Technically," Sean said, "it's okay if she holds my hand." He followed close behind her, leaving Tommy alone at the mouth of the chasm.

"Just being safe is all," Tommy said to himself. "I like to be prepared. Nothing wrong with that."

Something twitched in the bushes twenty feet away. A shiver shot up his spine, and he hurried ahead to catch up.

The visitors stepped into the shade of the huge sandstone. Within the narrow confines of the chasm, the temperature felt noticeably cooler—at least by two or three degrees. The opening between the two rocks was fifteen feet or so at its narrowest point, but widened to thirty or more at its broadest.

The group stayed close together, especially Tommy. He nearly tripped on Sean's shoes several times as they walked deeper into the gap.

When they reached a point where the opening grew much wider, Sean branched off from the group. "I'm going to check this side. There are some shrubs blocking the view of the rock. Reece, you and Tommy take the other side."

"Good idea," Reece said. "Come on, Tom."

"So we're just going off the trail. Perfect. Good things always happen when you veer off the path." He muttered the sarcastic words to himself.

Adriana joined Sean on the right. They crept forward, carefully eyeing the base of the rock for any signs of what could be art. After a few minutes of looking, he stopped and shouted over at the other two.

"You guys find anything?"

"Pretty sure we would have let you know!" Tommy yelled.

"No need to be a smart aleck!"

"Then don't ask obvious questions!"

"You two are like a married couple sometimes," Adriana said.

Sean smirked. "Jealous?"

She shrugged. "Maybe a little." The corner of her mouth creased up the right side of her cheek. "Back to work, mister."

"Yes, ma'am."

They moved forward, scouring the stone for any signs of ancient drawings, but nothing appeared. It was only another three minutes before they heard a shout from the other side of the chasm.

"Sean?" Tommy shouted.

"Yeah!"

"I think we found it!"

"Be right there!"

"No, wait!"

Sean and Adriana exchanged a surprised expression and then ran out from the bushes and rocks, across the path and to where Tommy and Reece hovered around something on the rock wall.

"What is it?" Sean asked as they approached.

"See for yourself," Reece said and pointed at the wall.

They followed his finger to a point on the rock about waist high. The drawings were subtle, barely noticeable compared to most they'd seen in the past—probably due to exposure for a few thousand years. They were definitely man-made designs, though, and two of them stood out more than others.

Figures of people were etched into the rock, all standing around a bunch of squiggly lines. Again, there were several circles within circles, just like they'd seen with the last clue at the Baiame cave.

"What are they doing?" Adriana asked, putting her hands on her hips.

"From the looks of it," Sean said, "it's a bunch of people standing around water." He motioned to the wavy lines. "I mean, I'm just guessing those represent water. My expertise on Aboriginal drawings is a bit meager."

"No, that's a pretty common thing," Tommy said. "While their art may differ in many ways, if I was Mathews, that's what I would have thought it meant. Keep in mind, we're tracing his steps, not the steps of the people who left these here."

"Good point. Now my question is, what is that?"

At the base of the monolith, the flat surface of a creamy white stone poked out of the ground.

The other three looked where Sean pointed. The foreign rock almost blended with the color of the sand surrounding it, but not perfectly. It was shielded from the path by a few large bushes, and even if someone had noticed it, they likely wouldn't have thought anything of it.

Sean and the others knew better.

"Where light turns dark," Tommy said in a low tone.

Everyone took another moment to gaze at the odd rock before Reece spoke up. "So, dig it up?"

"Definitely. We'll need something to dig out the packed earth around it." Tommy bent down and then crouched to get a closer look. He shifted his feet to the right and brushed his back against a nearby bush.

A sudden hiss and crinkle of dried grass behind him froze Tommy in place. "Guys? What was that?"

The other three looked behind him and immediately saw the danger. A long snake with blended black and light brown scales coiled next to the bush only four feet away from where Tommy crouched, terrified.

"Is that what I think it is?" Tommy asked. His legs were already burning from being in a baseball catcher's position.

"Tommy," Reece said, "stay perfectly still."

"Easy for you to say. My quads are on fire."

"Don't move," Reece ordered in a deeply serious tone. "That's a fierce snake."

"Fierce snake? That doesn't sound good."

"It's a Liru. Locals call them Mulgas or King Browns. If you stay still, he won't come after you. Most of the time they don't bite people."

Tommy's voice trembled. "Yeah, you said most of the time. That means some of the time they do bite people."

"Don't you worry about that, mate. I got this one." Reece unbuckled the button on his knife sheath and flipped it to the side. Inch by inch, he carefully drew the knife—the whole time keeping an eye on his prey.

"Would you mind terribly hurrying it up a little," Tommy hissed. "Just shoot the thing."

Sean and Adriana had initially had the same thought, but Reece wasn't drawing his pistol for a reason. In the rocky chasm, a bullet could ricochet in unpredictable ways. They saw Reece's reaction and trusted the more experienced man's wisdom.

Just in case, however, Sean had his weapon at the ready.

Reece pinched the knife tip with his thumb and forefinger. The blade was a long hunting knife. Tommy remembered thinking it was a tad excessive when he first saw it. Now he wished Reece carried a long sword.

"Stay still," Reece reminded. He raised the knife over his shoulder and eased his right foot back to get a steady position. "It's still there, Tom. He's lookin' at you. Just relax."

"My legs are about to give out." Tommy said. Sweat poured down the side of his horrified face. His legs began to tremble violently.

"Steady." Reece sized up the snake one last time. "Steady, Tom. If I miss, it will just piss him off."

"Not helping, Reece. Can you just kill it already?"

Reece's arm whipped forward like a catapult. The shiny blade flashed through the air, only turning over once before the tip sank through the snake's neck just behind the head. Tommy fell forward against the base of the monolith, his legs still quivering.

"Did you get it?"

Reece swallowed and then gave a nod. "Yeah, I got him."

Tommy looked over at where the other three were staring. Reece's knife stuck out of the ground with a writhing serpent between the handle and dirt. Tommy got up and staggered over to where his companions watched the dying snake trying in vain to wiggle free.

It took nearly four minutes before the reptile stopped moving. When it finally appeared to be dead, Reece took a deep breath and stepped over to retrieve his knife.

"Wait," Tommy said. He put out a hand to keep his friend from getting too close. "You sure it's dead? I mean, give it another minute or two."

Reece flashed him a toothy grin. "He's a goner, Tom. Won't be bothering anyone again."

He reached down and pulled the knife out of the ground and kicked the dead serpent several feet away. It didn't move other than a few nerves in the tail causing it to flick around now and then.

Reece eyed the blood on his blade and then wiped it off with some leaves from the bush.

As he put the knife back in its sheath, Tommy stared at him with silent admiration. "You know, for a second there I thought that thing was going to get me. Is that a very poisonous snake?"

"Mulgas? Sure. That snake has some of the deadliest venom in the world."

"You said they don't bite people very often. Were you just saying that?"

"Nah. They don't. Only a handful of blokes die from Mulga bites every year. That being said, their venom can kill ya in about forty-five minutes if they do get ya."

"It's a good thing you're so experienced with that knife," Sean said.

"This thing? I've never used it like that before."

Tommy's face grew instantly concerned. "Wait. What do you mean, like you've never killed a snake with it like that before?"

"Nah, Tom. I mean I've never even thrown it like that before. Much less to kill a venomous snake. To be honest, I wasn't sure if I could do it or not. I'll have to remember that little trick. Now, you blokes want to get something to dig up this piece of rock, or are we going to stand around here all day talking about snakes?"

Tommy stared in disbelief at Reece. Sean bit his lower lip to keep from laughing.

"It's not funny, man. I could have been killed," Tommy said.

"Oh don't be so dramatic," Sean said. "You heard Reece. It would have taken you forty-five minutes to die."

"Thank you. Very helpful. Now can we please just try to not talk about the snake anymore and dig this thing up?"

Chapter 17
Uluru-Kata Tjuta National Park

Finding anything useful in the way of digging tools was a chore in and of itself. Sean offered to run back to the vehicle to get some things, but Tommy insisted they didn't have time. The setting sun to the west wasn't slowing down, and dusk would be on them soon.

They still had a good ninety minutes of daylight, but Sean decided not to chase the point. Instead, they found some sticks and small rocks that served the purpose albeit slower than actual tools.

As they cut away at decades of packed dirt, the group realized the white stone was almost a perfectly shaped rectangle. It measured about two feet in length and eighteen inches across. Fortunately, they didn't have to dig very deep to figure out what it was.

Almost twenty minutes into their work, Sean stopped and pointed. "It's a lid," he said.

Adriana leaned over his shoulder and spied the inch-thick stone top. "And a matching box underneath."

"Would be nice if we had something to pry it off," Sean said, casting an accusatory look at Tommy. "Like, I don't know, a crow bar?"

Tommy sighed. "You may have to go get one of those," he resigned. He ran his finger along the seam between the stone container and the lid. This seam is too tight for us to use our fingers."

"And I don't feel like breaking my knife," Reece added.

Sean didn't put up an argument. He turned and trotted back toward the path and a minute later was out of the chasm and back on the main trail. The sun dipped low on the horizon, much lower than he believed it to be when he checked the time while digging.

It was getting late.

He picked up the pace and jogged back to the car. There were only a few tools in their gear bags for doing any sort of excavation: brushes, some small spades, nothing that would really help to lift the stone lid. The car's tire iron, however, did have a nice flat edge to it that would make getting leverage on the heavy object a little easier. Lifting it up enough, on the other hand, might prove impossible."

Sean grabbed one of the spades—just in case—and the tire iron, and started back for the chasm. Something glinted on the eastern horizon, and he froze in place.

"What's that?" he muttered. He kept staring out into the growing darkness to see if he could figure where the burst of light came from. His eyes narrowed, and he put the bridge of his hand against his forehead to shield it from the waning sun. "Must be seeing things."

From time to time, Sean's instincts were a little too on edge. He heard noises in the night that turned out to be nothing. That didn't keep him from staying awake for another hour on those nights.

He started back toward the gap and stopped again to give one last look. He searched the horizon close to where he'd seen the glint. Still nothing. Maybe it was an animal, a stray dog with a shiny collar, perhaps. Sean shook it off and hit the trail.

It took him less than eight minutes to get back.

"What took you so long?" Tommy asked.

Sean decided not to bring up whatever it was that had distracted him. No need to worry the others over nothing. "Thought we had more digging supplies than this."

He handed the tire iron to Reece. "Care to do the honors?"

"Sure."

"Why not me?" Tommy protested.

Sean's eyebrows knit together. "I don't want you to hurt yourself. And that stone looks heavy."

"It can't be that heavy." He crossed his arms and did his best to sound offended.

"I didn't say it was."

Adriana covered her mouth to hide the laughter.

Reece pressed the iron against Tommy's chest and stepped in front of him. "Excuse me."

Reece bent his knees and shoved the iron's sharp edge against the tight seam between the two pieces of stone. He had to wiggle it back and forth before it worked into the opening. Tommy and Adriana watched with intense anticipation. Sean, however, kept looking over his shoulder back toward the entrance to the chasm, just in case.

Reece tried to pry the lid up, but the iron's edge slipped out. He grunted in frustration and started over again, working the slim piece of metal back into the gap. The second time, he shimmied it back and forth in a wider arc until the flat piece was deep into the seam. He looked over at the others. "Be ready when I get this thing up," he said. "Brace it with your spades if you can. Then we can all get a grip underneath it and lift it up."

The others nodded. Sean and Adriana crouched down to the lid and held the little tools close.

"Ready," Sean said.

"I feel useless," Tommy said, still sounding pouty.

"You are. Okay, Reece, do it."

Before Tommy could retort, Reece lifted the tire iron. He used as much leverage as he could and—at the same time—kept shoving the thing forward so it wouldn't slip out. As soon as the heavy lid was a few inches off its seat, Sean and Adriana wedged the flat ends of their spades under it. Reece pulled the iron out and dropped it on the sand. The lid stayed elevated, propped up at a tenuous angle.

"Should probably go ahead and get this thing open all the way," Reece said. "Don't know how long those little shovels are going to hold."

Tommy stepped in next to him and grabbed the underside of the lid. "What are you waiting for?" he asked.

Reece grinned and gripped the lid. The two grunted and lifted the flat stone. Moving it was slow at first, but when they got it high enough, Sean had room to grab a corner and help. With his assistance, the thing went up easily, and a moment later, the lid reached its zenith and toppled over, crashing to the ground on the other side.

Dust erupted on all sides and sent up a cloud around the immediate area for a minute. The visitors waved their hands around to clear the air faster. When the dust finally settled, they all leaned in a little closer, staring into the white stone box. It was empty.

For a few seconds, the group didn't believe—or didn't want to believe—there was nothing in the chest. The drive, the effort to lift the lid, all the time they'd wasted, and for what? To find nothing?

Sean put his hands on his hips. "I have to say, I expected there to be something, anything."

"You don't think there was something in there before and somebody came along and took it, do you?" Adriana's question was the same one Reece was considering.

"No," Tommy said. "You can tell from the ground around the lid that it hadn't been touched in a long time, several decades at the very least. I'd say the last person to see this thing was Mathews himself."

"So why is it empty?" Reece asked.

Sean took his eyes off the chest and looked back at the chasm entrance. Darkness was settling across the land to the east. They were running out of time and needed to get to Alice Springs for a warm meal and a comfortable night's rest. He rubbed his eyes at the thought, the fatigue finally catching up to him.

As he was returning his attention to the disappointment at hand, he glimpsed the lid lying a foot or so away from the chest. He was standing close to it but hadn't noticed anything unusual when the top fell over. How could he have? An eruption of dust had blocked his vision, and their focus instantly switched to what might be inside the box.

Now he could see clearly. Something was written in the stone on the lid's underside.

"Guys," he said.

The others followed his gaze and realized what had caught Sean's attention. They looked at the lid and saw the words cut neatly into the surface.

In the royal valley the boomerang's water flows into the underworld, another secret kept.

"Royal valley?" Sean said. "What does that mean?"

"No idea," Tommy answered.

The only symbol that accompanied the words was the outline of a boomerang etched into the stone just above the cryptic sentence.

"Underworld?" Adriana spoke up. "Perhaps it's referring to a cave. Many native religions believe caves are the gateway to the underworld."

"Good point," Tommy said. "But we still need to know where it is." He turned to Reece. "You have any ideas?"

Reece had been more silent than usual. He stroked the scruff on his face with a forefinger as he considered the riddle. "Nothing comes to mind. Never heard of a place called the royal valley. Sounds like a place that I'd remember." He stopped himself.

"So you've never heard of it? You've been all over the place down here."

"I know. I'm racking my brain to recall if I've ever heard anybody else talking about it. Sorry, guys. Afraid I'm not much help on this one."

"No worries," Sean said. "We can figure it out when we get back to the hotel."

"Or over breakfast," Tommy added. "I'm wiped."

Reece thought for a second. "Right. Maybe a good night's rest will jog my memory. We can do some searching online and see if there's anything like that in the region."

"Fair enough. How far back to Alice Springs from here?"

"Not too far. It's just east of here. I'm including our walk back to the car and all. The staff at that hotel is really good. I've used that place before to stage some tours for travelers."

"I can't wait to get into a nice comfy bed," Tommy said. "That's going to feel amazing." He leaned closer to the lid and took three pictures with his phone. The LED light flashed brightly in the rapidly darkening chasm.

Again, Sean surveyed the area. Something had him on edge. He wasn't sure what it was. Things were too quiet.

"You okay, Sean?" Reece asked.

"Yeah," Sean tipped his head up. "Just thinking...and keeping my eyes open."

After the group put the lid back in its place and kicked some loose dirt and sand over it they walked back out to the chasm entrance. To the west, the sun dipped behind the horizon beyond Uluru.

"That's an incredible view," Adriana said.

"Sure is," Reece agreed. "Looks like we're getting out of here just in the nick of time."

A sudden rustling sound in the bushes ten feet away nearly caused Tommy to jump out of his skin. Before he could climb Reece's back, a little lizard appeared on the edge of the trail. The reptile looked around as if deciding which way it should go next. Humans, apparently, were no concern.

Tommy leaned over to get a closer look at the almost cute animal. As he bent down, a loud boom echoed across the plains. A huge chunk of rock exploded from the monolith in a burst of debris and sparks.

Sean and Adriana dove to the ground. Reece took an extra second before he reacted and dropped as well. Tommy was already hunched over and simply dropped to the dirt.

"What was that?" Tommy said.

"Someone shooting at us," Reece answered.

"Thank you very much. Yes, that much I get. But *who* is shooting at us?"

"Not sure," Sean said. "Thought I saw something earlier."

"Wait a minute." Tommy was incensed. "You *thought* you saw something? When were you going to tell us about it?"

"I figured it was nothing. No need to get you all worked up over something that isn't there. Besides, you'd have blown it off anyway. Probably called me paranoid."

"Now when was the last time I called you that?"

Sean started to respond, but Adriana cut him off. "Would you two mind terribly if we figured out a way to get out of here alive?"

"Yeah," Sean said. "I doubt the shooter is where he was before. We'll need to figure out his position and then flank him."

"What if there is more than one of them?" Tommy asked.

"One thing at a time. Reece..." Sean extended his hand. "Give me your hat."

Reece didn't question the request, though he wondered what Sean had in mind. Ten seconds later, he found out. Sean took one of the spades and stuck the tip inside the hat.

"Everybody stay down," he whispered. Sean held the tool at the tip of the handle and eased it up to mimic someone raising their head. He propped himself up on his elbow to make sure the hat would come into view.

Another gunshot rang out. The round tore through the hat and knocked it to the ground.

Sean turned his head in the direction the sound had come. "Got you."

"Tommy, you three head back toward the car. Don't go all the way there. Just go that direction. Stop halfway. In five minutes, I want you to snap another picture with your phone. Make sure the shooter can see the flash."

"Then he'll start shooting at us again," Tommy protested.

"Stay down, and he won't hit you. The flash will draw his attention. All I need is one more shot to pin down his location."

"So you're using us as bait?"

"Would you prefer to go after the sniper hiding in the weeds? Maybe there's another snake you can make friends with?"

Tommy hesitated for a second and then answered. "Fine. But I still don't like the idea of being used as bait."

"Remember. Five minutes, and then hit the flash."

"Yeah, yeah."

"I'm coming with you," Adriana said.

Sean drew a deep breath, ready to deny her request.

"It wasn't a question," she said before he could respond. "If the shooter sees you, you'll need someone else to flank him."

He knew better than to suggest she could get hurt. Adriana was fully aware of how much

Sean cared for her. She didn't need any chivalrous demonstrations. She was correct, too. Having one more person to flank the shooter wasn't a horrible idea.

"Fine," he said. "Go around that way. I'll take the center."

She gave a nod and scurried off in a low bear crawl. Sean looked back at the other two and shrugged. "What can you do? She's stubborn."

Reece's eyebrows were high on his forehead. "Good to see she's got you right where she wants you, mate."

He chuckled quietly and crawled down the path with Tommy tucked in right behind.

"She definitely does," Sean said to himself.

He looked out toward the coming darkness. There was no sign of the sniper—not yet.

As soon as the gun fired a second time, Sean had pinpointed the general vicinity of the shooter. He'd done the drill enough times blindfolded to be able to zero in on someone's location to within about fifteen feet. And that was in pitch darkness.

He crept forward into the bushes, saying a silent prayer he didn't encounter any more snakes like the one Tommy accidentally discovered. Gunmen he could deal with. Snakes hiding in the dark were something altogether different.

Sean kept his back down as he moved like a lion stalking its prey. The clock was ticking. He knew that Tommy would be on time. Sean figured the shooter was close to a hundred yards away from their position at the front of the chasm. Five minutes was more than enough time to cover that distance at a bear crawl. Sure, it would be exhausting, but he'd done it before. The problem was that he wasn't able to bear crawl the entire distance.

In several places, the ground elevated to the point where he had to get down and belly crawl, slithering forward a few inches at a time. The earth was rocky, too, and several times a jagged stone stabbed at his knees and hands.

His muscles started aching, especially his legs and abs. While he kept in good shape, it had been a long time since Sean had done anything this grueling.

Four minutes in, he'd only covered about seventy-five yards. He'd have to hurry if he was going to get to the area he believed the shooter was hiding. Of course, there was the possibility the sniper had moved. It's what Sean would have done if the circumstances were reversed. Sure, he never wanted to give up a good spot, but if you took a shot and missed, it was imperative to get moving.

Based on the proximity of the two shots the gunman already took, Sean figured the shooter had no plans on leaving until all his targets were dead.

He slowed his pace with twenty seconds left on the clock and crept forward, focusing on making sure his movements were silent. As far as he could estimate, he was within twenty to thirty feet of where the sniper had taken the other shots.

The sun was completely gone in the west. The dark sky to the east began sparkling with stars and a crescent moon in the distance. Sean waited, crouching like a predator about to pounce. He didn't know the exact position of the shooter. As soon as Tommy flashed his light, that would change. Sean just hoped he hadn't misjudged things.

Something shifted in the dirt about twenty-five feet away. It was subtle, almost unnoticeable, like a shoe grinding on pebbles in the dirt.

The next second, a searing bright flash burst through the area from fifty yards away. There was a quick movement, and then the shooter fired.

Chapter 18
Uluru-Kata Tjuta National Park

The muzzle erupted in a burst of flame. It was farther away than Sean had anticipated but still within the general area he suspected. He moved forward toward the silhouette that now stood against the starry backdrop. The long barrel of the rifle remained motionless, pointing out toward where the flash had come just a moment ago.

Sean closed the gap fast, keeping low as he rushed at the target. The shooter suddenly swung his weapon around, aiming right at Sean. The American dove to the ground and watched as the gunman's weapon suddenly jerked upward as he fired. The round sailed harmlessly into the night.

The sniper shook his head and grabbed the back of his skull with his free hand. He kept his senses enough to spin around and locate the person who'd thrown the rock at him.

Sean used the moment.

He lunged forward and plowed the man in the back with his shoulder. The shooter grunted and dropped his weapon. Sean felt his own gun dangling in the holster, but he didn't dare fire the weapon. Adriana was there in the dark somewhere. A stray bullet could hit her. This fight he'd have to win with his fists.

The gunman rolled over and swung at Sean's midsection. Sean straddled him for a moment. He slugged him with a right and then a left. The shooter's face was broad. In the pale moonlight, Sean could see the guy was strong—the type that hit the gym five times a week just because he enjoyed pain. The third punch was caught by a strong fist. The man's fingers wrapped around the back of Sean's hand and pushed it back.

Sean desperately threw a hammer fist. The gunman caught his wrist and squeezed with a vise-like grip. Sean felt himself struggling to push back. Then, with a big heave, the shooter kicked his legs up and caught Sean in the upper back with a knee.

The blow sent a deadly surge of pain through Sean's spine. He grimaced and felt his muscles weaken for the briefest of moments. The next thing he felt was his body being tossed through the air as the shooter flung him across the open space.

He landed in one of the nearby bushes, breaking little branches that scratched his skin on his drop to the ground. He winced again and tried to roll over, but the gunman gave no respite.

The man stalked over to the American. He started to reach down to grab Sean by the foot when another rock struck the man in the back of the head. He wavered for a second and then turned around. Adriana stood at the edge of the clearing in a fighting stance. The gunman's right eye twitched as anger coursed through his veins. He charged her with no warning, running full speed at the woman who'd just delayed his kill.

Sean reached for his pistol, but it wasn't in the holster. It must have fallen out in the struggle. He scrambled to his feet, desperately looking for the weapon.

"Honey?" he said. "Shoot him."

It was too late. The assassin surged at her with a roar. Her right hand whipped forward again at the last second, flinging another stone at the big man's face. The projectile struck true, hitting the attacker squarely in the nose. Now the shooter's size worked against him, and his momentum carried him forward even as his head rocked back. He lost his balance and tripped—knees skidding on the rocky soil.

Adriana coiled to the side and then unleashed a swift roundhouse kick to the side of the guy's head. The top of her foot made a sickening sound against the man's skull just above the ear. He fell sideways, still grabbing at the wounded nose with one hand and covering the new wound to his head with the other.

She didn't wait for him to recover.

Adriana leaped into the air, bending her feet underneath her body and leading with her knees as she fell. The kneecaps drove deep into the gunman's back. He gasped at first and then started coughing hard, desperate to catch his breath again. Adriana spotted a rock sticking out of the ground a few inches from the shooter's head. She grabbed his thick black hair and smashed the man's skull against the stone.

The gunman's body went limp. She released his hair and let the head drop to the ground.

Sean had scrambled his way out of the bush and rushed over to aide Adriana, but she'd already finished the job.

He noticed his pistol lying on the ground and picked it up. "Thing isn't supposed to come out of its holster that easily." His comment was more for his own benefit than hers. He motioned at the unconscious gunman. "You think he's dead?"

Adriana pursed her lips as she evaluated. "No, I don't think so."

"If he's still alive, he's gonna have a massive headache tomorrow." He checked her over. "You okay?"

She laughed and raised a dubious eyebrow. "Yeah, I'm fine. But you look a little beat up."

"That's what happens when you get your butt kicked." He stepped closer to the shooter and bent down. A quick search of the man's pockets only produced a thousand dollars in cash and a car key with a remote entry device."

"No ID?" Adriana asked.

"No. But he had to get his car somewhere. Only question is where he would have parked it."

Sean pressed the unlock button on the fob. He didn't notice anything right away, so he hit the lock button and spun around. That's when he saw the yellow lights flash another hundred yards or so away. The car was nearly invisible, especially in the cover of night. The gunman clearly wanted to stay as low profile as possible.

"We should check it out, see if there's anything else that might help us solve this whole case."

"Yeah, but what about him?" Adriana jerked her thumb back toward where the man's body had been just a moment before.

Now he was gone.

"What the?"

A dark silhouette jumped out of the shadows, lunging toward Adriana from behind. Sean shoved her out of harm's way as the big man plunged a knife down over his shoulder.

The blade missed Adriana's shoulder by inches. She rolled to the ground from the force of Sean's push and got up to see the knife that almost caught her off guard.

The gunman's momentum carried him at Sean. Keeping his balance, he reversed the attack and slashed the knife's edge upward to rip Sean's abdomen, chest, and throat in one deadly move.

Sean did the only thing he could. He fell backward, letting the blade's tip pass harmlessly by. He hit the ground—flat on his back—and kicked his right foot up as the attacker stumbled forward. His shoe caught the guy squarely in the groin. The gunman doubled over and groaned in agony. Sean kept driving his foot upward—now lifting the guy like a shovelful of dirt. He used the assassin's momentum and managed to get him off the ground, effectively tossing the guy eight feet beyond where Sean lay .

The would-be killer crashed to the ground in a clumsy roll. A fresh roar of anger escaped his lips. Sean pushed himself up off the ground and charged. The gunman regained his composure and stood up. His knife's handle protruded awkwardly from his side. Sean realized he must have fallen on it. The wound wouldn't be immediately mortal, but being so far away from medical attention...it might do the trick.

The big man yanked the knife from his body. He grimaced as fresh blood spurted out and splattered on the ground. His head trembled, and his face filled with rage. He roared again and raised the knife in defiance, motioning for Sean to come at him with his other hand.

"You know," Sean said, "I'm too tired to keep doing this."

He drew his pistol from its holster and fired a single shot into the man's chest.

The assassin took a step back and then another. He looked down at the new hole in his body and touched it with his index finger, almost as if he was curious. Then he winced and collapsed onto his back. His eyes stared up at the stars as the last few gasps of life passed through his lips.

Sean and Adriana rushed over to where the dying man lay and stopped a couple of feet short.

"I don't suppose you'd be willing to tell me who sent you," Sean said.

The gunman's lips quivered. His eyes searched the starry sky—for what, Sean and Adriana didn't know.

"Tell me who's behind this," Sean said with more force. "Where is Annie? Who has her?"

The man's breathing quickened for a moment, and then ceased completely. His eyes fixed in their sockets, unblinking.

Sean sighed.

"Did you really think he was going to give us any information?" Adriana asked.

"No," Sean said. "But you never know."

Tommy and Reece burst out of the bushes on the other side of the clearing. Sean spun around with his weapon raised, but he immediately recognized his friends.

"That's a good way to get shot, sneaking up on someone like that."

Both of them raised their hands at first and then when they realized Sean knew who they were, put them back down.

"We weren't exactly being quiet," Reece said.

Sean shoved the pistol back in the holster. "I know. We heard you when you were a good eighty feet away."

Tommy looked to Adriana for confirmation. She nodded. "It's true. You two aren't the quietest."

Reece pointed at the dead man on the ground. "I see you got the shooter."

"Did you get anything out of him?" Tommy asked.

"Unfortunately, no," Sean said. "He was pretty set on not speaking. Tough sucker, though. Didn't want to have to shoot him, but he didn't leave me much choice. Plus, I really need to get some sleep."

Tommy had his weapon in his hand and put it back in its place alongside his belt. "I don't suppose he has any identification or anything."

"Actually, we found the keys to his car over there." Adriana motioned to the general area where they'd seen the yellow flashing lights earlier.

"Oh, that's what that was," Reece realized. "We were wondering what was going on with that other car out there. Saw the lights flash and thought maybe there was a camper who'd strayed off the beaten path."

"We were just about to check his car for clues," Adriana said.

"Good idea," Tommy said. He faltered and then motioned for the others to go ahead. "Lead the way...you know, since you guys saw where it was and all."

Sean turned on his phone light. "Still worried about the snakes?"

"No...okay, yes. But you would be too if one almost bit you on the butt."

"Pretty sure the snake didn't strike at your butt."

Sean spun around before his friend could retort and started walking the direction he'd seen the flashing lights. He hit the button on the fob again. Once more, the lights blinked. Sean adjusted his direction accordingly and marched ahead with the other three right behind him. The lights from their phones danced along the ground as the group moved. Sean kept an eye out for snakes—just in case.

He wasn't as worried about them as his friend. That didn't mean he should be careless.

The group reached the car after only two or three minutes of walking. It was a five-door hatchback, gray with black interior. The color scheme made it perfect for keeping the vehicle hidden at night in the outback. That part was probably not in the shooter's plans. There was no way he could have known he'd be going after his targets at night. Or was there?

"Hardly a luxury car," Adriana said, staring at the modest commuter vehicle.

"Yeah. Strictly for utility purposes," Reece agreed. "See a lot of these from bikers and kayakers."

"Probably a rental," Sean said. "These guys are assets. They never use their own cars. That would leave a trail."

"Doesn't a rental leave a trail?"

"Not if you use an alias. The systems have made it increasingly more difficult to do those kinds of things. Pros still know how to get it done. They have connections for their connections. When you know the right people, strings get pulled."

"Remind me never to cross you," Reece joked.

"That would be a good idea," Tommy said.

Sean opened the front passenger door. He sifted through the glove box and found some paperwork. As he suspected, it was a rental agreement—signed for by a Jonathan Stout. No way that was the guy's real name.

Tommy opened one of the back doors and found a black book bag sitting in the floorboard. "Find anything?" he asked.

"Just the rental agreement. The guy was definitely working under an alias. No question about it, he was a pro. What you got back there?"

"Found a black backpack. Looks like something I used to carry around in college."

Black backpack? Sean thought.

"What's in it?"

"Haven't opened it yet."

Sean stood up out of the car and looked in the back seat where his friend was hunched over. Tommy started to unzip the main compartment to the book bag when Sean tried to stop him.

"No, wait."

Something beeped. Sean grabbed Tommy and jerked him back.

"Get down!" Sean yelled at the other two.

Adriana and Reece dove away from the vehicle and covered their heads. Sean expected an explosion, but none came. He looked back into the hatchback at the book bag. He frowned and patted Tommy on the shoulder.

"False alarm. Must be the guy's watch in the bag. For a second there I thought it was a—"

A sudden burst of bright white flashed from the backpack, and the car erupted in flames. The concussion blast hit Sean like a dump truck, driving him back fifteen feet through the air. He hit the dirt and shielded his face with his forearm from any falling debris.

He rolled over and stared into the burning wreckage for a second. Next, he checked to make sure Adriana and the others were okay. She and Reece had jumped for cover behind a boulder only twenty feet away from the car. They rose slowly from behind the big rock, both safe from the blast. Tommy wasn't far from Sean, lying on the ground with his hands over his head.

"You okay, buddy?" Sean asked over the crackling roar of the fire.

"Yeah," Tommy said, though his tone didn't sound so sure. "I'm okay. Just won't be going to the symphony anytime soon. Jeez, that was loud."

Reece and Adriana came out from their hiding place and joined the other two.

"I guess he had it booby-trapped," Sean said.

"Ya think?"

"We won't find anything of use to us now," Adriana said. "Might as well get back to the hotel and get some rest...if we can."

"Right. Good luck sleeping tonight, everyone."

Chapter 19
Sydney

"The shareholders aren't happy with your latest reports, Bernard. We were promised things would be better. So far all you've managed to accomplish is the same results as your predecessor."

Twelve sets of eyes stared at Bernard from their seats around the boardroom table. The sun had set nearly an hour ago. Its waning light filtered through the thirtieth-story windows and mingled with the sterile glow of the room's fluorescent bulbs.

But a white-hot light raged inside Bernard's chest—a fire, really, and one he had to temper for now. While he was the chairman of the board, things could change rapidly in the world of capitalism, especially in the oil sector.

The dozen ingrates around him were a greedy flock of vipers. Every single one of them would sell their own children if it meant another yacht in the Caribbean or another chalet in the Alps.

The man who'd spoken was a wealthy Aussie who'd made his initial money in real estate. When oil started becoming more prevalent in Australia, he was at the front of the line to get his share of the profits. A thin, bird-like character, he had a high hairline and a slender, pointed nose. His eyes, however, were piercing. When he wanted answers, he expected to get them quickly.

"Have you lost money?" Bernard asked. No one in the room responded. "No. You haven't. Every single one of you, to a man, has made 15 percent more than you did last quarter. You got a huge increase, and you're going to complain about it?"

"He's right, Bernard," another man to the right said. "You promised us we'd get an incredibly high return on our recent investments. Fifteen is good, but it's nothing close to what you said we could get."

The recent investments the man spoke of were an injection of funds the board had pooled together in order to purchase more land to the northwest of Adelaide. Reports had indicated large amounts of shale oil in that area. The problem was the owners weren't selling. They had no interest in becoming billionaires. Threatening them would have adverse effects and only make acquiring the land more difficult.

Fortunately, a solution to the problem had fallen right in Bernard's lap. He just needed a little more time.

"Gentlemen, of course you're right. I did make bold promises. And I have no intentions of letting you down."

"Your *intentions*...won't get us the money we were promised, Bernard." The man who spoke this time was one of the two oldest in the room. He was worth an incredible amount of money, and he carried the mantle of the board's respect. When he spoke, people were expected to listen. "You said we would get 1,000 percent return on the money we gave you. We don't care about your measly little 15 percent gains. We would have had that anyway. It's not like people have stopped using petroleum in the last ninety days."

The room erupted in a chorus of "Hear, hear" and "That's right."

Bernard put out both hands to try and get some order. It took more than a few minutes for the other twelve men to quiet down. When they finally did, Bernard stepped out from behind his seat and walked around the room. He touched the back of every chair as he passed by, biding his time before he spoke.

Every pair of eyes stared at him, waiting impatiently to hear his explanation.

"You men know as well as I do that things can change rapidly in the free market. One day, you're at the top of the food chain. The next, you're begging for scraps. It doesn't take much to be knocked off the pedestal." He stopped at the other end of the table and put his hand on the initial protestor's shoulder. "And make no mistake, gentlemen, we all have a target on our backs."

"We want results, not metaphors and long-winded speeches," the old man said.

Bernard pointed a finger at him and gave a curt nod. "Right you are, Jerry. Right you are. You all have risked a large amount of money, and you deserve to get what's coming to you."

"So when are you going to make it happen?" the second speaker asked. "And don't tell us to be patient. We've been plenty patient."

It was all Bernard could do to keep from yelling at the top of his lungs to shut them all up. There was a better way.

"Gentlemen, you have truly been patient with me. You really have. And I appreciate you putting your trust in what I have to offer."

He paced over to the window and stared out. The entire wall was covered in glass. The view of downtown was spectacular. The famous opera house stood next to the harbor about a half mile away. Holmes gazed out at the many buildings, streets, and sidewalks. People rushed around, filling their busy lives with whatever menial tasks they felt necessary. They were oblivious to the power play going on above. Holmes let his eyes stop on the building across the street. Most of the lights were off, save for a few here and there where people were burning the midnight oil.

Bernard paused for a second before he continued. He held up his hand and hit a button on a little remote. The lights dimmed, and a projector cast a map onto the far wall. The highlighted area was in South Australia, outlined in red. There were other locations highlighted in greens, blues, and yellows.

"The area in red," Bernard said, "is where our research teams have discovered an enormous deposit of shale oil."

Bernard's counterpart started to interrupt again, so he raised his voice and continued. "You will notice the areas surrounding it are some of the well-known oil deposits where drilling has already commenced or is about to. Some of those locations belong to us. That one in red, however, contains more than double what all the other areas hold combined."

"Yeah, it's also on land that's held by natives," a new voice chimed in. "You'll never get to that oil, not even if you waited a thousand years."

"What are you planning, Bernard? Some kind of drilling scheme where you go in sideways?" The chubby man who'd spoken up second laughed at his own joke.

The rest of the room joined in.

These laughing fools, Bernard thought.

Bernard put his hands behind his back and waited for things to die down again. When the noise settled, he continued. "Good one. Very clever." Bernard pointed at the man sitting at a middle seat. "To answer your question, Jaime, no, we are not planning on some sort of sideways drilling contraption to go in underneath the Aboriginal land." He paused again to let the drama build. "They are going to give us the land for free."

The room fell into deep silence. Bernard wasn't sure what to expect

"You're off your rocker, Bernard," one man finally said.

"He's lost his mind," another added.

Bernard held up both hands again to signal silence. "Please, hear me out. I know it must sound crazy to you, but I have received information about the location of something extremely important to the Aborigines. They would give anything for this relic. Soon, it will be in my possession."

"And what is this relic you're talking about, Bernard? Do you have it with you?" the old man asked.

"Regrettably, no. But I will have it in my possession soon, probably within the next twenty-four to forty-eight hours."

Jerry had lost all control. He stood up and pointed an angry finger as he shouted. "You talk about things that are out of your control as if they have already happened. I can't believe we're actually having this conversation! Relics? Have you gone mad? We are an oil company, Bernard. We sell oil to the world. Last I checked, we're not in the archaeology business. It sounds like it's time for us to make some changes to this board." He looked around into the other faces at the table. Several of the men nodded in silent agreement. "We gave this imbecile enormous amounts of money, money from our own pockets, because he promised us an astronomical return. You know what I think? I think he conned us. Where is that money now, Bernard?" He turned to the chairman who remained calm, staring straight at his accuser. "Where is it? Huh?"

Jerry put his hands out wide and waited for an answer.

Bernard's lips creased. He knew exactly where the money was. He'd taken over a billion from the men in the room. His intentions hadn't changed since he conceived the plan. Some of the money had gone to finding new deposits in the ground in South Australia. That was no cheap venture, either. It was time intensive, and the people who did that kind of work were highly paid. Still, that left Bernard with a large sum left over. He considered it an entry fee for the other men in the room, a way of paying dues to a membership that would give them incredible returns.

Now they were challenging him and his plan. Shortsighted fools. He'd known it would eventually come to this. Unlike the other men at the table, Bernard always thought two or three steps ahead, keeping his focus on the long game.

"As I was saying," Bernard finally spoke, "we will be able to negotiate for the land in the next forty-eight hours, although it could take up to a week before the preparations can be made. I think we can all agree that a week is not much time to wait when it comes to the tens of billions you will reap from this venture."

"He can't answer the question," Jerry said, ignoring Bernard's spiel. "You know what I think, Bernard? I think you stole our money. And now it's sitting somewhere in the world with no way for us to get it back."

Jerry was an instigator, an irritating flea itching the dog. Were they somewhere else—a dark alley, perhaps—Bernard would shoot the idiot in the face and leave his body in a dumpster. The thought caused a brief moment of pleasure as Bernard considered the irony of a billionaire's dead body in a heap of garbage. An assassination, however, wasn't an option. Bernard kept his composure, though, because he already had a plan for Jerry—and for the rest of the men in the room.

"Your money is safe, Jerry. All of your money is safe," he said to the others. "If you would like to get it back, all you have to do is tell me, and we will abandon the entire operation."

Several of the men grumbled, suggesting that was exactly what they wanted. One at the other end of the table in a corner seat spoke up. He was younger, in his midforties, with cropped black hair and a sharp jaw. "What about the money you spent on research and all that? I suppose we just take the loss?"

"No," Bernard shook his head. "I'll absorb that."

Surprised expressions washed over the room like the wave at a football game.

Jerry remained unimpressed. "That's very generous of you, Bernard. But I think we can all agree that Mr. Bernard has worn out his welcome as the chairman of this board. The decisions he's made over the last year have been reckless and imprudent to the finances of this company. The mere fact that he is willing to give up on this wild scheme of his shows that he is not committed to the company and its shareholders."

Most of the men nodded and voiced agreement to the statement.

"I believe," Jerry went on, "it is time we name a new chairman."

Bernard didn't hear any protests coming from the men in the room. They were unanimous in their thoughts. He knew they would be. It was all part of his plan.

"Very well," Bernard said. "If you want me to step down as chairman, I will. It is clear that our vision for this company and its future projects are not on the same track. I can accept that. I will resign effective immediately, and you can choose a new chairman."

"What about our money?" the old man said.

"You'll get your money. It will take me a day to get the transactions arranged and have it sent back into your accounts. I trust none of the information has changed?"

No one said anything, which meant it hadn't.

"Good. I'll begin the transfers in the morning."

Jerry stared at Bernard with suspicion. "How do we know you're not just going to leave the country with our money, disappear somewhere?"

Bernard cocked his head to the side and shot him a look like the guy was nuts. "Honestly, Jerry? Where am I going to go that a room full of billionaires couldn't find me? With all your resources, I'm sure there's nowhere I could go."

Jerry didn't say a thing. He actually grinned at the comment, probably because he knew it was true. It was remarkable what a few billion dollars could get.

"Gentleman, I apologize that this hasn't worked out. It's getting late. If you have no further business, I'd like to go ahead and retire for the evening. It seems tomorrow morning has a good deal of activities that will require my attention."

One by one, some of the other men stood up and stepped away from the table. They filed out of the room and walked slowly down the hall to where two brass elevator doors waited. Jerry was the last to leave. He fired a sinister look at Bernard as if to say, "Got you."

Bernard hung his head for a moment, feigning despair.

Down the hall, the two elevator doors opened, and the men stepped on board. Bernard drifted out into the hall and watched as the last of them entered the lift.

"Do you want to ride down with us, Bernard?" one of them offered.

"No," he waved a dismissive hand. "It would be awkward."

The guy shrugged and let go of the button holding the elevator in place. The brass doors closed on both lifts. Bernard took a step toward the end of the hall and watched. Something shook the building for a second, like a small explosion. A sharp screeching sound came from the two elevators as the emergency brakes engaged. Bernard glanced down at his $50,000 watch and then heard the next sequence of bangs as the brakes were blown one by one.

He imagined the men in the lifts had taken a collective breath when the brakes momentarily saved their lives. He couldn't hear their screams as the elevators plummeted to the bottom of the shafts, but he knew that's what was happening. An enormous crash rocked the building as the two lifts hit the ground after dropping nearly twenty-seven stories. Everyone inside the elevators would be dead, most killed instantly on impact. Maybe one or two had miraculously survived, though it was doubtful.

Bernard spun around and walked casually back to his corner office overlooking the city. He'd give it ten minutes or so before he made his way to the elevators to begin his act.

Normally in a meeting like this, there would have been several assistants or secretaries sitting in the proceedings. If that had been the case, the execution wouldn't have been possible. So Bernard requested the meeting be kept private. That meant only the board, no one else.

The security guard on duty had—no doubt—already responded to the emergency. Within the next few minutes, he'd make his way down to the basement and discover the wreckage of two crushed elevators.

It would be called an act of terrorism.

As chairman of the board, Bernard would call for swift justice for the villains responsible for such a horrific act. He would attend all the funerals, possibly even speak at some of them.

Tedious? Certainly. He cringed at the thought of all the time he'd have to waste in the coming weeks.

Time, however, was exactly what he'd just bought. And now he had full control of everything.

Chapter 20
Alice Springs, Northern Territory Australia

"Reports are coming in now that there may be as many as twelve deaths in the horrific incident that authorities are now calling a terrorist attack. Two elevators were bombed in a downtown Sydney office building earlier this evening. Experts say that these elevators had security measures built in to stop the cars in case of an emergency, but for some reason the brakes failed. Investigators are on the scene, but it's unclear when we will have any answers."

Sean and the others watched the news report with grim fascination. The television displayed dozens of police cars, several fire trucks and ambulances, and emergency crews rushing around the outside of a tall building.

"That's awful," Adriana said in a hushed tone.

The screen switched to a man in a suit with his tie slightly loosened. He had dark circles under his eyes and rubbed his head as he spoke. "I...we just adjourned a board meeting," he said, choking on some of the words. "I went back to my office to finish up some work, and I heard a loud explosion. A minute later, I heard the crash. I...I had no idea what had happened at first." The guy fought hard to keep the tears from gushing. "I can't believe they're all gone. It doesn't make any sense. Who would do something like this? Those men have families, friends. And now they're gone." He pushed the microphone away. "I'm sorry. I can't right now."

The camera went back to the reporter, a blonde woman wearing a ruffled purple blouse. "That was the company's chairman, Bernard Holmes, just minutes after the attack. We'll bring you more on this story as it develops."

"Crikey," Reece said. "Maybe Sean is onto something with his whole fear of heights thing."

Sean absently nodded.

"Whoever those terrorists were, they knew exactly where those men would be, and when they would be there," he said.

"What?" Tommy asked, still staring at the television.

"If it was a random terrorist attack, they would have hit in the middle of the day. Why bomb an elevator at night when no one is in the building?"

"I guess they knew someone was in the building."

Sean pointed at the screen. "See that?"

There were images coming in from the basement where both sets of elevator doors had exploded when the cars hit the bottom.

"Both elevators fell. Why two?"

"I don't know," Tommy shrugged. "I suppose you're going to enlighten us?"

"It's just weird, is all. Seems awfully strategic, taking out the entire board of directors of a major company like that. Not a terrorist's style."

"They attacked corporate America in 2001."

"True, but the timing of this one had to be absolutely perfect. Whoever did this knew those men would be on the elevator when they were. And they knew all of them would be there."

"Well, they missed one," Reece said. "That crying chairman sure is a lucky bloke. Good thing he's a workaholic; otherwise he'd be at the bottom of that wreckage."

Sean stood up and walked over to the blankets he'd piled on the floor in the corner. "Turn that off. We need to get some rest, and watching that isn't going to help. I'll take first watch. Tommy, you're next."

They'd rented two rooms, but with the events surrounding the sniper earlier, the group decided it would be best if they all stayed in one place.

Tommy switched off the television and climbed into his bed. Reece was already lying down and shimmied under the covers. Both men had offered their beds to Adriana, but in spite of their insistence, she declined, instead choosing to sleep next to Sean on the floor.

Reece reached over and turned off his lamp, plunging the room into darkness. Adriana curled up next to Sean and put her head on his chest. Within minutes, everyone was asleep, leaving Sean alone in the dark with his thoughts.

He'd done this sort of thing many times in the past. Some of his missions required him to stay up twenty-four hours, and more than a few of them put him in places where he had to fight off sleep to stay alert. Now it seemed like more of a struggle than before. He wasn't twenty-six years old anymore.

Gravity tugged at his eyelids, and several times he had to shake his head to keep himself awake. Thirty minutes into his shift, Adriana rolled over, turning her back to him. He felt around next to him until his fingers touched the familiar cold metal of his Springfield's barrel.

He grabbed the weapon and stood up. Sitting down wasn't helping. Since everyone was asleep, he figured moving around a bit would keep the blood flowing and force him to stay awake for the next ninety minutes.

Sean tiptoed over to the desk against the wall and set his weapon down on the surface. He'd cleaned it earlier while everyone else was getting ready for bed—an old habit from his days with the government.

Might as well walk around out in the hall, he thought.

He took a glance back into the pitch darkness and then padded toward the rim of light surrounding the hotel room door. Something clicked, and he froze in place. The noise came from out in the hall. He crept over to the door and looked out through the peephole. The corridor immediately beyond was empty. But he'd definitely heard something. Maybe it was one of the neighbors coming in from a late night of partying at one of the resorts.

Sean had slipped into a pair of cargo shorts and a T-shirt earlier, so he wasn't worried about being indecent if he stepped outside. Curiosity got the better of him, and he reached for the door handle. Just to be safe, he twisted it down slowly, careful not to make a sound.

The door latch was well made, and the bolt slid out of the housing without even the slightest squeak.

Sean eased the door open and poked his head out the door. A black combat boot disappeared into the room next to his. It was the other room he'd rented. Someone knew Sean and the others were there.

He swallowed and made a split-second decision. If he stayed there, he might be able to get the jump on the men when they realized the room was empty and decided to check the second one, but it could also jeopardize the safety of his companions. If he went on the attack, however, he'd have the element of surprise.

Sean went with the second option.

The best defense is a good offense, he thought.

He pulled the door closed, twisting the outside handle as he did so that the bolt wouldn't click when it shut. It would also lock automatically and buy his friends some time in case they heard anything and woke up.

He crept over to the other door and waited. The men inside had closed it behind them keep any light from the hallway from spilling in and to prevent any potential witnesses from happening on the hit. Sean had seen this sort of thing before. Heck, he'd done this sort of thing before—except when he did it, it was to rid the world of horrible people.

He stopped on the other side of the door and waited. They'd use sound suppressors if they were smart, or possibly knives. Guns were easier, faster, and much more effective. But even with the silencers attached, they produced a muffled pop that could potentially draw unwanted attention.

Sean pressed his back against the wall and waited. Something made a noise inside, like one of the guys had bumped against a dresser. Sean imagined they were rummaging through everything to make sure no one was there, though it would have been pretty obvious as soon as they stepped through the door.

The door latch started turning and brought Sean's attention back to the hallway. When the handle was pointing down, the door started to slowly open. The long black tube of a sound suppressor was the first thing that inched its way out. Mistake number one for the assassins. The killer wouldn't be anticipating an ambush, and their grip on the weapon would be somewhat relaxed.

Sean's hand snapped out and squeezed the barrel. He twisted and yanked it with the full force of his muscles. The movement caused the assassin's trigger finger to pull back, and the muzzle puffed, sending a round harmlessly into the floor. Sean wrested the weapon away within a second because holding on would have broken the other guy's wrist. He flipped the gun around to fire, but the man lunged at him and smacked his hand to the side. In the same movement, the villain twisted his torso and smashed Sean's cheek with a roundhouse punch.

Sean stumbled back for a moment but immediately recovered and raised the weapon again. He fired. The bullet zipped by the target as the man ducked to the left and snapped his foot up. The boot struck Sean's hand with such force that it jarred the gun from his fingers and sent it tumbling through the air until it landed two doors away.

Another man stepped out of the room with his weapon drawn. He tried to get a clean shot, but his partner was in the way, launching another assault at the American with a flurry of jabs.

Their faces were covered with masks, but Sean could see from the pallor of their skin they were likely from Eastern Europe. The cold, lifeless eyes were another giveaway. He'd encountered men like that before, men who'd been mercenaries in conflicts all over the world. They bounced around in various uprisings and then disappeared again, only to resurface when they needed more money.

Sean deflected the repeated punches, left, right, and back again. Even as tired as he was, he moved with lightning precision. The attacker twisted his hips slightly, a dead giveaway that he was about to kick. Sean finished the last block and stabbed his hand down to catch the man's boot as it swung at Sean's midsection. The assassin's eyes went wide for a split second, surprised at the American's counter. He quickly adjusted and jumped into the air, swinging the other foot around hard at Sean's face.

Sean knew that would be the guy's only play. Anticipating the desperate kick, Sean lifted the foot in his hand with all his might. The attacker's jump did most of the work. Sean just helped him over the top.

The guy flipped into the air. He went head over heels so fast that he made it a full turn and a half. While impressive, it was also fatal. The attacker landed squarely on his head. A snapping sound cracked from inside his neck. For a moment, it seemed like everything was happening in slow motion. The assassin wavered and then fell hard onto the floor in front of the other gunman.

Sean took two fast steps toward the wall as the remaining assassin fired his weapon in rapid succession. He'd reacted too slow. Sean jumped at the wall, took another running step off it, and launched at the attacker. The man tried to raise his weapon to get a point-blank kill shot, but Sean kicked the gun loose and then planted a hard punch on the guy's jaw that ended with a whap! four inches behind the target.

The man tripped and stumbled back. Sean didn't let up. He grabbed the man's shirt before he could fall away. Between yanking him forward and the power behind Sean's fist, the next blow was a little more than even Sean expected. His fist smashed into the man's face and sent the nose bone into his brain. Blood gushed out of the nostrils for a moment before Sean realized fully what he'd done.

He let the man's shirt go, and the body dropped to the floor. The attacker's eyes rolled into the back of his head, showing nothing but white.

Sean felt his body trembling, still pumping adrenaline through his veins. He swallowed hard. His right hand involuntarily wiped his forehead. It was then he saw the blood on his hand.

The man with the broken neck gurgled something from behind. Sean spun around and looked down at him. "Who do you work for?" Sean asked.

The attacker's breaths came in short bursts mingled with the sound of fluid in his lungs. All he could muster was a low groan.

"You're not going to say anything, are you?"

The guy wheezed but said nothing. His neck was bent at a grotesque angle. He was surely paralyzed. From the lack of movement, Sean guessed from the neck down.

Sean knelt down next to him and grabbed the guy's hair. "You tell me who you work for, and I'll put you out of your misery. Or you keep quiet, and I let you live like this for the rest of your life. Is that what you want? Forty years of life like this?"

Saliva and blood oozed out of the corner of the man's lips. He said nothing, not anything

Sean could understand at least. The guy wasn't going to give up the goods. Maybe he couldn't speak. Or maybe the pain was too much. Either way, there was no reason to keep him alive. The last thing Sean needed was this guy to live and talk to the authorities. Who knew what crazy stories he would concoct?

Sean held the man's hair tight and then jerked the head upward. Something crunched in the man's neck, and Sean let the head drop to the floor. It was a sickening sound. Sean never cared for that part of his former job. Killing up close was something only weirdoes enjoyed. Well, killing in general. He never cared for it, but he knew if he didn't use that talent to his utmost ability, the bad guys he went after would use theirs. Innocent lives depended on Sean.

That thought was interrupted by his hotel room door opening. Tommy rushed out first with his pistol in the air. He was followed by Adriana. She held her weapon at the ready and swept the corridor to make sure all the threats were neutralized.

When Tommy realized no one else was left, he lowered his weapon and passed his gaze between the two bodies.

"What did you do?" he asked.

Sean's breath slowed. "These two went into our other room. From the looks of it, they were here to kill us."

"Sound suppressors," Tommy said, seeing the attackers' weapons. "I thought I heard something out here."

"Yeah. Just the sound of gunfire. Totally normal," Sean said.

"I'm glad you're okay," Adriana said and put her arm around Sean's back. He squeezed her for a second, and then she let go.

"Me, too. I'm glad you're okay."

"Hello, I'm okay, too," Tommy said, waving a hand around.

Sean sighed. "I guess we need to call the police. We'll need to hide our guns first. Somehow I doubt they'd like the fact that we brought them into the country."

Reece stepped into the hallway and looked at the two dead bodies. "Whoa, mate. Did you just do this?"

"Afraid so."

"Wow. Thanks for inviting me to the party."

"You needed the sleep. But I'll tell you what. You get first shift next time."

Chapter 21
Sydney

Bernard Holmes walked into his kitchen and opened the stainless steel refrigerator door. He'd known it would be a long night when he planned the mass execution of his board of directors. He must have spoken with at least a dozen investigators, not including normal cops. Then there was the media. He did one television interview with the reporter, two with the local papers, and one with a guy Holmes was pretty sure just had a blog.

It didn't matter. The more people seeing him devastated by the tragedy, the better. He pulled a bottle of water out of the refrigerator and unscrewed the lid. He finished half of it in less than four seconds.

Holmes set the bottle down on the counter and ran his fingers through his hair. He didn't have as much as he used to. Seemed like he was losing more every day. He needed a drink. It was late, though, and the last thing he wanted was his buzz to wear off in the middle of the night and wake up at 3 a.m.

"I should have been an actor," he said to himself.

His head ached, and his reddened eyes were sore. Forcing himself to cry during most of the interviews had taken an extraordinary effort. He found it useful to put his mind in a place where he actually cared about something, and then imagine that something being ripped away. For Holmes, it was easy.

When he was twenty-six, his wife had been ripped away from him in a car accident. The driver wasn't drunk. He'd fallen asleep at the wheel. It could have happened to anyone. Then there was the irony of where Holmes now worked, as chairman of a company that produced the very thing that propelled automobiles.

Holmes never recovered from the accident. He threw himself into work, into making himself into something untouchable. To numb the pain in his heart, he dabbled with drugs, but that never touched it. Buying companionship helped him forget things for a little while, but his guests always left in the middle of the night, taking their compensation with them and never looking back.

In his thirties, he realized how much time had gone by and how pointless life truly was. It was nothing but a series of events, some good, some bad, and in between there were choices to be made.

Holmes chose to stop caring about anyone.

The day he consciously made that decision, he started to feel better. His focus went purely to building his empire, to crushing anyone who got in his way, and to eventually becoming one of the wealthiest men in the world.

Part of it was for the money. After all, cash bought things that produced pleasure. The real reason behind it all, though, was that as long as Holmes was building something, he didn't have to care about anything else or anyone.

He worked tirelessly. An efficiency expert to the core, he cut out the fat from his business systems and used it to fuel his one-man empire.

The only thing that stood in his way had been the board of directors. "Shortsighted old fools," he said. "They got what they deserved. To think they were going to try to cut me out. I built their company into what it is. Ungrateful. That's what they were. Ungrateful, greedy swine."

Holmes's only regret was that he couldn't see the look on that insolent Jerry's face as he plummeted to his death. What he would have given to hear Jerry's screams. Holmes imagined it was like a little girl squeal. Jerry talked big, but Holmes knew those types. They were little dogs with a big bark. Nothing more.

That dog would bark no more. And now Holmes had total control.

His phone abruptly started ringing in his pocket, rousing him from his thoughts. "Tell me you have good news."

"I do."

"That's a relief. I was starting to think you were running into problems."

"I am. I have good *and* bad news."

"Pfft. You know, just once I would like to get only good news. Seems like life has a rule about that or something. You can only get good news if you take it with bad."

"I assume you want the bad news first."

"Actually, no. Let's start with the good."

"I checked with my source; you're completely in the clear. We've put out some social signals suggesting a known terrorist group is taking credit for the attack earlier today. Next thing the authorities will find is traces of an explosive that is a calling card from that group. We've already nabbed the fall guy. He'll be dropped off at police headquarters with a dud bomb attached to his chest and his tongue cut out. He won't make it five steps before they shoot him on the spot."

Holmes changed his mind about that drink. He stepped over to the liquor cabinet, grabbed a bottle of a chic single malt scotch, and poured it into an empty glass. After a long, steady sip, he set the glass down and let the liquid streak down his throat before speaking again.

"Good. And the bad news?"

"The Americans are proving to be a problem. They took out three of my men earlier tonight. I'm going to have to handle this personally."

Holmes had been afraid of that. He knew about Sean Wyatt's reputation with the IAA. Before that, he couldn't learn much. It was a history shrouded in secrecy. That usually meant he worked for either a government entity or an extremely shady organization. Didn't matter. Both of those career paths made him extremely dangerous, which was why Holmes hadn't put Jack directly on the job. Jack was one of the few people Holmes trusted.

"No," Holmes said. "Bring in someone else. I heard about some guys out of Serbia who were looking for work."

"That's who Wyatt killed earlier today."

Crikey. "Then we get others. Money is no object. You hear me? Spend whatever it takes to get the best out there. Track Wyatt and his cronies, and sic those dogs on them. I don't care if you have to bring in a whole strike team, make it happen. We need the location of that relic. Everything depends on it."

A moment of trepidation passed between the two.

"I'll bring in the guys who did the elevator job," Jack said. "Their skills go beyond just demolition and explosives."

"Just make sure that you get them on it immediately. And tell them not to destroy anything that might help us in our search. They can't just walk in and blow up the evidence along with the targets. We need anything they've found totally intact."

"Understood. They'll be thorough, but careful."

"Good. Keep me updated."

"Of course, sir."

Holmes ended the call and set the phone on the counter. He stared at the golden liquid in his glass for a second and then took another huge gulp, finishing off the rest. The burn going down his throat was only slight, the way good scotch was meant to be. He took a deep breath and poured another glass.

These American meddlers were becoming a real problem, he thought. Maybe it was time to start using a little leverage.

Chapter 22
Alice Springs

No one in the group slept well during the rest of the night. After a group effort to take the bodies down to the trash bin and dispose of them, they decided to leave the hotel and try sleeping in the car at one of the camping areas nearby.

At nearly five in the morning, Reece woke suddenly after a restless half hour of sleep. He looked around in the darkness and rubbed his eyes. Unable to go back to sleep, he pulled out his phone and quietly opened the door. He stepped out into the cool early morning air. His brain raced—something that happened more and more frequently lately. Most of the time he was overly concerned about his bills and payments that were past due. At the moment, he was thinking about something else.

He carefully shut the door to make sure he didn't rouse the others. It was his turn to keep watch, so the others were dipping in and out of consciousness. Even taking turns with guard duty didn't produce any kind of relaxation.

Reece tiptoed away from the car and pressed the home button on his phone. The screen lit up and cast a bright glow onto his face. He winced at the sudden light and turned away for a moment, looking up at the stars to adjust his vision. As he gazed into the heavens, he remembered why he loved the outback. Billions of stars, planets, solar systems, and galaxies twinkled in the black canvas overhead. A thin gray line streaked across the horizon to the east, a sign that the dawn was on its way.

He looked back to his phone and then back at the others still sleeping in the car. "Come on, Reece. Think."

At the hotel, they'd only taken a few minutes to do some online searches for any information on the royal valley from the riddle. Their efforts had been in vain. There were any number of interesting things that came up. One of the more frequent results had to do with the Valley of the Kings in Egypt.

Reece tapped the screen and entered his search query again. Still no hits that made any sense regarding Australia and a royal valley. He lowered his phone and looked up again at the stars.

"Maybe you're being too direct," he muttered. "Think about it. This is a riddle, remember? Mathews wouldn't have made it so obvious to give the actual name of the place. It's more likely a description of what it looks like. Or maybe..."

What if it's a synonym or something like that?

The thought popped into his head as if from nowhere. "What's another word for royal? Royalty, no that's the same thing."

Think, Reece. Think. What kinds of people are royals?

"Kings, queens, princes, princesses, dukes, earls..."

He typed in prince's valley but didn't find anything useful. Next he tried queen's valley. Still nothing. Then, as he was typing in the word *king,* it hit him.

"I'm not looking for a valley. It's a canyon. Kings Canyon!" He nearly yelled the last part of his epiphany. "That's it! Kings Canyon!"

He tapped away furiously on his phone. A moment later, the search results for Kings Canyon appeared. He scrolled through some of the images, nodding with every one that passed.

Reece had been to Kings Canyon many times throughout his life. It was a place he knew well. He took tour groups there from time to time.

He stopped on one of the images of a waterfall that spewed into the canyon basin. Where the water flowed over the rocks, the ravine curved around sharply like a boomerang.

Reece's eyes widened. "That's gotta be it. The boomerang, the waterfall, that has to be the place."

He spun around, full of excitement. He wanted to wake the others, but as he looked through the window saw they were still asleep. How they slept in a car like that, he didn't know. Just as the thought occurred to him, Tommy roused in the passenger seat. His eyes pried open and blinked wearily.

He saw Reece standing outside the car with his phone and flashed a curious expression. "What?" he mouthed.

Reece couldn't keep it in any longer. He quietly opened the door and motioned for Tommy to get out.

Tommy shook his head slowly back and forth and opened his door. Sean and Adriana didn't move, though he had a feeling Sean was wide awake and simply faking sleep. Something about his friend was always on full alert, even when he was "resting."

"What?" Tommy asked as he continued rubbing his eyes.

He stepped around to the front of the car and met Reece in front of the hood.

"I've got it, Tom. I know where we need to go next." He could barely contain his excitement.

"Really?" Tommy perked up.

Reece raised his phone and showed the screen to Tommy. It took a couple of seconds for Tommy's eyes to adjust to the bright screen, but when they had, he narrowed his eyelids and stared at the images.

"Kings Canyon," he said quietly. "So we were looking for two wrong things."

"Seems that way. I got to thinking, the bloke that left these clues wouldn't be so direct to tell us the name of the place to go next. Where's the fun in that?"

"Good point."

"So I thought of what royals are called or what they do."

Tommy grinned at his friend and slapped him on the back. "Well done, mate," he said in a terrible fake Aussie accent.

Reece raised an eyebrow. "Don't do that again."

"What? I do pretty good accents."

"Nah, mate. You sound too Pommie."

"Pommie?"

"Yeah, you know. You sound British, which is fine if you're hanging out in London. Here in the outback, though, you sound like a bit of a fool."

Tommy appeared crestfallen. "Really? I thought it was pretty good."

"Let it go, Tom. We've got bigger things to think about. Gotta get a move on if we want to reach Watarrka by midmorning."

"Watarrka?"

Reece flashed a playful smirk. "That's where the canyon is."

The drive west took the companions through the Northern Territory high desert. It reminded the Americans a little bit of Arizona in some places.

Sean had spent much of their travel time trying to figure out how someone had tracked them once they left Milbrodale. Once they were out of Alice Springs, he took fifteen minutes to do a thorough sweep of the vehicle to make sure there were no homing devices attached. He also went through the extra step of switching off the car's satellite connection as well as making everyone turn off any kind of GPS on their phones.

There was another possibility that he considered, but that would take some resources. Then again, if someone was paying men to kill them, that was just the kind of person who might have that kind of wallet.

Fortunately, the Americans had someone like that on their side, too.

"Hey, Alex," Sean said. "How's the vacation?"

"It's fine. You do realize the time difference between where you are and where we are, right?"

"Yeah. I know."

"Must be pretty important, then," Alex yawned.

"I'll get right to it." Sean stepped away from the car and walked toward an outcropping of shrubs. He stared out at the rolling high desert and then took a look back at his friends to make sure they were out of earshot. "I think someone might be tracking our credit card use. There any way you can figure that out?"

Alex paused as he considered the question. "You mean, someone is following you by looking at where your cards have been used?"

"Yeah, maybe. Not sure yet. We had a run-in with some guys, a couple of incidents."

"Did you pick up a bug?"

"I checked the car. No homing devices on it. And nobody has followed us. Trust me, I would have noticed. Out here in the outback, there isn't exactly a ton of traffic."

"Okay, so I can do a check on that and see if there were any anomalies with your transactions. Might be that someone did a periscope on you."

"Periscope? Like the app?"

Alex chuckled. "No, although I do like that app. No, a periscope is what a hacker does to see if an account is worth tapping into or not. When you use a card, it sends a signal to the bank, they send one back, and information is exchanged. Even though they use some of the best security in the world to protect their customers, whenever there is a transfer of signals, that transfer can get a hole poked into it. When that happens, a hacker can periscope in and have a quick look. It doesn't take long. They just get in, see what they want, and then pop back out again."

"But that leaves a trail, right?"

"There's always a trail. Some trails are harder than others to find, but yeah, we can check it out for you. Haven't been doing anything else down here."

Sean still had a beach house in Destin that he'd let the kids use for their vacation time.

"Sounds like you're having a good time. Do yourself a favor and go to The Donut Hole for breakfast in the morning before you head out to the Caribbean. You won't regret it."

"I don't really care for donuts," Alex said.

"Neither do I, but trust me. Their breakfast is worth it. Let me know what you two dig up."

"Okay, will do."

Sean ended the call and glanced back at the others. They were staring out at the spectacular view of red rocks speckled with green bushes and patches of grass. Down in the canyon, thick stands of trees sprouted up, providing a beautiful contrast between the red desert stone and dirt and the lush emerald leaves. A small river flowed through the canyon's bottom, cutting around piles of fallen rock and trails for hikers.

One side of the canyon looked like it had been sliced off by a huge blade, its colorful strata not unlike the Grand Canyon, which had eroded over time and gradually revealed layers upon layers of sedimentary rock.

Sean walked back to the car and looked out at the setting. "Pretty view," he said.

"Yeah," Reece agreed. "I've come camping up here lots of times. Tourists are always pleasantly surprised when I bring them here. They didn't know such places existed down here."

"Australia is a big place," Adriana said. "It's full of all kinds of beautiful things."

Tommy had a sense of urgency to his tone when he spoke. "So where, exactly, are we supposed to go to find the next clue? You said there's a waterfall and we should look there first?"

"Right," Reece said. "We'll head down the canyon trail and then make our way to the falls. Shouldn't take us long to get there. Once we're there, we can have a look around."

"When you say it shouldn't take us long, are you talking about five minutes or two hours?" Tommy asked. "Because I get the feeling it's closer to the latter."

Reece laughed. "No, it's about a thirty-minute hike in from here. So relax, Tom. It's mostly downhill, too."

"Coming back won't be," Tommy muttered.

Everyone grabbed their gear bags and an extra bottle of water they'd picked up at a gas station before entering the national park. Reece warned them that the air in the high desert was pretty dry, so staying hydrated was of utmost importance.

Sean took a few sips of his water before they set out on the trail.

Adriana walked over to him and leaned in close. "What did the kids say?"

Sean hadn't wanted to alarm the others, but they needed to know what measures he was taking to figure out how the assassins had been able to track their movements.

"They may be looking at where we use credit cards. If they do that, they can follow a trail and connect the dots. One way or the other, we use cash from now on. Okay?"

She nodded. "You going to tell those two?"

Sean smirked. "Eventually."

They rejoined the others and looked to Reece for the next move.

"Lead the way, mate," he said in a fake accent.

"Hey, well done, Sean." Reece turned to Tommy. "See, that's how you do an Aussie accent."

"Oh, come on," Tommy protested. "That sounded exactly like the way I did it."

"Nah, mate. But keep working on it."

Incensed, Tommy threw his hands in the air. "It sounds the exact same."

"Okay, on we go," Sean said. "Sorry, buddy. Your accent does sound a little Pommie."

"What is with you two and the whole Pommie thing?"

Reece led the way to the trailhead and began the descent into the canyon. Sean and Adriana followed close behind, leaving Tommy muttering words in his bad accent in an attempt to practice.

"Still sounds the same," he said to himself and hurried to catch up.

The lean path leading down into the canyon would have been a problem for Sean had it been any narrower. As it was, he clung to the inner rock wall like an infant grasping its mother, keeping his right hand touching it at all times. As they reached a bend in the trail and rounded the turn, he switched to his left hand, to keep that feeling of stability.

It was a habit that he'd carried since childhood. Whenever he found himself in a high place, Sean had to touch something solid that made him feel like he was grounded. His fear of heights had been a curse as long as he could remember. He'd tried doing any number of things to get rid of it: therapy, rock climbing, rappelling. None of it had worked. As long as he had a little room like he did on this path, he could still move. There were times, however, when he'd been nearly paralyzed with fear.

His mind drifted back to an episode high in the mountains near an old Buddhist monastery. A staircase cut into the stone—hundreds of feet above the ground—had nearly been his kryptonite. It took him an incredible amount of time to navigate, but in the end he'd done it.

For some people, that might have been enough to shake him of his fear. Not for Sean.

"You okay, buddy?" Tommy asked. There was a hint of ribbing in his voice, but he knew better than to give Sean too much of a hard time. He knew his friend loathed his phobia.

"Yeah," Sean said. "Better with every step closer to the bottom. You gonna be okay coming back up?"

"I guess asking for a donkey to ride back is out of the question."

The two shared a short laugh.

Reece proceeded at a rapid pace, leading the group through a series of turns until they reached the bottom where the path stretched out in two directions. A sparse river ran downhill to the left. He waited for Sean to bring up the rear since Tommy had long since passed him, hiking quickly down the canyon side, seemingly unafraid of the potential danger.

"Which way?" Adriana asked when they stopped at the foot of the trail.

Reece pointed to the right. "Waterfall is that way. Not far now. Probably another fifteen-minute walk."

He took a gulp of water from his bottle and then shoved it back in his rucksack. The others did the same and followed their guide as he navigated around the rocks and bushes.

The temperature in the canyon was much cooler than up above. The rays of the morning sun had yet to bake the basin's rocks completely. Plus the little river provided a cool flow of air just above the water as it ran along the path.

The group heard the waterfall before they saw it. The water crashing over rocks and splashing into a pool below gradually grew louder until they finally rounded a bend in the canyon. Then the canyon opened up into a wide U. Short trees grew sporadically along the water's edge leading to a pool about forty feet across. Big rocks jutted up out of the ground close to the standing water and reminded Sean and Tommy of a few places they'd gone swimming near the mountains of Tennessee.

"Kind of like the secret place back home," Sean said as the group's march stopped next to one of the big rocks.

"Yeah, I was just thinking the same thing," Tommy said. "Shame we're in a hurry. Would be a nice place to go for a swim."

Reece took in a deep breath and sighed. He pointed at an area to the right where the path narrowed and continued up around the rocks until it disappeared behind the mist. "You can see the trail keeps going over to there."

"It's definitely shaped like a boomerang," Adriana said. She took in the scenery. "Quite the little getaway spot."

"Yeah. Nothing out here but nature and more nature. City people like to come out here to relax. On the weekends, this place will have quite a few visitors taking a dip."

Sean remained focused on the mission. "I'm going to take a look behind the falls," he said and started up the short hill path. "Hang back for a second."

The others watched as he made his way above the pool. He stopped where the trail narrowed and tested out his footing. Turning his body to face the rock, he secured his rucksack a little tighter against his back and then shimmied to the left, carefully moving a few inches at a time until he disappeared behind the falling water. He was only gone from view for a minute before he reappeared and started making his way back.

When he was back on the wider path, he turned his body and walked back to his companions. Before he reached the rocks where they stood, he shook his head.

"There's nothing back there."

Chapter 23
Watarrka National Park, Northern Territory
Australia

"What do you mean there's nothing back there?" Tommy asked.

"Just what I said," Sean answered. "There's a little overhang back there, not much of a cave. Just a recession, really. But that's it."

Puzzled, Tommy took a step toward the hill path. "You're sure there's nothing? You weren't up there very long. Maybe there's a secret entrance or something."

Sean snorted a derisive laugh. "Trust me, you can go up there if you want, but you'll find the same thing I did."

"Take a look at these drawings over here," Adriana pointed at some rock art on the canyon wall still enveloped by shade. "Maybe there's a clue."

The others had been so focused on the waterfall, they'd not seen the drawings on the other side of the water.

"How did we miss that?"

"Maybe you were thinking about skinny dipping," Reece joked.

They migrated over to the water's edge to get a closer look. Several depictions of ancient people were painted into the stone. Outlines of white hands were smattered all over in seemingly random places on the scene. A boomerang hovered over the entire section of art.

"Boomerang," Sean said. "This has to be the right place."

They peered at the artwork—half in admiration, half in an attempt to unlock the code potentially hidden within.

"The riddle Mathews left mentioned the underworld. Notice how one of those people in the drawing is horizontal underneath a few wavy lines?"

"Oh yeah," Tommy said. "You thinking what I'm thinking?"

"Unfortunately, yes. Looks like we're going to have to take that swim after all."

"Swim?" Reece asked. "You don't think there's something in there, do you? If there was, someone would have found it by now."

"You make a good point," Sean said, slipping his shirt over his head and unbuckling his belt. "But it can't hurt to check."

Tommy started undressing as well.

"Right in front of a sheila?" Reece said, still watching in disbelief.

"Don't be shy, Reece," Adriana said.

He turned around to find her in a sports bra and underwear. For a second, he was caught off guard and spun around to avert his eyes.

"What's the matter?" Sean asked. "Her underwear covers more than some bikinis I've seen."

"Fair point." Reece cleared his throat and glanced at Tommy. "Boxers, huh? I always figured you for a briefs kind of guy."

"Not sure how to take that. You coming with us or not?"

Reece sighed. "All right, fine." He began taking off his shirt as the other three dove in.

Tommy surfaced and screeched like a little schoolgirl.

"Cold?" Reece asked.

Tommy nodded. "Yeah, but it feels good. Come on in."

Reece looked around at the gear bags lying on the ground by the rocks. "You know, I think I'm going to hang up here and keep an eye on the stuff. Go ahead and check it out. Let me know what you find."

"Suit yourself," Sean said as he dog paddled in place.

A second later, he twisted around and dove under the water.

He kicked his legs hard and used an underwater breaststroke to swim closer to the churning water of the falls. White bubbles foamed violently for a solid fifteen feet around the base of the falls, making visibility impossible at the epicenter. Sean swam over to the left of churn and examined the underwater rock. After fifteen seconds of looking, he resurfaced and took a breath.

He ran a hand over his face and looked back at Reece still standing on the rock. The big Aussie put his hands out as if to ask if Sean had seen anything. His lips were moving, but Sean couldn't hear him over the constant sound of water crashing into water. He shook his head, and a second later, Tommy and Adriana popped up next to him.

"You guys see anything?" Sean shouted above the sound.

Their heads both tossed left and right.

"No," Tommy said. "The water coming off the top makes it impossible to see anything straight ahead."

"Should we check the other side?" Adriana asked.

"Yeah, just in case. But I've got a feeling whatever it is we're looking for is gonna be behind that mess." Sean jerked his thumb at the white foaming water.

He and the others swam around the churning liquid, and once they were on the other side, dove down again. Thirty seconds of analyzing the rock on the right produced the same results.

Sean pointed to the surface, and the three shot back up again for more air.

Reece put his hands out again, hoping they'd had better luck. Sean shook his head again. Reece was saying something once more, but they couldn't hear him.

"Only one more option," Sean said.

"I don't know, man. That's an awful lot of power right there." Tommy stared into the bubbling mayhem. "Seems a little dangerous."

"Don't worry, buddy. I know what I'm doing."

Before Tommy could protest further, Sean kicked a couple of times and paddled over to the rock face. He grabbed a slippery edge and shifted his hands to the left, moving a few inches at a time.

Tommy and Adriana watched as he neared the point where the water pounded the rock and the pool below.

"You think he knows what he's doing?" Tommy asked, tilting his head to the side.

"No, but you know him better than I do."

Sean's left hand disappeared into the falling water. His head and body followed next. A second later, his right hand was gone as well.

Under the falls, Sean found a momentary respite from the falling water that seemed to come down in a crescent shape. It wasn't much, maybe ten inches at most, but it gave him a second to evaluate the situation.

If there was some sort of hidden underwater cave in the rock, it had to be directly below his feet. He wondered how strong the water pressure was and if he could escape it if he fell backward into the whitewash. Then another thought occurred to him. *How do I get out if there is a cave down there?*

Only one way to find out.

He lowered his body several inches, gripping the wet ledges like a rock climber descending a mountain face. When his chin touched the water, he took ten short breaths and then a long, deep one.

Sean let go of the rock and dropped fully into the water.

The low, constant sound of the churning water filled his ears. He narrowed his eyes, hoping that would help him see, though it did little to aid his vision. Everything was a roiling white mess. He kept his hands against the rock to use as a guide, feeling his way along as he continued to go deeper into the pool.

He stopped abruptly. His left thumb was the first to feel it. Then fingers on both hands grasped it. He ran his hands along the underside of something that felt like a natural arch carved into the rock.

Sean lowered himself a little more and poked his head into the hole, still gently pushing his finger tips along the ceiling. He felt his shoulder hit something hard and jagged. The opening was only about two-and-a-half feet high and maybe three feet wide, possibly a tad less. He was pretty much going on feel alone at this point.

His lungs started tightening, and Sean knew it was time to go back up for air. Holding his breath for long periods of time had never been one of his better skills. He could go for maybe eighty seconds if he really pushed it, and that was if he wasn't moving much.

He pulled himself up the rock face and broke the surface of the water amid the deluge coming off the falls. He pressed his body against the rocks to keep the force of the falling water from pushing him back out into the pool.

After a couple of quick gasps, he lowered back into the water, this time hurrying to the cavity he'd discovered. When he felt his toes hit the bottom edge of the hole, he flipped his head down and pushed through the opening. He couldn't see much, though it was easier to see in the little tunnel than it was out in the pool. Ahead was nothing but dark, still liquid. He felt his back scrape against the roof. It stung for a moment and made him feel claustrophobic. Visibility grew fainter as he swam from the light, deeper into the underwater cave. Thirty seconds in, he knew he was going to have to turn back soon if he didn't find another opening.

His internal clock hit forty seconds, and still he pushed forward. He swallowed hard to help fight off the natural urge to breathe. At the fifty-second mark, he'd all but passed the point of no return. Every survival instinct in him said to go back. Sean pressed on.

One minute.

He felt his lungs begin to squeeze again. *Go back,* he thought.

Sean knew it was too late for that. This tunnel went somewhere. It had to.

He felt along the ceiling with his right hand, pulling himself faster with his left along the bottom. Seventy seconds in, his right hand pushed ahead. This time, however, it didn't brush against rock. It punched through the dark liquid and up.

A shaft.

Fueled by a desperate hope, he pulled himself into the new opening and pushed his feet off the bottom as hard as he could. He'd either burst through the surface and into a cavern, or he'd hit his head and die from blunt force trauma.

Either option was better than drowning.

His lungs ached as he shot upward. He winced, fighting back the urge to inhale. Then he suddenly felt the familiar touch of air on his face. He opened his mouth wide and let the air in, in huge gasps. He panted for nearly a minute as he hovered in the water, treading with his arms and legs. When he finally caught his breath, Sean spun around in the darkness, letting his eyes adjust.

He couldn't see anything. The room was pitch black. The realization that he needed some kind of light set in. He'd have to go through the underwater tunnel again. Fortunately, he knew exactly how to do it. The first run was exploratory. Coming back a second time, he could go much faster.

The only thing he could see was the faint glimmer of daylight poking through the tunnel below. Really it was more like slightly brighter darkness. It was enough to guide him back, though.

Adriana and Tommy exchanged a worried glance. Reece was shouting something to them but was still too far away for them to hear.

"You think he's okay?" Tommy asked.

"I'm guessing if he wasn't, we'd see his body floating in the pool right about now."

Her answer sounded callous. Tommy knew what she meant, though. Adriana cared about Sean as much as anyone, if not more. She didn't want anything to happen to him. If she believed he was okay, Tommy should, too.

That being said, he still stole a look over his shoulder to see if anything was floating in the water.

Sean's head popped up right behind him, nearly scaring him up onto the rocks.

"Ah!" Tommy shouted and grabbed the next ledge up.

Sean shook his head to get rid of any excess water and then rubbed his face and eyes.

"Did you find it?" Adriana asked.

Sean nodded. "I think so. But it's a dangerous little swim. You have to go in through an underwater tunnel. Figure we can do it in about a minute. Maybe fifty seconds. You can hold your breath that long, right?"

"Easily," she said. Adriana had developed that skill over years and years of practice, beginning when she was a child.

"Tommy, what about you?"

"Eh," Tommy said, hesitating. "Not sure that's a good idea. First off, tight spaces. Secondly, underwater tight spaces. Third, I probably can't hold my breath for thirty seconds."

"Okay, that's a no for him." He turned back to Adriana. "Looks like it's just you and me, babe."

Tommy rolled his eyes. "You guys are starting to make me sick."

Chapter 24
Watarrka National Park

After Sean and the others swam back over to Reece, he explained what he'd discovered in the underwater tunnel.

"Sounds like you're going to need light," Reece said.

"Yeah, you can't see anything down there. Pitch black. I've got some dry bags I can use. And I think the flashlight in my gear bag is waterproof up to a hundred feet. So it should be fine."

"For a second there I thought you were going to ask me to go down there with you," Reece said, relief filling his voice.

Sean chuckled. "Would be a tight fit for you, big 'un. Besides, no need to have too many cooks in the kitchen."

"We'll hang back and keep watch in case more of those goons come our way," Tommy said. He pointed at a position behind some rocks on the other side of the little river. "We should be able to see anyone coming down the trail from over there. Plus the rocks and trees will give us some cover."

"Good idea, mate."

Sean slipped his phone into the dry bag along with his pistol. He noticed the look Reece gave him at the latter. "Not necessary, but I really love this gun."

"Can't say I blame you."

Sean tied the dry bag to a rope to loop around his ankle and then looked over at Adriana. "Ready?"

"Let's do it."

They jumped back in the water and started paddling over to the falls.

Reece turned his head and raised an eyebrow. "When's the wedding?"

Tommy snorted. "With those two? Maybe eighty years from now."

When Sean reached the rocks, he tightened the loop around his ankle to make sure he didn't lose the dry bag.

"So here's the deal," he said when he finished with the little rope. "You go under the falls, and then in the center there's a place where the water doesn't really hit you. From there, you drop straight down. It's probably close to eight feet under when you'll find the cave opening. Once you're in, pull yourself as hard as you can until you reach the shaft. Wait twenty seconds before you come down. That way I'll be able to shine my light down the shaft for you so you'll see it easier."

"Sounds good," she said. Then she pulled close and pressed her lips against his.

While pleasantly surprised, he still had to ask. "What was that for?"

"Do I need a reason?"

"No."

"Good. We'll say it's for luck, you know, for the benefit of our audience." She ticked her head to the left at the two guys still standing on the rocks.

Sean didn't need to look over his shoulder to see Tommy's disgust. He could feel it from across the pool.

"Good enough for me," Sean said. "See you on the other side."

He worked his way back across the rocks and into the deluge once more, disappearing from sight. Once he was in the middle, he let himself drop down into the water and pulled his body down using the rocks. The maneuver saved him valuable seconds, and in a brief moment he was back at the tunnel entrance again.

This time, Sean used the rock to his advantage, pulling his weight through the submerged corridor faster than he could swim. Gripping the flashlight in his teeth kept both hands free as he reached for a handhold and then another until he made it to the shaft. Just as he'd done before, he twisted his body around and used his feet to kick off the floor and up to the surface.

When he broke through to the air, he still had plenty left in his lungs. Knowing where he was going made all the difference. And to think he'd almost drowned before.

Sean dog paddled in place—remaining over the shaft—and aimed the beam of his flashlight down into the water so Adriana could see it. The light diffused somewhat, but it would do the job.

About thirty seconds later, he noticed movement in the shaft below before Adriana suddenly burst through the surface. She blew out the air from her lungs, spitting a little water as she did so. Then she shook her head and smoothed her brown hair back against her head.

"Not too bad if you go through it fast," she said.

"Tommy would never make it."

"You're probably right."

He turned his body, shining the light around the underground pool to see if there was a good place to climb out. Over to the left, it appeared the rock gradually sloped into the water. Something else caught Sean's eye about five yards away from that spot.

"You see that?" he asked.

"Looks like cave art," she said.

"Let's have a look."

The two swam over to the shore and found climbing out to be a trickier bit of work than expected. The sloped rock was slippery, and the two explorers both nearly fell as they tried to keep their footing.

The water dripped off of them, echoing off the stone in the cave and blending with another sound.

"Is that an underground stream I hear?" Sean asked. He flashed his light around the room.

"Sounds like it. There must be a fissure in the riverbed above."

Standing on solid ground, Sean untied the cord around his ankle and opened the dry bag. He produced three glow sticks, cracked them, and tossed them on the floor. They cast an eerie green glow onto the wall, revealing the rock art the two had seen from the water.

"Why'd you bring your gun?" Adriana asked, seeing Sean's pistol in the bag as he removed his phone.

"Force of habit," he said as he winked. "Never leave home without it."

She rolled her eyes and moved over to the rock where the paintings stood out like ghosts etched in stone.

"Come on, Agent Wyatt," she joked. "Let's take a look at these."

He joined her and crouched by the wall. "More of those odd-looking beings," he said, running a finger next to one of the shapes.

Creatures with narrow bodies and huge round heads dotted the rock, covering a span of about ten feet. There were twelve of them in total, and again the white hands appeared in random places across the ancient canvas.

"What is with these hands?" Sean said. "They've been at every place we've seen so far."

Adriana looked at him, puzzled. "You mean you don't know what those mean?"

He shook his head. "No. I have no idea. Do you?"

"No," she said with a frown. "Just surprised you don't. That's kind of your thing, you know, history?"

"Sorry. I've been a little busy lately, you know, spending time with the woman I love?"

"Aww," she said with a grin. "I know. And I appreciate that." She changed the subject back to the artwork. "So what does all this mean? There are lots of those circles again. I take it whoever put this here is conveying more passage of time?"

"Most likely. That much we do know, at least now. But there's nothing else." A look of growing concern washed over his face. He pointed his light to either side of the drawings. There was nothing else to see. "I don't understand. Mathews should have left something here for us, a riddle or clue of some kind."

Adriana picked up one of the glow sticks and held it out at arm's length. She stepped cautiously over the rocks, shining the green light on the wall as she moved. "I don't see anything," she said. Eventually, she came to a point where the path ended abruptly in a rock face.

Sean aimed his flashlight back in the other direction and searched the opposite wall for any signs of something Mathews could have left. He, too, found nothing.

"I don't get it," he said as Adriana rejoined him. "It should be here, right? Or am I crazy?"

"The jury's still out on that one," she said. "But you're right. There should be something here. Maybe we're just not thinking about it correctly. What was it the last riddle said again?"

Sean's nearly eidetic memory sprang to life. "The boomerang's water flows into the underworld, another secret kept. We found the secret room. Stands to reason whatever Mathews put here would still be here." He had a gut-wrenching thought. "Unless someone got here before us."

"Maybe," Adriana said. "Or maybe the secret isn't here in this cave. What if it's in the water? After all, the clue suggests that the secret is kept there, not up here."

The realization hit him. "You're right. This whole time I thought it had to be up here in the cave, but that's not what the clue says at all. It's in this pool." He flashed her a look of admiration. "Very impressive, my dear."

She leaned close as if to kiss him. "Why, thank you." Then she yanked the flashlight from his hand and fired a flirty smirk. "Let me take a look. I can hold my breath longer than you."

"I don't suppose telling you no is an option."

Adriana was already tiptoeing cautiously to the water's edge. She glanced back over her shoulder. "You know it isn't."

Before he could protest further, she jumped back in the pool and disappeared below the surface.

"There's no debating with her," he said to himself.

Sean watched her swim all the way to the pool's bottom, following the light as much as he could in the rippling dark liquid. It was difficult to tell what was down there. The water was remarkably clean and free of debris, which made visibility less of an issue for the swimmer.

The light danced off the submerged rocks below as Adriana made her way around the semicircular pool. He noticed her abruptly stop and hover over something. She was halfway around the grotto, and he had no way of being able to tell what she'd found. He didn't have to wait long.

Sean watched as the light streaked toward the surface. Her head breached the air and she spewed water away from her lips. After two short breaths, she turned to where Sean was sitting on the rocks next to one of the glow sticks.

"There's a dead body down there."

The ghastly report caught Sean off guard. "Maybe you should get out of there."

She shook her head. "Whoever it was, they've been dead a long time. I'd guess over fifty years. It's just a skeleton, really. Probably drowned trying to come through that tunnel. I guess they didn't know how far back this thing went."

"You sure you don't want me to look around?" Sean asked.

"No, I'm good. Going to check around the rest of the perimeter."

Again, Adriana tipped over and dove headfirst into the water. Her feet kicked the surface as she knifed down into the blackish pool.

Sean could do nothing but watch as she made her way around the base of the wall. Only a few yards to the right of where Sean was perched, she stopped again. The light fixated on something—what it was, he couldn't tell. She'd been down for about a minute, maybe more. He wished he'd set a stopwatch to keep track.

It started jerking around violently. Sean's heart pounded. His gut told him the worst had happened, that she'd caught her foot in a rock or something and couldn't get it free. He stood up, ready to dive in to her rescue. As he steadied his balance, the light stopped its radical gyrations and went still.

A single horrified thought pierced Sean's mind. *Adriana drowned.*

Chapter 25
Watarrka National Park

Sean jumped out and into the water, making sure he put enough distance between himself and the rocks that he didn't injure himself. Desperation coursed through his veins as he dove downward, cutting through the water with hard, powerful strokes. He pushed his muscles to the max as he kicked and paddled down toward the light near the bottom.

As he drew close to the lithe, white figure, the flashlight suddenly turned up toward him. Adriana blew bubbles out of her nose and then pointed at something in her hand. Then she motioned to the surface with her index finger.

Sean was so relieved he nearly sighed in spite of the fact that he was twenty feet under water. He gave a nod and watched her ascend before he kicked off of the pool floor toward the surface.

The two broke into the cool cave air and hovered for a moment in the water, kicking their legs to keep them above the gentle waves.

"You okay?" Sean asked, trying to cover up the near-irrational concern he'd felt just moments before.

"Yeah. I'm fine. Why'd you come down there?"

Sean felt embarrassed. "I...I saw the light getting yanked around like something was wrong...so I...I jumped in because I thought you were in trouble."

An appreciative smile crept onto Adriana's face. "That is so sweet. You know I can hold my breath longer than that, though."

"I know. I just...I didn't know how long it had been, and I started to worry."

She pulled close to him and gave him a kiss on the cheek. "It's good to know I have a hero for a boyfriend. Now let's see what this thing is."

She held up a stone cube about the size of a baseball.

Sean stared for a moment at the object.

"Come on," she said, and then she paddled away toward the shore. He followed quickly after.

They sat on the slope with their feet still in the chilly water as Adriana passed the cube to him. She pointed the flashlight at it, revealing engravings on four sides of the stone's surface.

On one side, letters and an ampersand spelled out *J & M C*. Another side featured what looked like an animal paw. The third image looked like it had been defaced, nothing more than a divot dug out of the stone. The last engraving was the shape of a boomerang.

"Well, there's another boomerang," Sean said. "Starting to see a pattern here."

Adriana continued to look at the object. "What do the others mean? You think the letters have something to do with Mathews?"

"Maybe. We need to get back to the others. Been gone a while."

"Don't want Tommy to worry?" she said in an almost seductive tone.

He shrugged. "Yeah. And I'm not totally convinced we're out of the woods yet with whoever was following us."

"You and that intuition. It never shuts off, does it?"

"Sometimes I wish it did."

He tucked the rock into the dry bag, tied it to his ankle like he'd done before, and jumped back in the water.

The two made their way down the shaft and through the tunnel, returning to the daylight that mixed with the churning white water of the falls. Instead of going left when they made it out of the underwater corridor, the two turned right and headed for the landing close to where Tommy said he and Reece would wait.

Sean popped up first and spotted the two exactly where they said they'd be. Adriana wasn't far behind him and caught up as he swam slowly toward the shore.

"Did you find anything?" Tommy asked eagerly. He'd been sitting on a small rock next to Reece. Their spot was situated in the canyon's shade. Even so, Tommy had already dried off completely due to the warm, dry air.

"Yeah, but we don't know what it is."

He found a place where the rocky ground ascended onto shore and trudged up to the others. Once out of the water, Sean disconnected the cord around his ankle and then removed his gun and the odd cube.

"Take a look at this," he said, tossing the rock to Tommy.

Tommy nervously caught the cube after almost fumbling it to the ground. He stared at the still-wet object with Reece looking at it over his shoulder.

"Another boomerang," Tommy said.

He flipped the cube over and examined the other engravings. "Not sure what these letters represent. Any ideas?" he asked Reece.

"Not off the top of my head, but that paw print I recognize. Looks like a wallaby's foot."

"You recognize that?"

"Of course I know that. I'm an adventure tour guide. Part of that entails tracking animals sometimes."

Sean was impressed. "You hunt animals for sport?"

"Nah, mate. Well, not wallabies. Really, I only take a few hunters out every year, but I don't like it. Only do it for the money."

"What happened to this part?" Tommy asked as he turned the cube again. He pointed at the place where it appeared the image had been dug away.

"No idea," Sean said. "We found it like that."

"I guess whoever put it there wasn't happy with the way it looked so they took it off."

"Seems odd," Reece said. "The rest of it is so perfectly done."

"Here, hold this for a second," Tommy said to Reece and handed him the cube. "I want to take a few pictures.

Reece held out the stone with the divot facing up. Tommy took his phone out of the gear bag at his feet and took the first picture. "Okay, now turn it."

Reece started to twist the cube, but a loud bang stopped him. The sudden noise was accompanied by a bullet ripping through Adriana's upper chest. Blood splattered onto Sean's side. He looked into her shocked face. Adriana's eyes went wide with shock, and then she fell over backward into the water.

"Adriana!" Sean shouted.

Tommy reacted, shoving Reece behind the nearest boulder. He charged at Sean, diving at his friend who desperately reached out his hands to grasp at Adriana as she splashed into the pool. Another shot boomed from above. Tommy's shoulder struck Sean in the midsection and drove him behind another giant rock just as the second bullet smashed into the rock where Sean had been standing.

Tommy hit the ground hard with Sean on top of him. Sean struggled, but Tommy wouldn't let him go, keeping his weight pressed down on his friend.

"Stay down," Tommy ordered. "Don't do anything stupid."

"Adriana...I have to save her, Schultzie." Sean's protests were muddled. He still hadn't fully comprehended what happened.

Tommy felt like he was riding a crazed bull. Sean fought with every ounce of his strength, but he couldn't get his friend off of him.

"It's an ambush, Sean. There's a sniper up there on the other side. And he's got us pinned down. You go out there, you're a dead man. We're in a kill box."

Sean's breathing increased. "Where's Adriana?"

Tommy poked his head around the boulder and saw Reece tucked down, out of the sniper's view. He pulled his head back before the gunman could see. There was no sign of Adriana.

"She's gone. Reece is behind the rock next to this one. I need you to focus, buddy."

Sean searched his friend's eyes for answers. Usually Sean had an idea for every situation. This time was different. Sean's emotions poured out of his eyes that kept twitching left to right as if searching Tommy for answers.

"Let me go," Sean said. "I don't care if I get killed. I love her, Schultzie."

Tommy gripped his friend's shoulders tight. "I know you do. But you walking out there and getting killed isn't what she would want. Right now, we have to get out of here. You, me, and Reece. You hear me? We have to move, or we're all dead. We need a plan."

Sean still held his weapon in one hand. Tommy's gear bag was sitting twenty feet away, close to the water. Adriana's was next to it, meaning they only had one gun between the three of them, and only one magazine of ammunition. No chance he could go for the other bags. The sniper would cut him down. At the moment, Sean didn't care about that.

To make things worse, Sean knew they were up against a skilled sniper with nothing more than what equated to a pea shooter. His .40-caliber was plenty of gun when it came to a short-range firefight. Hundreds of feet away from the target, it would do little more than scare the other guy.

Tears welled in Sean's eyes. He started to speak but had to choke back the words. Finally, Sean pushed his mind back to the way it was when he worked for Axis—to times when he'd lost comrades in the field and had to push on without them. This was different, way different. The mental exercise strained his faculties to their utmost. He sniffled and then realized what he had to do.

"That's it," he said, more to himself than to Tommy.

"What's it?"

"Do as I say, and we might just get out of this." Sean swallowed hard, shoving down his emotions to the back of his mind as much as possible.

Tommy stared at Sean with uncertain eyes. "You just came up with a plan? Like, right now?"

"Yeah. But you're not gonna like it. Listen to what I say." He leaned around to the side of the boulder, keeping his head out of view and tucked away behind a bush growing right beside it.

"Reece," he hissed.

"Oy," he said, using common Australian slang.

"You and Tommy do exactly as I tell you. When I start shooting, you two sprint to the water. Get in, and don't come up for air as long as you can stand it. Swim downstream. I'll catch up to you."

"There's no way you can hit him from here," Reece said. "You're good, but even you have limitations."

He wasn't wrong.

"I'm not trying to hit him, although if I get lucky I'll take it. I just need to buy you guys a few seconds to get in the water. Once you're in, make sure you stay a few feet below the surface. Bullets lose most of their force within a foot or so of hitting the water."

"What about you?" he asked. "Who's going to cover you?"

"If I do it right, I'll buy enough time for myself, too. Just get to the water when I start shooting." Sean didn't say what he was really thinking. He didn't care if the shooter moved for him or not. His plan was to get Reece and Tommy to safety. If he died trying, so be it. Sean was in a reckless place now, a place where personal safety was no longer an issue.

He turned around and found Tommy crouching right behind him. "I don't like it, Sean. You don't even know where that guy is."

"I will."

Sean reached out his hand and jiggled the base of the bush. Another shot boomed from the top of the canyon. Sean peeked over the top of the rock and immediately ducked back down.

"Got him," Sean said through gritted teeth.

"What do you mean, got him?" Tommy tried to imitate his friend's voice.

"I just need the general area. He may move around a little, but I have a feeling he likes his spot. I saw the gunsmoke lingering in the air from some rocks across the way. He's got a shooting hole for his gun. I'll put some rounds close to his position. He'll have to duck for a minute."

"There's no other way out of this, is there?"

Sean leveled his head and locked eyes with his friend. "Other than a dead sprint down the trail? No. And if you want it that way, I'm game for that, too."

"Operative word being *dead*. No, I'll opt for the swim."

"Right. So you ready?"

"What, now?"

"We could wait for the sniper to get bored and come down after us... Yes, now."

Reece whispered back to them, interrupting their conversation. "Whenever you're ready."

Sean motioned to him with a flick of his head. "See? He's good to go. When I fire that first bullet, move."

"But..."

Tommy couldn't voice the rest of his protest.

Sean crawled over to the other side of the boulder and took up a position on both knees. From this range, he doubted how accurate he could be. Hitting the target would be improbable. Even pinging a few rounds within a yard or two of the sniper's spot would be unlikely. Sean's entire escape plan depended solely on his experience with people. And that experience told him that guys with guns usually ducked for cover when someone else started shooting at them. It was the natural survival instinct built into every living person on the planet. Only the most well-trained individuals could ignore it. Sean hoped this sniper wasn't one of those.

He took a deep breath and let it out slow to reach total calm. It was an exercise he'd learned a long time ago: take a deep breath, count backward from ten, slow the heart rate, unleash the fury.

For Adriana.

Sean reached the number one in his mind and stuck his weapon around the boulder's edge. He raised it fast and squeezed the trigger. "Go!" he barked at Tommy.

Sean adjusted his aim slightly—higher and to the left. The first round sent a poof of rock and dust off the canyon wall. He fired again. The second shot was much closer to the sniper's position and had the same effect on the stone as the first. Reece hit the water with a splash as he launched out headfirst into the pool close to where it flowed downstream.

Tommy tripped on a rock and tumbled to the ground. He rolled a foot or two and came to a stop close to the water's edge. He was out in the open, easy pickings if the gunman above was still taking aim.

Sean kept moving and fired again. No rock debris or dust this time. The bullet must have sailed over the target and into the bush beyond. He marched forward with an insane look of fearlessness in his eyes.

Tommy struggled to his feet and plunged into the water. A second later, he disappeared below the surface.

Sean's weapon popped again, the fourth round much closer to the target than any of the others but still a yard away. He stole a glance into the rippling water. No sign of Adriana. Reece was drawing close to the short drop-off where a patch of rapids churned and pushed downstream. He could see Tommy's pale skin moving quickly toward the drop-off as well—not far behind Reece.

Sean shot again. He noticed movement behind the rocks above. It wasn't much. Just the shadow of a leg moving by the shooting hole. But it told Sean what he needed to know. The sniper was on the move.

Sean continued toward the water's edge. Tommy was gone now. Sean realized Adriana's body must have floated downstream. He didn't have time to wonder. The thought fueled his rage, and he shot again. Over and over again he popped off repeated shots, peppering the rocks above in the direction he'd seen the movement. As he emptied his magazine, he moved faster and faster toward the water's edge until he felt his feet licked by the cool liquid.

He counted the rounds until he reached the last one. The water was up to his shins. Sean saw the sniper's barrel poke around the side of his rock fortification. One more step in the water, and Sean squeezed the trigger again. The last bullet smacked into the big boulder, sending the sniper ducking for cover and pulling his weapon out of view.

Sean didn't hesitate.

He dove into the water as quietly as possible and frog paddled downward until he felt he was deep enough. He kicked out with his legs, going as hard as his muscles would allow. Something struck the water nearby, mere inches to the left of his shoulder. The big-caliber bullet jittered for a foot or so and then fizzed out, falling limp toward the pool floor. Another zipped through the water a foot in front of him. Again, the water snubbed the round's force and sent it drifting to the bottom.

That did little to ease Sean's concern. He'd done the research long ago about bullets and water. He didn't necessarily want to put it to the test in this kind of situation.

Ahead, the water churned noisily. He was almost to the rapids. Another round struck the water next to him, then another. The sniper was getting desperate, firing shots faster than he could aim.

At the edge of the pool, the pool's floor sloped up to the point where the space between it and the surface was marginal. If the shooter was on target, there wouldn't be enough water between Sean and the bullet to slow it down.

Sean kicked harder. His legs started to burn. He was almost there. Speed would be crucial. A fast target was a hard target.

He reached the lip of the pool where the water dropped over the rocks and rushed down the river. He winced, anticipating a bullet into his spine as he felt his body slide over a smooth river rock.

Sean was close enough to the surface that he could hear the gunshot. It never came, and he splashed into the next section of the river and the onrushing current.

Chapter 26
Watarrka National Park

Sean tumbled through the white water, if he could call it that. In East Tennessee, the Ocoee River offered much more treacherous waters. This was more like the Nanthahala in North Carolina—a river Sean also knew well—deep enough to keep his body covered but no real danger as far as the undercurrents were concerned.

Fortunately, that part of Australia had gone through a wetter-than-usual summer, and the river pushed downhill at a rapid rate.

Sean saw Tommy's head bobbing out of the surface thirty yards ahead. He knew Reece was probably just beyond. Sean forced thoughts of Adriana out of his mind and kept paddling forward, only slowing his effort occasionally to look back up to the canyon's ridge for any signs of the shooter. They were moving so fast, he doubted the guy could keep up on foot for long, especially with such a big weapon. By the time the sniper reloaded, they would be nearly out of range, and nearly impossible targets in the unpredictable current.

After five minutes of swimming steadily with the current, Sean caught up to Tommy. Reece was only forty feet away.

Sean gasped for air. He'd exerted a good deal of energy during the swim. His muscles felt like Jell-O.

"Any sign of her?" Sean asked, his voice still in a panic.

Tommy shook his head as he floated downstream on his back. "I'm sorry, Sean. I've been watching the shore, but I haven't seen her."

Sean couldn't fight back the emotions any longer. He sobbed uncontrollably, mixing his tears with the river water on his face.

Tommy reached over and grabbed the back of his friend's head. "I'm so sorry, buddy." He couldn't think of anything else to say. Silence was probably best. Any words right now would just stir up more emotions.

Reece had slowed his progress up ahead, and the two Americans gradually caught up. The big Aussie flapped his hands to keep steady on his back as he floated next to the others. He said nothing to Sean. It was the same dilemma Tommy faced. What could he say to a friend who'd just seen the love of his life gunned down right in front of him?

They reached a calm point in the river where the currents slowed.

"What are we gonna do now?" Reece asked Tommy.

"Where does this river go?" Tommy answered with a question.

"Through the outback, mostly. Not much out here."

Tommy thought through the issue. "We can't go back to the car. They'll be waiting for us."

"Not like there's much to go back for anyway."

"True," Tommy nodded. "I know. Passports, your ID, weapons, everything. It's all gone."

Sean remained quiet, though he still clutched his Springfield in one hand. It was the only possession they had left. At least Reece and Tommy still had clothes on. Sean was in his underwear.

"Wait a minute," Reece said, a glimmer of hope in his voice. "I have a friend a few miles from here. His name's Rick, Rick Teague. He's a bit of a hermit, but he might be able to help us. If we ride the river a little further, we can get out and go on foot. Won't take us long."

The plan sounded good enough, considering the circumstances. "What does your friend do?" Tommy asked.

"Not sure anymore. He used to be a businessman in Adelaide. Then one day he walked in to his boss's office, pissed on the desk, and walked out. Since then, he's just been living out here."

Tommy raised a suspicious eyebrow. "Wait, how long have you known this guy?"

"About five years. Actually, I only met him once. Accidentally stumbled on his property while driving a group around. He was kind enough to help me get the Land Cruiser out of the mud. Said if I ever needed anything to just ask."

"So this guy is more of a one-time acquaintance than a friend."

Reece cocked his head to the side. "Yeah, I guess that sounds about right. But he's a good guy. We can trust him."

"I don't trust anyone," Sean said.

It was the first time he'd said anything in several minutes. "Well, you trust us, buddy." Tommy patted his friend on the shoulder.

Sean didn't respond. He simply stared off into the distance.

The three floated through the still waters and back into faster currents.

"We don't have much choice," Reece said over the sound of rushing water. "We've got no money, no ID, no credit cards, nothing. And Sean there has no clothes. Our only chance is Rick."

Tommy sighed. "Fine. A bad plan is better than no plan at all," he muttered.

After another fifteen minutes in the water, the canyon gradually shortened until the men found themselves on the desert plains that stretched beyond.

Reece pointed to a sandy, rock-strewn beach to the right. "Over there. Make for that shore."

Tommy and Reece paddled their way over. Sean hesitated for a moment. He would have been fine with the river taking him far away from here. Adriana was here. Was she at the bottom of the river? Or had she drifted to shore somewhere and he'd just not seen her? Sean considered staying in the water, if for no other reason to keep the hope alive that he might find her. His eyes desperately scanned the shore on either side of the river, thinking maybe she'd washed up on the rocks.

She was gone. Deep down, he knew that was the reality. Sean didn't want to admit it. He'd failed. All the people he'd protected over the course of years, the lives he'd saved, ran through his mind. But he couldn't save hers— the life that mattered most to him.

Reluctantly, Sean started stroking his way over to the beach. The current wasn't strong, and he easily spanned the distance. Tommy and Reece were already on dry land, sitting on some rocks to catch their breath. Sean felt the first rock under his feet and gained a foothold as he struggled out of the water a few dozen yards downstream. River water ran off the tip of his nose as he stared at the ground. His fingertips and elbow dripped constantly for a minute. His boxer briefs were soaked.

He slowed his breathing and let his muscles rest for a moment. He fought the emotions back again and refocused his mind on the one thing he could control: that was the moment and his next move. Even though those were things he could normally command with willpower or desire, this was different. The sickening pain filled his chest again and tightened his stomach.

She can't be gone. The thought kept running through his mind. *She has to be alive.*

His imagination started going through wild scenarios where Adriana somehow made it to shore. If she could, maybe she'd get help. He choked thinking about it. He knew it was all just fanciful dreaming. If she'd been able to miraculously make it to the river's edge, she'd still be bleeding and in desperate need of medical attention.

Tears rolled freely down Sean's cheeks. He squeezed his fists against his knees, hoping the moment of pure rage would make him feel better. It did little to stem the utter heartbreak pulsing through his being.

A bird chirped in the distance, barely audible above the sound of the rushing water. Sean looked toward the trees on the other side of the river. A bird—possibly the one he'd heard whistling—took off, flying in an up and down pattern through the air until it disappeared into the forest.

He and his friends needed to do the same. Sean knew it, but he was paralyzed with grief. The idea of escaping the killer didn't register in his mind. All he could think about was Adriana.

Sean twisted his head toward his two friends sitting with their arms folded across their knees. Tommy, unsurprisingly, was still panting for breath from the short swim to the beach. They'd been uncharacteristically quiet since their narrow escape. He couldn't blame them. Sean knew Tommy well enough to know that his friend wouldn't say anything stupid. Reece would follow that lead.

The urge to jump back in the river and go looking for Adriana downstream resurfaced. *Maybe she's just around that bend,* he thought. Or maybe he should run back up the shore and get a higher point of view to see better. He searched the beach and noticed a thin trail leading back toward the canyon.

Common sense took over, and Sean shook off the irrational thoughts. For a man who was used to taking action to get things done, doing nothing felt like having a thousand-pound weight sitting on his chest.

Again, he took a sidelong glance at his friends.

"They'll come looking for us," Reece said. "We're safe for now, but we need to get moving."

Sean could tell his friend didn't want to say anything. Reece's reluctance further proved his friendship. Sean couldn't think about leaving, though. He had to find Adriana, even if she was dead.

Dead. He shook his head violently to rid it of the thought.

"Sean?" Tommy said, full of hesitation. "He's right. We need to get going. If we sit here, we'll get picked off one by one."

Sean honestly didn't care. He didn't want his two friends to die. But concern over his personal safety was no longer present. In a strange way, he almost hoped the sniper found him sitting there on the river beach. Nothing mattered anymore.

"Sean? We have to move."

Tommy's persistence bounced off Sean like a marble striking a tank. "Go on," he said in a voice that was almost absent from his body. "Leave me here."

The other two exchanged nods and slowly got up from the ground. As they trudged toward Sean, he saw his pistol on the ground next to him.

Tommy and Reece stopped a couple of feet from Sean. They both wore anxious expressions on their faces.

"I don't mean to be a jerk about this, brother, but Adriana knew what she was getting into. She was stubborn. We loved that about her. But you dying out here in the wilderness isn't going to bring her back. And I somehow doubt that's what she'd want you to do."

The words stung. Sean winced again, like the pain was taking another swing at him.

"I can't move on," Sean said. "Not without her. I at least have to find her."

"Tommy's right, mate," Reece said in a solemn tone. "I know how much you love her. But sticking around here...it's suicide. We need to get to my friend's place and hunker down for the night."

"Yeah," Tommy agreed. "I can guarantee you Adriana wouldn't want you to sit around here and get killed. You have to keep going, no matter how hard it may seem. Live for her, if for nothing else than to get back at the guys who did this."

The last line struck a chord in Sean's head. *Yes. They have to pay,* he thought.

Sean slowly stood up. Mud and sand clung to his skin. He didn't care. There was only one thing on his mind. It beat like a steady drum. Until he had it, he would think of nothing else.

Revenge.

Chapter 27
Watarrka National Park

Jack leaned over and picked up the cube stone from the rocks. He examined the different sides and pursed his lips in silent consideration. Five other men—Jack's personal henchmen—stood around as Jack turned the object over so he could see the different engravings.

"The big one dropped that when I started shooting," a muscular man with blond buzz-cut hair said. He stood off to the side, allowing his employer to have a look around. His right hand gripped the barrel of a rifle propped against his hip.

Dark droplets of dried blood smattered the loose rocks around the pool. Jack bent down and rubbed a finger on it. The blood was still slightly sticky. He rubbed two fingers together and then moved to the water to dip his hand in.

"Shot her in the chest," the sniper said. "She fell into the water."

Jack stood, washing his hands of the blood. "Where's the body?"

"Washed downstream. She's at the bottom of the river by now. Fish food."

"Where are the other bodies?" Jack asked. His tone had taken on a stern, irritated sound.

"I know what you're getting at," the man said in a sharp English accent. "Don't worry. They're dead too." The sniper lied about that part. He wasn't about to tell his employer—a man who paid handsomely for results—that he'd let his quarry get away. "Fish food, all of 'em."

"Are you sure?" Jack didn't look the man in the eye. He merely stared into the pool.

There was a slight pause before the shooter answered. "Yes. Of course I'm sure. That's why you hired me, right? Because I'm good."

"You know who I work for?"

The question seemed to come from out of the blue. The sniper wasn't sure how to respond at first. After a moment of thought, he said, "Sure, Jack. You work for Mr. Holmes. That's no secret."

"Exactly. And do you know why it's no secret?"

The second question was considerably harder than the first. The gunman clutched the barrel a little tighter, just as a precaution.

"Can't say I do, Jack. If I were a man in your position, I'd probably keep my identification under wraps."

Jack spun around abruptly and faced the sniper. He still held the stone in his hand. His eyes wandered to the gear bags on the shore. "What's this?" he gave a sideways nod at the stuff.

The shooter shrugged. "Just their stuff. It was sitting there when I opened fire. They didn't have time to get it. I guess they figured they didn't need it. They made for the water, I shot 'em in the back, and now they're gone. No worries."

Jack considered the answer for a moment. He rubbed his chin, still staring at the bags. "I want to make sure I got your story straight. You killed the woman, and she fell in the water."

The sniper nodded.

"The other three went in after her?"

"Right."

"And you shot them in the water. Were they trying to save her?"

"Beats me. Alls I know is, they're dead. Just like you wanted."

Jack drew a long breath in through his nose. He let the air seep out of a tight hole between his lips that almost made a whistling noise. "That's true. I did want them dead. And you know what else I wanted?"

The shooter hesitated and then pointed at the cube. "That thing?"

"Precisely," Jack said in a sharp tone.

"So you got everything you wanted. It's like a Christmas a month late for you." The gunman attempted to smile to ease the tension, but it was an unnatural gesture—especially for a hit man.

"Getting back to the question and your answer, I allow people to know my identity because I want them to be afraid."

"Afraid?" The sniper shifted uneasily.

Jack took a step toward him. "Yes. Afraid. You see, I can't have people lying to me. And if anyone fails to do what I ask, it's important they know that there will be consequences. Just like there would be consequences if someone were to try to kill me. I'm one of Mr. Holmes's most trusted friends. Should anything happen to me, he would find out. And then he would find out who did it."

"Good to have friends in high places." The guy tried to sound gruff as he said the words.

"Absolutely."

Jack moved over to the gear bag closest to his feet and bent down. He picked it up and stuffed his hand inside. He pulled out a pistol and gave the weapon a good once over before checking the rest of the bag's contents. Surprisingly, there was a wealth of things inside: passports, driver's licenses, credit cards, a spare magazine, and several other items.

Jack flipped open the passport and held the driver's license inside so the images lined up with each other. "It seems our friend Tommy Schultz won't be needing these again, eh?"

"Not unless he's resurrected."

Jack stuffed the identification and the cards in his back pocket. Then he shoved the pistol into his belt. "Might as well keep this since he won't be needing it. Right?"

"Sure," the sniper agreed.

"You don't happen to know what any of these mean, do you?" Jack held the cube out suddenly, and the hit man jerked back for a second, startled.

His head twitched back and forth. "No. Can't say I do."

Jack bit his lower lip for a second and then pointed at the paw. "You see this paw here?" The sniper nodded. "That's a wallaby."

"If you say so. What does it matter?"

"Well, wallabies are kind of a big deal here in Australia. My guess is, whoever hid this cube here wanted us to know that the next place we should visit has wallabies."

The gunman was totally lost, so Jack kept talking.

"Now, if I was a guy trying to leave bread crumbs for someone else to follow, I'd need to let them know about the general vicinity of where they should go next. That makes me wonder what those letters mean." He pointed at the set of letters cut into the stone. "I don't suppose you have any idea about those either."

"You pay me to kill people, not solve old puzzles for you."

"Fair point. I don't pay you to figure these sorts of things out. Fortunately, I think I have someone who might be able to help me with it. So I really won't be needing you anymore."

"Good, then," the sniper said. "I'll just collect my hundred grand and be on my way."

"The money is in the truck," Jack said, pointing at the trail. "We should get going before any tourists happen to show up. Wouldn't do well for them to find a bunch of guys with guns here, now would it?"

The gunman picked up his rifle and turned toward the trail. He never saw Jack take a big step toward him and raise the cube high over his shoulder. The first blow from the corner of the stone knocked the sniper to the ground, sending a sudden sharp pain through his head from the back of his skull. His vision blurred. He could feel the rocks and dirt under his fingertips. Something in his head told him to grab his gun, but he couldn't feel it.

"I don't deal with liars," Jack said as he crouched over the gunman.

The man didn't feel a thing after the second blow that rendered him unconscious. Jack kept going, driving the now-bloody corner of the cube into the back of the sniper's head until his arm gave out. He stood up, still holding the dripping stone, and then sauntered over to the water's edge to wash it off. When it was sufficiently clean, he tossed it to one of his men.

"Hold onto that," Jack said. "We need to get that back to Sydney so our friend Miss Guildford can have a look at it."

"What about him?" one of the other henchmen said and pointed at the dead sniper.

"Throw him in the water," Jack said. "Let him float downstream with the others."

Chapter 28
Northern Territory

Sean sat at the wooden table with his hands folded, staring straight ahead at a candle flickering in the dying light of dusk.

They'd made it to Rick Teague's place in under forty-five minutes. That wasn't to say the journey was easy. They had to hike over rough terrain, dirt roads littered with sharp rocks, and then there was the heat. Temperatures had climbed to their zenith before the three men arrived at Rick's cabin.

Tommy and Reece had offered Sean their shoes several times, but he refused, choosing instead to walk the entire distance barefoot. After ten minutes of walking on scorching hot earth and slicing one of his feet on a rock, he accepted Tommy's socks, but nothing else.

The physical pain was a welcome respite from the emotional stabbing in his heart.

"You want something to drink?" Rick asked, setting a glass of water next to Sean's elbow.

"Whiskey if you got it."

Rick, a fifty-five-year-old guy with a scruffy graying beard and overly tanned skin nodded. "Sure. I've got whiskey."

Rick scurried over to a cabinet he'd built with his own hands and pulled down a bottle of Jack Daniel's.

He'd built the entire cabin on his own, from the foundation to the roof over their heads. It was an impressive achievement, and the results were better than could have been expected. There were a few things that would have raised an eyebrow here or there, like the bathroom that was only separated from the rest of the living room by a shower curtain. Then again, Rick lived alone and probably didn't have many visitors.

Considering that last fact, the house was remarkably clean—probably a remnant of his OCD past still coming through.

"Anyone else want a whiskey?"

"I'll have one," Reece said, raising his hand.

Tommy stared across the table at his friend. "You don't drink, Sean."

Rick returned with three tin cups, all with generous amounts of amber liquid sloshing around inside.

He set one in front of Reece, Sean, and Tommy.

Tommy put up his hand as if to say he'd pass.

"I am tonight," Sean said in response to his friend's comment. He raised the cup to his lips and tipped it back.

He swallowed every drop and then reached over, took Tommy's cup, and poured the contents down his throat before the burn of the first shot could hit him.

Tommy raised both eyebrows, surprised at his friend's actions. "Okay, so now I guess we're at a frat party?"

"You'd be drinking too," Sean said. He held out one of the empty cups toward Rick, who was standing close by, still holding the bottle. "Mind if I have another?"

"Go right ahead," Rick said as he poured a double.

Reece sipped his drink and watched as Sean downed his third.

Letting out a long sigh, Sean held his cup out again for another refill. Rick started pouring again, now unsure if he had enough left in the bottle to quench his visitor's thirst.

"I think that's enough, Sean," Tommy said. "You're gonna get sick."

"I'll decide when it's enough." Sean looked at their host. "Am I drinking too much of your whiskey?"

"Not at all," Rick said. "Plenty more where this came from. Though, I'll have to go out to the shed to get another bottle at this rate."

Sean pounded two more drinks before he slammed his cup down on the table and sniffled.

"Had enough?" Tommy asked.

Sean didn't answer. Instead, he got up out of the chair and walked outside, letting the screen door slam behind him. He'd put on some shorts and a T-shirt Rick stored in boxes. The sandals were from a time when Rick took beach vacations. They were a tad big on Sean's feet, but fit well enough to warrant wearing them.

"Your friend," Rick said, sliding into Sean's seat, "had a rough day?"

"You could say that," Tommy answered. "Just watched his girlfriend get shot right in front of him."

"Crikey." Rick thought for a minute and then turned to Reece for his next question. "What were you all doing out here anyway? Taking these Americans on a tour of the bush?"

"We were looking for something."

"Looking? Found, I'd say. That is, if you were looking for trouble."

"A friend of mine went missing. And someone tried to kill me, shot up my whole house. I barely got out alive. All because of an email she sent."

"Email? What kind of email?" Rick took a sip of his drink.

"His friend—a woman named Annie—found something we think leads to a treasure of some kind."

"Treasure?" Rick's ears perked up.

"Yeah. We don't know what it is, only that some guys over a hundred years ago went looking for it. They spent a good amount of time trying to find it, but had to give up in the end when one of them took ill."

"So you're looking for a treasure, eh?"

"We're not treasure hunters, per se," Tommy said. "I run an artifact recovery agency out of Atlanta. It's our job to preserve important pieces of history for the rightful owners—or governments."

"Ah," Rick said with a nod. "So the treasure for you is just making sure these artifacts are kept safe."

Tommy was somewhat surprised the man understood what he was talking about. After all, he was a hermit living out in the middle of the Australian outback.

"Yeah, pretty much."

The room fell silent for a couple of minutes before Tommy pushed the chair away and walked over to the kitchen counter. The room was dimly lit, both from a single lamp that hung in the ceiling overhead and multiple candles throughout the building. Rick preferred to stay off the grid. Why, no one knew.

Tommy grabbed a jar of rice and opened the lid. He looked inside at his phone. He'd been surprised to find the device still in his pocket after the trip down the river. The thing was completely soaked, though, and would need to sit in rice overnight if it was going to have any chance of being usable again.

"So this treasure," Rick broke the silence, "I suppose there was some kind of map or something that led you out here to Watarrka?"

Reece relayed the whole story up to that point—how they'd visited the museum in Sydney, the Baiame Cave, and Kata Tjuta before coming to the canyon. He told what happened at the waterfall and how someone was trying to kill them with a long-range rifle.

Rick listened intensely until Reece finished the story. When the tale was done, Rick nodded and finished his cup of whiskey. He poured another and offered one to Reece, who accepted with a nod.

"You sure you don't want one, Tom?" Reece asked. "Wouldn't hurt."

"I don't drink, but thank you."

"More for us, eh, Reece?" Rick said. The two clinked their cups together and took another draw.

Tommy sat back down at the table and looked out through the screen door. Sean was nowhere to be seen.

"I should go look for him," he said.

"Nah, mate," Rick disagreed. "There's nothing you can say to a man who has had that kind of day. All you can do is let him be. Let him think about what happened. And let it either kill him, or make him stronger."

"He's my friend."

"And that is exactly why you must leave him alone." Rick raised a finger at Tommy. "Now, from the sounds of all these clues you've been finding, it sounds an awful lot like you're looking for something the Aborigines call the Golden Boomerang."

Tommy's right eyebrow shot up. "Golden boomerang?"

"Mmm hmm."

"Never heard of it."

"Me either," Reece said.

"Most people outside the Aboriginal cultures haven't. Shoot, most Aborigines haven't heard of it. Only a select few get the knowledge of the boomerang passed down to them from their elders. Keeping it secret is how they keep the thing safe."

"If it's a secret, how come you know about it?" Reece looked skeptical as he lifted the cup to his lips.

"That's a legitimate question. Can't say I wouldn't be wondering that myself if I were you." He took a draw from his cup and then set it back on the table, smacking his lips as he swallowed the warm liquid. "When I first moved out here, I became friends with some of the tribesmen. They were kind enough to teach me about their culture and their beliefs about the world around us. And not just the world—the entire universe.

"Of course, their belief systems vary a great deal. Different tribes believe in different deities, but there is usually some kind of crossover that brings it all together."

Tommy and Reece listened closely as the man continued.

"One of the deities from their religion is a creator god called Baiame. You mentioned before that you visited his cave close to the east coast."

The American nodded.

"On that cave wall, you no doubt saw a few boomerangs—one a little closer to the deity than the other."

"Yeah. We weren't really sure about what that meant."

"Well, I'll tell you. One of them represents Baiame's own boomerang. The other is the one he gave to the people, one to keep—so to speak."

Reece's curiosity piqued. "Why did he give one to the people?"

Rick drew in a deep breath through his nose and then sighed. "The legend says that it was a promise to the people that their god would always be with them. And it was also to guarantee that he would return again someday."

"Return?"

"Yes. As with most religions, there is a common feature in that the people are usually awaiting the return of their god. It's true in most mainstream religions, and in several even more ancient ones."

"Okay," Tommy said, "so this boomerang was left as a promise to the people that Baiame would watch over them and someday come back to do what exactly?"

"I'm a little fuzzy on that part," Rick said. "Most religions believe they'll be taken away to some kind of paradise. I'm not sure what the Aborigines believe Baiame will do."

Silence fell on the kitchen for a minute before Reece spoke up again. "I'm sorry, Rick. I don't mean to sound skeptical. Tell us again how you got them to cough up this information. You mentioned the tribesmen took you in, but for a secret this big, it seems sort of far fetched that they would have just told an outsider like yourself."

"Very astute," Rick answered. "As it turns out, a couple of them really like their whiskey. They also happen to be some of the older guys who are privy to things others are not. We got drunk around a bonfire one night, and they started talking, probably a little too much. I doubt either of them has any recollection of what was discussed the night before. And I have no intention of letting them know they gave up such an important secret."

The story seemed plausible enough, especially considering the amount of whiskey

Rick apparently had on hand. Still, they were talking to a guy who'd walked out of a high-paying job one day to move into the Australian bush.

Tommy wanted to know more details, partly because he still wasn't sure about the story. "How big is this golden boomerang?"

Rick leaned back in his chair and flicked the cup's handle with a finger. It made a clinking sound that echoed throughout the room. "No one knows for sure. At least they didn't mention that to me. I'd assume it would be about the size of your average boomerang. That is, if the thing exists."

"You're not sure?" Reece asked.

"No," he said. "I'm not. This world is full of myths and legends. A handful of them are true. The Aborigines can't agree on a single theology that brings all their gods under one banner. They don't fight about it like other religions or denominations, but there are still inconsistencies. I respect what they choose to believe. I've just never seen any sort of proof to make me think any of it is true."

His comments caused serious consideration for the visitors. Rick made a good point. The inconsistencies in the belief systems created a ton of doubt.

"You know," Tommy started, "most of what we do at my agency is all about finding things people don't believe exist. There are times when we come back empty-handed. More often than not, though, we make discoveries that change the way the world views history. One of the reasons I do what I do is to help dissolve those inconsistencies—like the ones you mentioned." He looked up at Rick. "I know that it's a possibility that this boomerang doesn't exist. But we have to keep looking. Not because we're looking for fame and fortune. We have to do it because a woman's life depends on it."

"And what will you do with it once you have it?"

"We'll give it to the Aborigine people. It belongs to them."

"Unless, of course, they already have it," Reece chimed in.

"Right."

Rick considered Tommy's explanation. He made a good case. Unfortunately, he didn't have much more information to give them. "I don't believe they have it," he said. "To the people, the boomerang is just another of their myths. It isn't real. If it were, though, it would be an incredibly important find to all of them, and would go a long way in uniting their theologies."

Something else had been on Tommy's mind during their conversation. "Do you have any idea who else might want something like that?"

Rick snorted. "You mean besides every other treasure hunter in the world?"

"Well, yeah."

Their host shrugged. "I don't know. Never thought about it. That sort of find would fetch a good sum, though. It's priceless."

"Yeah," Reece said, "but how many wealthy Aborigines do you know?"

"Good point."

"We've gone up against big-time collectors before," Tommy said. "Maybe they wouldn't try to sell it to the Aborigines. A historical item like that would be of incredible value on the black market." He paused for a moment. "Rick, do you happen to have a map sitting around?"

"Yep. It's under the table where I keep my truck keys."

Their host got up and walked out of the room, around the corner of the wall that divided the kitchen and eating space from the living room and front door. Twenty seconds later he reappeared holding a folded map in one hand. He tossed it onto the table in front of Tommy. "Here you go. What's in your head?"

Tommy grabbed a pen that happened to be sitting nearby on a counter and then opened up the map. "Okay if I make a few notes on this?"

"Sure. I don't use it much anyway."

Tommy spread the map across the table. He missed the feel of a physical map now that everything was available in a digital format. It took him a second to find what he was looking for. "Ah there it is," he said and circled the word *Milbrodale* on the map.

Next, he traced an invisible line over to Uluru-Kata Tjuta National Park and then circled it. He repeated the process and circled Watarrka National Park then stepped back to look at his handiwork. Tommy put his hands on his hips as he tried to connect the dots beyond the ones he'd already connected.

"You looking for a pattern or something?" Reece asked. He stood up and craned his neck to get a better view of the map.

"Yeah. So far, though, it's just a line. I don't know. I guess I was just reaching."

"Get some rest," Rick said. "Stop thinking about it for a while, and the answers will come."

"No offense, but I don't think I'll be able to sleep tonight. One of my friends—and the girl my best friend loved—was just killed right in front of us. I doubt Sean or I will be sleeping much for a while."

Trying to work through the puzzle surrounding the golden boomerang had momentarily taken Tommy's mind off the crushing sadness of Adriana's death. Now it came crashing down on him again. He slumped back into the seat and stared at the map.

No one said anything for a couple of minutes. Then Tommy lifted his head and looked over at Rick. "Pour me one of those drinks."

Chapter 29
Northern Territory

Tommy woke with a start. A familiar smell filled the air. For six or so seconds, his eyes showed him a blurry area lit by a bright light coming from the left. As his eyes adjusted, he remembered where he was, and the disorientation faded away.

He'd fallen asleep on Rick's couch the previous night.

Tommy wasn't accustomed to drinking alcohol, so it only took a few drinks for him to get plastered. The whiskey had also made him extremely drowsy, and before he knew it, he'd passed out.

He looked over at the opposing couch where Reece still slept. There was no sign of Sean.

Then everything from the previous day came rushing back. Adriana was dead. Sean hadn't even had a chance to say goodbye. Tommy worried about his friend. Sean had drunk enough booze to kill a small horse and then walked out without so much as a look back.

Tommy took rapid inventory of the rest of the room. Rick's house was simple, built by his own two hands. It consisted of a kitchen with a small eating space, a living room, and a bedroom and bath. All told, the building was only about 750 square feet, if that. The interior reminded Tommy of the tiny house movement that had taken the US by storm.

He sat up and paused. His head throbbed, and he put his hand over his face. After rubbing his eyes, he stood up. The world tilted slightly, and he had to put both hands out to steady his balance.

"I really am a lightweight," he said.

Reece stirred on the other couch. He turned his head the other direction and remained asleep.

Tommy tiptoed around the corner and into the kitchen. He was surprised to find Sean sitting at the table. The smell came from the stovetop where Rick was busily frying potatoes and eggs.

Sean's focus was on the device in his hands. It was Tommy's phone.

"Is it dried out?" Tommy asked, deciding not to bring up the night before.

"I think so. I'll know in a second."

Tommy nodded and waddled over to the table. He collapsed into a chair and looked over at Rick, who was busily stirring things in one pan and flipping things in the other. "Smells great, Rick."

Rick turned around and grinned. "Thanks. Breakfast will be ready in a minute."

Before Tommy could ask, Sean told him what he was doing. "We lost our only clue to the next destination yesterday. But we took pictures of it on your phone."

"Oh that's right. I almost forgot about that."

"If your phone isn't fried, we might be able to look at those images and figure out exactly what Mathews was trying to tell us."

Rick shoveled some eggs and potatoes onto a plate and then slid it in front of Tommy. "Pepper and salt are over there if you need it," he said, pointing at a series of shelves on the wall near the refrigerator.

"Thanks again, Rick."

The host filled another plate of food and set it down in front of Sean.

"Thanks," he said. "Not hungry."

"I know," Rick responded as he poured more scrambled eggs into the frying pan. "Maybe you'll change your mind."

Sean kept staring at the phone, as if waiting another minute or two would make a difference between the thing working or not.

He drew a deep breath and then pressed the power button. "Moment of truth."

Tommy slid his chair around to the other side next to his friend and then pulled the plate over. His appetite wasn't strong either, but he knew he had to eat. And if there was one thing Tommy could do, it was power through food while starving himself of emotion.

The screen flickered for a second, and both men held their breath. Then the little icon appeared in black and white, and a moment later, the passcode appeared.

"Looks like it's okay," Sean said.

"My passcode is—" Tommy started to say.

Sean was already typing it in. "I know it."

Incredulous, Tommy straightened up and glared at his friend. "What do you mean, you know it?"

Sean kept staring at the phone. "I know all your passwords, pretty much for this sort of situation."

"Wait a minute. All my passwords?"

"Yeah. Don't worry, I don't use them."

"But...how?"

"Let it go, Schultzie. I used to work for the government, remember?" Sean's tone was hollow, like a man who'd lost everything.

The phone's screen went to the home page, and Sean tapped on the camera. He scrolled to the most recent photos and tapped on the first one.

Rick scooped up some more of the food onto a plate and joined the other two at the table. He grabbed the salt and pepper shakers, sprinkled a little on his eggs and potatoes. After shoving a steaming forkful into his mouth, he looked at the device in Sean's hands.

"What are you looking at?"

Sean turned the phone around so Rick could see. It only took him two seconds to recognize what it was. "Ah, wallaby track."

Tommy frowned. "So everyone here knows it's a wallaby but us."

Sean ignored his friend's complaining. "We found this stone cube yesterday in an underwater cave at Kings Canyon. In our rush to leave, we dropped it. Fortunately, we took a few shots of it before...before everything went down." He struggled to finish the sentence.

He looked at the phone again and swiped the image to the left. "The cube had four distinct images wrapping around it. This is another one that was carved into it."

Sean twisted the device again.

Rick stared at the letters cut in the rock. "J & MC? What does that mean?"

"We have no idea. There's a boomerang engraved into it and then a fourth image that looks like it was destroyed."

"Destroyed?" Rick asked, chewing another mouthful of food.

"Yeah," Sean said. "See?" He displayed the defaced side of the cube to their host, who nodded.

"Ah yeah. Looks like they didn't want anyone to know what was there."

Sean flipped the phone around in his hand and gazed at the image. "See, that's what I don't understand. The cube was where the previous clue said it would be. That means it hadn't been touched since Mathews put it there. If it's the next piece to the puzzle, why would he gouge it out like that?"

"Maybe it was a mistake," Rick offered.

Reece yawned from the living room, interrupting the conversation. "You guys mind keeping it down? Trying to sleep in here."

He stretched and sat up.

"Saved you some food," Rick said. "Best eat it before it gets cold."

Reece reluctantly got up out of the couch and staggered into the kitchen. "That was a lot of whiskey," he said, grabbing his head.

"Hair of the dog in the cabinet if you want some more."

Reece put out his hand to signal his answer to that was no. As he fixed himself a plate of food, the others resumed their discussion.

"It's a good question," Tommy said. "Based on how well the other engravings were done, I'd be willing to bet the person who did them didn't screw up often. They were clearly at the peak of their craft."

"Exactly," Sean said. "Which makes me think it's something else."

"But what?"

Sean's head twisted back and forth slowly. "Not sure." He set the phone down next to his plate and looked at the map Tommy left on the table the night before. "I see you were working on something. Trying to figure out a pattern?"

"Yeah," Tommy nodded and forked some potatoes into his mouth.

"And?"

"And what? There's no pattern. Three locations. Three circles. The lines don't give us anything to go on."

Sean leaned back and put both hands behind his head, interlocking the fingers. He stared at the ceiling for a moment and then sat up straight. "We're thinking about this all wrong."

"How's that?" Reece asked, pulling up a seat next to Rick.

"We're trying to find the wrong answers in the wrong places. We need to go with what we know so far."

"And what do we know?" Tommy said.

"Each location we've been to has that Aboriginal rock art, right?"

The others nodded. Rick just kept eating.

"So it would stand to reason that the next place would have the same thing."

"Yeah," Reece agreed, "but there are dozens of those spots all over the country. How do you know which one to go to?"

Sean moved his plate out of the way and picked up the pen lying in the center of the map. "Give me some of the other locations, places where you've taken tourists before where there was rock art."

Reece swallowed a mouthful of food. The question caught him off guard. "Off the top of my head?"

"Yep."

"Oh wow. Um..." He struggled to think. His head still pounded from the hangover. Plus he was hungry. Not a great combination for tapping into his memory banks.

"Just start with the last one you went to," Tommy said.

Reece nodded. "Okay, yeah. I can do this." He picked up a bottle of water sitting next to him and took several big gulps. He let out a satisfied sound and then started pointing out locations on the map.

"Here," he said, tapping on a spot. "Here," he said again. "This one."

Reece went over the entire country of Australia in two minutes and gave them a working list of seven places he knew had rock art. A few were to the far west, beyond the big desert.

"There are more, I'm sure," he said. "But these are the ones I've seen."

"That's a good start," Sean said.

"Yeah, but now what?" Tommy asked. "We've got all these locations and no idea which one to visit next."

"Maybe." Sean slid the phone onto the table and flipped back to the image of the paw then swiped to the lettering. "Do any 'of these locations have wallabies?"

Rick's interest spiked. He leaned forward and spied the different spots. "I can tell you where there aren't any." He pressed his finger to the map. "These three spots definitely don't have any wallabies."

"You're sure?"

"He's right," Reece said. "You won't find any there."

"Okay, good." Sean drew a big X through each of the three circles. "That leaves us with four. Now think, what do these letters have to do with any of these places?"

The others were stumped. Their eyes went from one circle to the next and back again as they tried to unravel the mystery.

"A place that has wallabies and relates to those letters," Tommy muttered. He knew he wasn't going to be much help with Australian geography. That didn't keep him from trying.

Reece cut through the relative silence that had seeped into the room. "Wait a minute. Show me those letters again."

Sean turned the phone so the screen was facing the big Aussie.

"That's it. That's gotta be it," Reece exclaimed.

"What?" Tommy asked.

"Here." Reece stuck his finger on one of the circles in South Australia. "The Flinders Ranges."

"What makes you think that's the place?" Sean said.

Reece had to collect his thoughts while he fought the headache reverberating through his skull. "J & MC. At first I thought that meant some kind of company. It's not. It's a tribute to John and Mary Chambers. There are lots of places named after the Chambers in South Australia. Chambers Creek, Chambers Valley, and most importantly...Mount Chambers Gorge."

"What's so special about that gorge?"

"Don't you see? There are rock paintings there. Lots of them. Dozens and dozens of circles like we've been seeing."

The others were listening, but still needed more convincing.

"The paw," Reece said, "there's a rare breed of wallaby that lives in the Flinders region." He looked to the ceiling and smacked his hip to coax the answer from his mind.

"The yellow-footed wallaby," Rick said. "Nearly went extinct a long time ago from people hunting them. They've made a comeback. That wallaby is native to the Flinders Ranges."

"Yes!" Reece nearly shouted and pointed at their host. "That's it. Yellow-footed."

"Okay," Sean said. "But what if this is just an ordinary paw? Wallabies are in three other places on this map."

"Right. But the real key is the side we thought had been cut out, the one we believed was a mistake." Reece swiped the screen to see the image in question. "That's no mistake," he said. "It's a topographical map of the Flinders Ranges."

Sean flipped the phone around in his hand and looked at it. Rick stood and looked over his shoulder, moving like a sloth in the trees.

"He's right," Rick said. "Wouldn't have thought it unless you told me, but that's definitely an overhead view of the mountain range."

"Looks like a massive crater," Tommy said as he leaned over Sean's other shoulder.

"That's Wilpena Pound, one of the big attractions to the national park. That has to be the place. Mount Chambers Gorge. We have to go there next."

Sean sucked in a big breath and let it out through his nose. His head rocked back and forth. "Okay. Let's do it."

Ten minutes later, the visitors loaded into Rick's old Land Cruiser and prepared to leave.

The plan was to get back to Reece's place, grab some more supplies, ammunition, and a vehicle, and then head to the mountains. It was a long drive, but Rick didn't seem to mind.

"Not like I'm doing anything anyway," he said as he stuffed a bag in the back of the SUV.

The engine grumbled to life, and a puff of smoke spat out of the tailpipe. Sean lingered near the house for a moment, looking out in the direction of Kings Canyon. Tommy walked over and joined his friend, putting his arm around his shoulders.

He'd debated saying anything, but couldn't help himself. "You gonna be okay?"

"The woman I love is out there, Schultzie," Sean said. "Her body is at the bottom of that river or washed up on the shore. So no, I'm not okay. I have to leave her here because no matter how hard I look, I won't find her. I know that. I have to live for the rest of my life with the image of her dying right in front of me.

"All the skills and abilities I have...I couldn't save her. I have to live with that. Don't give me some speech about how it wasn't my fault, how she chose to come with us. I already know all that. It doesn't make it feel any better. And it doesn't heal the pain. No, I'm not okay. And I won't be. Even after I kill every single person responsible for this, I won't be."

"I know," Tommy said. A tear escaped his left eye and streaked down his face. "I know.

Killing the men who did this won't change the past. That said, we're going to kill them all."

Sean gave a solemn nod. "Yeah. We are."

Chapter 30
Sydney

The corner of Annie's mouth trickled a thin line of crimson down to her chin. A distinct taste—like iron—covered her tongue. During her imprisonment, the men holding her captive hadn't touched her save to throw her in the room when she arrived. Even then it had been a gentle push.

All that had changed.

Desperate men did desperate things. Apparently, that included striking a woman.

It hadn't been a full-on punch to the jaw—just a backhand across the mouth. Her face stung, though. The man's hand who struck her was broad and strong. The knuckles caught her lips at the precisely correct angle.

She did a quick inventory of her teeth with her tongue. They were all intact.

Annie swallowed and stared into the eyes of the man they called Jack. She'd been afraid for the first several days in her cell. As time wore on, her resolve steeled, and anger slowly overtook the fear.

"I already told you," she said, "I don't know anything about those things." Her obstinate tone didn't do her any favors with her captor.

Another backhand struck her cheek this time and opened a narrow cut. Annie winced and clenched her teeth as a fresh surge of pain fired through the nerves in her face. The new gash began seeping blood parallel to the trickle coming from her lips.

"You can hit me all you like," she spat. "That isn't going to jog my memory of something that isn't in there."

Jack stared down at her.

He'd noticed the change in demeanor his prisoner had gone through. In this cocoon, she'd experienced a metamorphosis from a frightened little creature to a defiant older woman who had nothing to lose. *But she still has one thing left to lose*, Jack thought.

He pulled a pistol out of his belt. Then he screwed a suppressor to the end and pressed the long barrel to the top of her head.

Annie strained against the ropes holding her to the chair. She could feel the twine cut into her wrists and ankles. The knots were too tight. She couldn't even move them a centimeter. These men knew what they were doing.

"If you have no information, then there's no use in keeping you around, is there?" Jack said. He felt the trigger tense against his finger. He also let her see the pressure on his trigger finger's skin.

"I don't care anymore," she said. "You're going to kill me anyway. Might as well get it over with so I don't have to hear your redundant questions anymore."

She's gotten braver; I'll give her that, Jack thought.

He also knew he wasn't to kill her, not yet at least. They needed information to solve the riddle of the cube. Annie was the closest thing to an expert they had. If she couldn't help, it didn't mean she was useless. Having a hostage was always a good leverage point to use in case of an emergency.

"I don't want to kill you, Annie," a voice said from the doorway.

Her eyes shifted to the man in the suit she'd seen before.

"I want to let you go," he said. "Don't get me wrong, I'll have to send you far away from here. You'll leave your job, your home, all of it. You can be put on a nice little island somewhere. I have property all over the world. All I need you to do is help me understand what these things mean."

He held out the stone cube and stepped farther into the room.

Holmes put a hand on Jack's shoulder and pulled him away. Playing the role of an angel of mercy was a new strategy. Holmes figured they'd tried everything. Maybe it would work. If not, they'd lost nothing but a little time.

"This side here," he said, pointing to the paw print, "we know it's a wallaby. But wallabies are all over the country in many places. As best as we can figure, this cube is telling a story."

"What story?" she asked, full of resentment.

"We believe the story is the place we're to go next in our search. Our problem is we don't know what this other side means. We need your help, Annie. If you help us, I will make sure you are put somewhere safe where I will never bother you again. Imagine the warm sun on your face, the sand between your toes. You've worked hard enough your whole life. You deserve a retirement like that. Don't you?"

Annie wasn't stupid. This guy was up to something. He'd gone from threatening to overly flattering bribery in no time flat. That meant they were getting really desperate. Maybe desperate enough to let her go if she helped them. *If* she could help them.

She stared at the letters on the stone. "I already told your lackey here, I don't know what those letters mean."

"I know, Annie. I know. But try to think about this in terms of the story that's being told. There is a place where wallabies live. And it relates to these letters."

She shook her head. "You don't understand. You don't have enough information."

"What do you mean?" Jack said. He'd set the pistol on a nearby table.

"I mean you two blokes are trying to do the equation without all the information. Can't be done. There's something you're not telling me, something that is key to understanding your little code."

The two men looked at each other with a questioning glance. Then they turned back to her.

"Like what?" Holmes said.

If she could have shrugged she would have. "I don't know. You tell me. What is another element to your search that you haven't mentioned? Where are some places you've gone, things you've seen there, unique physical features of the land, anything like that?"

Jack thought about her point for a moment while Holmes looked to him for answers.

"The areas we visited are all different," he said after a few seconds of thought.

Figuring out things of this nature wasn't necessarily Annie's strong suit. Her type-A personality was geared more toward what most of her career entailed—collecting information, storing information, and documenting things. Often, her job required a high level of organization and detail. Maybe her attention to detail could help her with this puzzle and get her out of this mess.

"What did you see at these places?" she asked.

Jack shrugged. "I don't know. There were big rocks, like Uluru and Kata Tjuta."

That was less than helpful. Annie started getting the distinct impression that this Jack character was more muscle than brains.

"Bring me a laptop," she said, surprising herself with how commanding her tone was. "I need to look at every location you've been to so far."

The two men froze for a moment, uncertain as to what to do. Holmes wasn't accustomed to taking orders. He looked over his shoulder at the man by the door and gave him a nod. "Get one of the laptops out of the office down the hall." He twisted back around and glared at Annie. "You'd better not be wasting our time."

She honestly didn't care if she was wasting their time or not. If so, that would be a happy side effect. But if she could actually figure out the solution to their problem, maybe Annie would have a bargaining chip.

"You'll need to untie me," she said to Jack.

Jack turned to Holmes for confirmation.

"Do it," the boss said.

Jack took a knife out of his pocket, flipped it open in an almost threatening manner, and then made quick work of the ropes he'd so diligently tied.

Annie felt the circulation pump back into her fingers and toes. She hadn't realized the blood had been mostly cut off from her extremities.

The door guard returned with a black laptop in one hand. He set it down on the table and then returned to his post. Holmes flipped the screen up, and the monitor flickered on.

Annie stood up and moved her chair over to the computer.

As she eased into the seat once more, Holmes gave her a warning. "You know that if you try anything stupid, like sending an email—even if it's just one letter—we will kill you right now."

She nodded. "Sending an email like that won't get me to the beach you promised," Annie said as coolly as possible.

Inside, her nerves had returned. The funny thing about giving people hope is that it takes away all anxiety. Knowing there might be an escape from a dreadful future can be a calming thing. Now, she felt a glimmer of hope return. It was a mere crack of light shining through a dark wall, but it was there. And it caused her fingers to tremble as she typed away at the keyboard.

"Where was the first place you visited?" she asked.

"It's a place near a small town called Milbrodale. There's a cave there with rock art. Baiame Cave." Jack's voice was deep and cold.

She typed in a few words and then hit the search button.

The search results appeared in only a few seconds. Images sat atop the top URLs for the given keyword phrases. Most of them were pictures of the cave drawings.

Annie clicked on one of the images and then scrolled through to a some of the others. Her eyes scanned the monitor, making sure she was getting everything.

"Where was the second place?" she asked.

"Uluru-Kata Tjuta National Park," Jack responded.

She typed in the name of the park and waited. Repeating the process, she looked through some of the images and stopped at one that featured rock art. "Hmm," she said. "That's interesting."

"What's interesting?" Holmes asked.

"Before you slapped me," she said to Jack, "you mentioned you went to three places. What was the third?" Annie didn't try to hide the contempt in her voice.

"Watarrka National Park, a place called Kings Canyon."

Annie typed in the terms again and hit the search button. Once more, images popped up at the top of the results. This time, however, she didn't click on them. She didn't need to. She'd already drawn her conclusion.

"The common thread you two are missing is the rock art. Seems fairly obvious to me."

The epiphany washed over Holmes. "Of course. We forgot all about the rock art. That's the missing connection."

"Yes. So if you combine that with the wallaby paw, my initial thought would be that you're looking for a place where wallabies live and where there's rock art."

"That could be any number of locations," Jack said. "There are wallabies all over this country."

Annie nodded. "I suppose that's where the letters on your rock come into play. J & MC might be a company of some sort. Or it could have been two people."

She stopped her conjecture and looked at the stone in Holmes's hand. "What about that?" she pointed at the defaced side.

"It's nothing," Jack said. "They dug it out to remove what was there."

Annie wasn't so sure. "Let me see it."

Holmes hesitated and then reluctantly set the stone on the table next to her. She picked it up. The weight of it surprised her. Annie turned it over and examined the odd side the two men believed to be a victim of vandalism.

She stared at the anomaly for nearly a minute before she spoke. "This shape. It's quite unique, like a crater. Notice how the sides of it slope up, though."

"So?" Jack asked. "Who cares? Obviously they didn't want us to know what was there."

"Seems like a strange thing to do if they were going to leave the other sides in good condition."

"Maybe they were in a hurry."

Annie shook her head. "No. You can see here that it took a good deal of time to cut the stone in this way. This thing wasn't defaced. This is a design."

Holmes jumped back into the conversation. "A design of what?"

"Well," she thought for a moment, "if my memory serves correctly, I think it's a place in South Australia."

She turned back to the computer and started pecking away at the keyboard.

"Wilpena Pound?" Holmes said.

"Yes. It's in a national park in South Australia." She hit the enter key.

Seconds later, images of a plateau with a crater in the middle appeared on the monitor. She clicked one of them and circled it with the arrow to emphasize her point.

"See? Looks an awful lot like that side of the stone."

The two men stared in astonishment.

"How did you know about this place?" Holmes asked.

"My parents took me camping there when I was a child. It's in the Flinders Ranges."

The men didn't say anything for nearly a minute. Then Holmes said, "So that is the next place we will go. We'll find the boomerang there."

"Or maybe another clue," Jack corrected.

"Right. Still, now we have something to go on."

Annie stopped both of them. "Don't be too sure about that."

"What do you mean?" Holmes said, looking distraught. "You just said that's the place."

"You're forgetting the letters on that rock of yours. You need to figure out what that has to do with this area. Besides, you don't want to go traipsing around the bush at Flinders. You could be there for weeks and not find anything."

The idea of them doing that nearly caused Annie to smile for the first time in a while, but she held it back. The longer they took to find whatever it was they wanted, the longer she would be in this box of a room. If she could help them, though, maybe they would extend a little courtesy to her.

"I want a room with a window," she said.

"What?" Jack grumbled. His face took on an irritated expression. He raised his hand to strike her again.

"Wait," Holmes said. "She's trying to help us, Jack. Take it down a notch."

"I know where you need to go next," Annie muttered.

"How's that?"

It was the ace up her sleeve. She considered not playing it, but given the circumstances, she needed to try.

"During my time in the museum, I came across more names than I care to remember. These were people who usually had some sort of importance in regard to Australian history. I didn't pay much attention to this particular pair of names at the time, but now it seems like they're the ones connected to the letters on your stone.

"How can you be so sure?"

"Because there are several areas named after those people."

Holmes grew tired of her game. "Annie, spit it out."

"I want a better room than this closet you've been keeping me in. Call it a down payment on the beach you're going to send me to."

Holmes rolled his eyes. "Fine, I'll put you in a nicer room. Now please, tell me what we're looking for."

She flashed a devilish grin and then spun back around. Her fingers flew across the keyboard, typing in the name of Mount Chambers Gorge.

"This is where you need to go."

Images of circles cut into dark red rock appeared on the screen.

"It's named after John and Mary Chambers. J&MC, as the stone suggests."

The men didn't speak for almost twenty seconds as they stared at the images on the computer screen.

Finally, Holmes cut through the silence. "Astounding. Good work, Annie. See? That wasn't so hard?"

Holmes turned and started for the door.

"Wait," she said. "My room?"

Jack picked up the computer and followed his boss to the doorway.

Holmes stopped mid-stride and spun around. "Jack, have Miss Guildford here moved to a better room. And get her a change of clean clothes."

Annie stared down at the table and smiled. She'd just given herself a way out.

Chapter 31
South Australia

The drive back to Reece's place seemed to take forever. To say the air conditioning in Rick's truck didn't work well would be a vast understatement. During the day, the four men spent much of the time sticking their heads out the windows to let the wind evaporate the perspiration from their faces and heads. Fortunately, half of the journey took place at night when the temperatures were much milder.

As soon as Tommy's phone hit cell service, it started vibrating repeatedly in his pocket. He fished out the device and checked the screen. He'd missed a half-dozen text messages plus three voicemails from Tara and Alex.

"Got something from the kids," he announced, breaking the long silence.

"What is it?" Sean asked.

Tommy held up a finger and mouthed, "One minute," as he listened to the first voicemail.

He finished it and then put the phone against his ear again, listening to the second.

"They found something. The hackers weren't using a periscope. They put a trace on your accounts. That's how those guys were following us. They tracked our purchases."

"We didn't buy much," Sean said. "Except at that diner in Richmond."

"And getting gas on the drive."

"By then they were already on our trail, could have been following us for hours."

"You didn't see anything unusual, did you?" Reece asked.

"No," Sean said. Admittedly, he'd been so tired, he kept dozing off on the ride out to Kata Tjuta. Though he never stayed asleep long on the journey, all those moments added up.

Tommy continued relaying information. "Alex said it wasn't any kind of traditional hacking job. He said it had to be done by someone on the inside of the credit card company."

Sean's forehead wrinkled as he frowned. "Most of them do operate on common systems. But for someone to have access to that...there would need to be significant resources behind them."

Tommy put the phone back in his pocket when he'd finished listening to the voicemail. "They're going to call me back if they find anything else."

"Sounds like they found a good bit," Reece said.

"Yeah. Unfortunately it doesn't tell us much, only that whoever is after us is adept at using computers."

"And has a ton of resources," Sean repeated. He stared out the window. "Back in the late 1980s there was a big hack job down here in Australia. Some hackers out of Melbourne used a worm to mess with a bunch of corporate computers."

"Alex said these probably weren't hackers, though," Tommy said.

"Right. Was just thinking out loud. Doing something like this requires knowing how to do it. I doubt a coder at the credit card company has it in for us. They were paid to tag our account."

"We've only used cash since we called the kids."

"Yeah, which we still need to do." Then out of nowhere, Sean had an epiphany. "Tommy, give me your phone. I need to make a call."

****

When they arrived at Reece's the next day, the men made a quick transfer of vehicles. They thanked Rick for his assistance and said their goodbyes before loading up supplies from the shed.

Reece had an assortment of rifles and handguns, nothing the Americans would pay money for back home, but definitely tools that would do the job in a pinch. Sean also asked if the big Aussie had any stump remover, sugar, and a few others items.

After Reece brought the ingredients to Sean, he disappeared into the house.

Curious as to what he was doing, Tommy went in after twenty minutes had passed and found Sean cooking up a strange concoction in a big frying pan.

"What are you doing?" Tommy asked.

Sean poured the thick mixture into a cardboard cylinder he'd taken from the battery pack of an old drill and then dipped a piece of string into the batter.

"Wait," Tommy said, "are you making fireworks or something?"

"Sort of. These are smoke bombs. They'll last about half a minute or so. Long enough to buy us some time if we need it."

"How'd you make the fuses?"

"Dipped them in a weaker variation of this stuff."

Tommy pouted his lips and nodded. "I'm impressed. That one of the things the government taught you to do?"

"No. I learned this on YouTube."

Before Tommy could ask his friend if he was serious or not, Sean set the six smoke bombs on a baking tray and then covered them with aluminum foil. "We should be going," he said as he picked up the metal sheet.

"It's gonna be dark soon. Should we stay here for the night?"

"Maybe," Sean said. "But seeing how this place has already been shot up once, I'm thinking a night in a few tents might be a better option. You know, in case they come back."

"Fair enough."

"Plus I don't want to waste any time. We get there, set up camp tonight, we can get up early tomorrow and get to work."

Sean's idea made sense, no matter how tired they all were of being in a car.

"At least my truck's got air," Reece said to the two Americans when they returned to the driveway.

"That's a relief," Tommy said.

"Yeah, it's not ice cold, but it's better than old Rick's truck. Should take us little over four hours to get there. I know a place that's not far from those petroglyphs where we can camp. We'll blend right in with all the other campers."

The three men watched the sunset on the western horizon from the road for the second time in twenty-four hours. The drive was mostly made in silence, just as the previous one. Conversation only happened when they needed to pull over for gas or bathroom breaks. On the four-hour journey, that only happened once.

They arrived well after dark at the Flinders Ranges. The big, jagged mountain peaks were bathed in bluish white moonlight against the backdrop of stars.

Reece steered the SUV down a gravel and dirt road into a camping area littered with tents and caravan-style campers. He passed plenty of vacant spots in favor of getting away from the family outings and tourists. Setting up camp away from everyone else would keep innocent people safe in case bullets started flying. It also gave the Americans and their Australian friend plenty of space to see or hear any approaching threat. Campgrounds tended to be loud, full of people singing or talking loudly around a fire. That wouldn't help anyone.

They found a place just three minutes past the last tent. It was a flat area about forty feet off the road, tucked between a few rocky mounds.

"That'll do," Sean said, pointing at the camping area.

Reece turned the wheel and guided the truck into the spot. The men got out quickly and took a look around. They were just out of earshot from the other campers. No lights impeded the incredible view of the stars. Sean stared up at them for a long moment, thinking of the times he and Adriana had sat under a sky like that nearly all night. The celestial bodies were so prominent now, he felt like he could almost touch them. A novel idea popped into his mind that maybe, just maybe, it was some kind of sign that he was doing what he was supposed to. He shook his head and refocused on the thing that was driving him. Revenge.

"You sure about this location, Sean?" Tommy asked. "Don't you want to have the high ground?" He pointed at the two mounds.

"In a fight, yeah. When you're trying to hide, no."

"What's your plan?" Reece asked.

"We've been cautious, so there's no way they would have tracked us with our credit cards the last few days. That doesn't mean these guys aren't going to show up here. We might as well plan on that happening."

"If they found the stone cube and were able to figure out its meaning, that is definitely possible," Tommy said. "Still, I think it's unlikely."

"We deciphered it," Sean said. "Remember what I always say: Plan for the worst. So put it in your heads that these guys are either already here or they're on their way."

Even in the darkness, Sean's steel resolve shone through in his eyes. "Keep the lights low. Try to do as much as possible in the dark. The fewer people know we're here, the better."

The men spent the next half hour setting up two tents and laying out a mattress in the back of the truck. Reece volunteered to sleep in the SUV. Sean wouldn't hear of it. He insisted the big Aussie sleep in one of the tents because he'd have more leg room. After a few minutes of coaxing, Reece finally acquiesced.

When Tommy and the Australian were in their tents, Sean crawled into the back of the truck and lay down on his back. He stared at the SUV's ceiling for more than a half hour while tears trickled down his face. While he was distracted, the reality that Adriana was dead seemed like fiction. He could push it away for short bursts of time, convincing himself that it hadn't really happened. Then the truth came crashing down on him again, and the cycle started over.

"Why her?" he muttered to himself. "Why?"

Sean considered himself a believer in a creator. Raised in a Christian home, he grew up with a firm foundation in spiritual teachings. Through the years, those beliefs changed and morphed into something he thought transcended religion.

Early on in his role with Axis, he'd struggled with taking lives of evil men. Then he came to realize that sometimes, the forces of good had to use weapons to protect the innocent.

The way he saw it, he was a sword of God.

He used to pray every day, usually just for a few seconds to give appreciation for his life and the things in it. Over time, he'd gotten so busy that a day or two slipped by where he simply forgot.

His spiritual life had taken a backseat.

Now, as he lay in the back of Reece's old SUV, surrounded by the smell of old upholstery and metal, he prayed again.

Sean didn't know what good it would do. He knew there was nothing that could bring Adriana back. She was gone. Really, he just wanted answers. Everything he'd ever learned about God was being challenged now.

Maybe that was justice for all the years of killing he'd done. All the lives he'd taken as judge, jury, and executioner drifted by his mind's eye. Judgment was upon him now.

He wiped the tears from his cheeks. "Is that what this is? Repayment for what I've done?"

Outside the open tailgate of the SUV, the desert was still, almost perfectly silent.

"Some kind of sign would be good," he said. "Or at least some comfort."

None came.

He waited another five minutes in silence and then said, "If you're there, I just wish you'd fix this for me."

Then he remembered back to a time when he was in training, only weeks before he became a full-time Axis agent. One of his superiors put him through a drill that seemed almost impossible.

It was meant to be difficult as a way to weed out the lesser recruits. In fact, it was so strenuous, only 3 percent of people in the training program made it through.

"Are we going to encounter anything this tough out in the real world?" Sean asked.

His trainer stared through him into his soul. The man never blinked, never cracked a smile as he spoke. "You will experience much more difficult things than this out in the field."

Sean had found that difficult to believe at the time. "Tougher than this?"

The trainer nodded. "Far worse. We put our recruits through this for two reasons. One, to test mental and physical fortitude. If you're captured in the field, you have to be able to resist torture of both kinds: mind *and* body."

"And the other reason?"

"We are higher beings," the man said. "We cannot depend on luck or external forces to help us. You have been given a conscious mind that determines your fate every single moment of every day you will live."

Sean considered the man's words. "So what you're saying is, don't hope for a miracle."

"Not at all," the man shook his head. "What I'm saying is, don't hope for one to come from somewhere else. Everything you need is readily available to you at all times."

Sean's mind snapped back to Reece's SUV. He took in a deep breath and let it out slowly. Outside, a light breeze rolled across the outback and blew cool, dry air into the truck. Sean wasn't sure if it was the sign he was looking for, but he'd take it.

Utter exhaustion took hold of him and pulled him down into the darkness where emotions no longer held sway. His eyes closed, and Sean fell into a deeper sleep than he'd had in a week.

Chapter 32
Flinders Ranges
South Australia

Tommy woke up at the sound of his phone vibrating on the nylon floor next to his sleeping bag. He reached over and took a look at the screen. His eyes were still blurry, and it took a moment for them to adjust before he could read it.

"Voicemail from Tara," he said. "Can't believe I have service out here."

He tapped the button and listened to the message.

"Hey, Tommy, it's Tara. Just wanted to let you guys know that we kept digging around but couldn't find out any more information about the people behind the credit card tracking. Sorry we couldn't be more help."

"That's disappointing," Tommy muttered.

He pressed his finger to the screen to listen to the second message from Tara.

"Oh, I almost forgot. The one piece of information we *were* able to obtain was that the credit card company recently went through a big merger. They were acquired by an oil company based in Australia. That company was also in the news lately for a major tragedy. Apparently, the entire board of directors was killed in a horrific elevator accident a few days ago. Only one of the men survived because he stayed behind to get some work done in his office. Now he controls pretty much everything. Seems a little fishy to me. Not sure if it helps, but his name is Bernard Holmes. Might want to check it out if you get the chance."

A rush of excitement coursed through Tommy's veins. It was a reach, but at least it was something. Up until now, they'd had nothing to go on.

If Tara's hunch was right, though, they may have just found the man behind it all.

Tommy thought about it again. Holmes's company acquires credit card company. Tara didn't say when exactly that happened. However, if this Holmes character was one of the principal owners, he'd have access to people who could put tracking tabs on certain cards.

The fact that twelve men from the board of directors were killed recently—while Holmes was left unharmed—also smacked of conspiracy. Was it a coincidence that when the entire board died, he got everything? Couldn't be.

Tommy would need more information. He tapped the screen again to return the call to Tara. A warning appeared on the screen. He was out of service. He should have noticed a moment before that he only had one bar. Out here in the bush, cell service would be spotty at best.

Still brimming with the new information, Tommy unzipped the sleeping bag and then the tent entrance. He slipped on his shoes and then unzipped the vestibule. He couldn't contain what he'd just learned and started yammering before he climbed out.

"Sean, Reece. Wake up. I just got a voicemail from Tara." He nearly shouted as the words spilled out of his mouth. "She seems to think some wealthy oil guy named Bernard..." Tommy stopped in mid-sentence as he stood up from the tent and realized he was not alone.

He looked around the campsite at the strange faces.

Six men wearing tan military-style gear with assault rifles surrounded the tents and vehicle, covering every escape point. Two of them held Sean and Reece at gunpoint. One of the six was standing next to Reece's SUV. He had a different look than the rest, cleaner. Tommy immediately identified him as the leader.

A second later, that suspicion was confirmed when the man spoke. "You were saying?"

Tommy didn't respond.

"Seems like you said you knew who was behind all this. That's unfortunate. Mr. Holmes would much prefer to keep his identity anonymous with this little operation. Not good for public relations."

The guy spoke with a sharp Australian accent. He had an athletic build, probably a former athlete turned goon because of a past injury.

"I see you met my friends," Tommy motioned to the others.

"Sorry, Schultzie," Sean said. "I don't know what happened to me. I never sleep like that."

Tommy couldn't believe these guys got the drop on Sean. He must have been completely exhausted for that to happen. Sean was always up early, and he was a light sleeper—something that Tommy assumed he'd picked up during his time working for Axis.

"If you would be so kind as to join your friends over there," the guy in charge said, "we were just about to execute them."

Tommy trudged over to where the other two were standing and took his place next to Sean. He didn't say anything to his friend about sleeping late into the morning. He'd just lost the most important person in his life. Tommy knew what that felt like. Those same emotions had racked his body for weeks after his parents were killed.

One of the other men stepped over and raised a pistol to the back of Tommy's head.

Right about now would be when Sean pulled some kind of miracle out of his rear, putting his super spy skills to work to take out all six of the bad guys, Tommy thought. His friend, however, didn't move. He just stared straight ahead with a blank look on his face.

"I know you," Reece said as he glared at the man in charge. "You're Jack Robinson. I used to cheer for you back in the day when you played rugby."

Jack fired a cynical smile at Reece. "Well, it's always nice to meet a fan. Unfortunately, those days are long gone, and I have to kill you now."

"What was it that happened?" Reece tried to keep the conversation going. "Blew out your knee and never recovered, right? ACL injury to the left knee?"

"That's right. After that injury, I was never the same. Luckily for me, I picked up some other work. And it pays much better. Now, as much as I appreciate this trip down memory lane, we have to be killing you. There's a treasure to find, and our employer is quite intent to get it soon." Jack turned and stepped away to keep from getting splattered with blood.

Tommy felt the muzzle press into the back of his skull. A hundred different ideas zipped through his brain. He grabbed one and ran with it. "You kill us, you'll never get that golden boomerang for your boss."

Jack cocked his head to the side with a quizzical look on his face. "Why would you think that? We have the cube. And we know exactly where to look."

"Yeah. But do you know how to decipher the petroglyphs?"

Jack paused for a second, which told Tommy everything he needed to know. The guy was in the dark.

"You're about to kill the only people in the world who can help you decode those ancient circles," Tommy lied. There were plenty of people who could do that, but he was betting this former rugger had no idea. He was out of his element. "You kill us, and you'll never find that boomerang. Then what will happen? I imagine someone like Holmes has enough money to replace you pretty easily. In fact, some of these guys working for you would probably be happy to take your place."

Jack's eyes narrowed. "So, you're going to throw empty threats at me in hopes of living a few more minutes?"

"I was thinking hours would be good," Tommy said. "Call it a survival instinct."

"He's serious," Sean finally spoke up. "Without us, that boomerang is as good as lost to antiquity. You said you have the cube. But what you don't have is what I found while we were in Kings Canyon."

Jack took a cautious step forward. "Ah, so the great Sean Wyatt speaks. I gotta say, mate, you don't look all that tough to me." He stopped a few inches from Sean's nose.

"Me? Oh, I'm not that tough. Not tough enough to play rugby with a guy like you."

Jack towered over Sean by three or four inches. Sean's instincts were to grab him and put Jack between himself and the gun in his back. In the two seconds that move would take, the gunman could easily put a round through Sean's spine. Part of him didn't care. Another part—the well-trained agent deep inside—knew he'd have to wait for the opportune moment.

"Speaking of tough," Sean said, "you always kill women by shooting them in the back?"

A puzzled look filled Jack's eyes. "What are you talking about?"

Sean searched the man for a lie, but there was none to be found on his face or in his voice. "You killed her," he said through clenched teeth.

Then it hit Jack as to what Sean was referring. "Ah. The girl. Yes, she is dead. But I'm not the one who killed her, mate. One of my men did," he said with a cheerful smile on his face that begged to be punched. If Sean hadn't had a gun in his back, he would have knocked that grin into the gorge.

A short snicker escaped Jack's lips. "If it makes you feel better, I heard she died quick."

He met the fury in Sean's eyes with a hollow stare and then stepped back. Jack looked down the line at each of the three men. "Very well. Let's see what you blokes know. I'll let you live for a few more minutes, at least." He turned to two of his gunmen. "Bring the trucks around, and load them up. We're going over to the rocks to have a look."

He twisted around and put his hands on his hips, staring at the three friends. "You try anything funny..."

"Yeah, we know. You'll kill us," Tommy cut him off.

"Right."

An SUV and a four-door pickup truck came around the bend three minutes after Jack's henchmen trotted down the road. The two Americans were forced into the truck bed first, followed by Reece. Two gunmen sat in the back with them, keeping their weapons trained on the prisoners while the driver steered the vehicle down the bumpy dirt road.

The drive from the campground to the petroglyphs only took fifteen minutes or so. It was still so early in the morning, they were the first vehicles to arrive at the heavily frequented site.

Jack hopped out of the SUV and motioned to his men to take the prisoners off the truck bed and herd them toward the trail.

His men did as told, forcing Sean and the others off the truck. They marched reluctantly to the trail head and beyond until the parking area was out of sight.

Reece led the way since he knew where they were headed. "Never thought I'd be coming to this gorge with a gun pointed at me," he said.

"You hang around us long enough," Tommy said, "you'll get used to it."

"No offense, Tom, but I'd rather not get used to having a gun aimed at me."

"It's an acquired taste," Sean said.

"Quiet, you three," Jack snapped from a few guys back on the trail. "Unless you want to cut that arrangement short now. I got no problem dumping your bodies down the gorge."

"Probably going to do that anyway," Sean muttered.

"Don't give him any ideas," Tommy said.

The men kept marching down the trail, by dried brush and diminutive trees until they reached a point where the trail opened. To their right, a wall of dark red rocks jutted up into the sky.

The surface of the stone wall was covered in dozens of circles, lines, white hands, and a myriad of other designs. Tommy drifted unconsciously over to the symbols and ran his fingers over the rock, making sure he didn't touch the art itself.

"So tell us what it all means," Jack said, standing a good three yards away from the American.

"It doesn't work like that," Tommy said. "Each of these symbols could have a different meaning. We have to interpret that first and then figure out how it all ties together with the riddle from the cube."

Jack considered his response and then pursed his lips. He shook his head. "No, I'll tell you how it's going to work. You get thirty minutes. By then, tourists will start showing up. Can't have that, now can we? So if you don't have this little puzzle figured out in a half hour, well...I'll just have my men go ahead and kill the lot of you."

"Half an hour? These things can take months."

"You have thirty minutes. And I already started the clock. You'd best get to it."

Tommy glanced at his friends. Reece and Sean looked back at him with sympathetic eyes.

"We'll do our best," Sean said for Tommy.

He moved close and stared up at the wall.

"Any ideas?" Tommy whispered.

"Yeah, but they all involve the guns these guys took from us at the campsite."

"Touché."

Reece stepped close. "What are you two talking about?"

"Fanciful dreams where we have guns, and those guys are all bleeding to death on the ground," Sean answered.

"Well, those kinds of things don't really get us out of this situation, now do they? I was thinking more in terms of understanding what we're looking at?"

"It's nonsense," Tommy said in a hushed tone so their keepers couldn't hear. "All of this, it's gibberish. There's no pattern to any of it. These circles point to these?" He motioned with his hand as he spoke. "And then you have these pointing off to another set." His hand waved again to other corresponding circles. "And I still have no idea what all these white hands mean."

"Stop worrying about those hands, and focus," Sean said. "We have to live long enough to make a move. I don't care if you have to make up the details."

The men spent twenty minutes studying the wall, desperately trying to understand the code embedded in rock. When twenty-five minutes had passed, Jack gave them a reminder. "You blokes have five minutes left. Then we'll just dump you in the gorge."

Sean took a step back and examined the dark red surface. There were circles on top of circles, like the entire journey up to this point would only end in mass confusion—as was represented by the art.

The only thing that seemed different in the drawings was the figure of a human that lingered high above the rest. At first, Sean didn't think much of it. He and the other two largely ignored the aberration because it lacked detail and wasn't really similar to anything they'd seen before.

Maybe it was time to give it a second look.

He gazed at the image, twisting his head back and forth.

Tommy was next to him, counting to himself. Sean figured his friend was trying to see if there was a numerical meaning to all the symbols.

Sean had noticed that the figure drawn into the rock had a strange body shape. While Baiame had been a skinny figure with long arms and legs, this one had those thin appendages, but the torso was swollen and rotund. Inside it was another large circle with several dots smattered on it. One dot in the middle was slightly bigger than all the others.

"What about that figure?" Sean said to Tommy. "Think it has anything to do with what we're looking for?"

"I was wondering the same thing," Reece said.

"I took a look at it earlier," Tommy answered. "It doesn't seem to be like anything we've seen. It's just random. Like everything else on this wall."

Sean frowned and looked back up at the figure. "Wait a minute. Think, Tommy. When all this started, we went to Baiame Cave. We're looking for the boomerang of Baiame."

"Right... Where are you going with all this?"

"The Baiame story, Schultzie. What does the legend say happened to this god?"

Tommy shrugged. "I don't know. I only read a little about it. According to the story, he left the people of Earth from the top of a mountain."

"Which mountain?"

Tommy's eyes went wide as he realized Sean had just unraveled the code. "Yengo," he whispered. "The story said Baiame ascended into the sky from the top of Mount Yengo." Then his temporary high vanished. "Even if that is the right place, it has to be a huge area. We don't know where to look once we're there."

Sean turned his head and spied the dots in the middle of the circle on Baiame's torso. "I do."

"Time's up," Jack said as he stepped forward toward the three friends. "Do you have the solution for me, or do we start dumping bodies into the ravine?"

"We know where to go next," Tommy said.

"Tell me. Maybe I'll make your deaths quick."

"No," Sean said. "See, here's the problem. We know where you need to go next, but you have no idea. I'm willing to bet you can't figure it out like we just did. So, as I see it, you're going to need to take us with you to the next location."

"I think maybe you're bluffing," Jack said after a moment of careful thought. "Maybe you don't know the solution to this riddle and you're just trying to bide your time, hoping my men and I slip up."

Sean stared through him. "Do you want your golden boomerang or not? I'm thinking your boss, Mr. Holmes, would rather have it sooner than later." He waited for a minute as Jack considered. "Or you could just kill us right now and then never find the stupid thing. I'm sure Holmes would be happy about that."

Jack clenched his jaw. "You do realize that you are going to have to tell us where we're going before we get there. Once you do that, what need do I have for you anymore?"

"I thought you might ask that," Sean said. "Even if I told you the name of the place you need to go, you could search for a hundred years and never find where that boomerang is hidden."

"And I suppose you know the exact location?"

Sean's head moved up and down. "Yeah."

"And you'll lead us right to it?"

"More or less."

Tommy and Reece watched the exchange like a fierce tennis match of words lobbed back and forth.

"For your sake, I hope it's more." Jack turned to his henchmen. "Back to the trucks. Let's get out of here before the visitors start arriving. Tie these three down in the back of the pickup, and keep a close eye on them. If any one of them tries anything stupid, shoot them."

Jack stepped close to Sean, again hovering over him like a statue. "If you're lying to me and wasting my time, I'll make sure you die very slowly."

Chapter 33
Sydney

Camera crews wedged in closer to the podium to try and get a better angle. Flashes went off across the room. Reporters sat on the edges of their seats, eagerly awaiting what the chairman would say. Some held up their smartphones to record the press conference. Laps were full of notepads with notes jotted down—questions to be asked of the petroleum giant's head man.

Bernard Holmes stepped out into the light from behind a dark blue curtain. He offered a solemn grin, keeping in character with the sadness he wished to portray. Much had been made of the recent elevator tragedy that killed his board of directors. He'd pretended to be reluctant about taking the reins on his own but promised to put together a new board from some of the more active shareholders.

Many called it a miracle that he'd survived. Others had said it was a lucky coincidence he'd stayed behind to do a little extra work in the office. Then there were a few who claimed the whole thing was a conspiracy—all engineered by Holmes so that he could gain total control of the company.

Those mouths were soon hushed.

In the old days, Holmes would have simply had the conspiracy theorists murdered. It was the way things were handled. Now—in the digital age—things had to be taken care of with subtler tactics.

With the resources Holmes had at his disposal, it was easy enough to make things happen rapidly.

One reporter who'd written an article about the Holmes theory was arrested for heroin possession just three days after the piece was published. Police dragged him out of his home, kicking and screaming as he tried to proclaim his innocence. Another writer was taken into custody after authorities—working on an anonymous tip—found ten gigabytes of child pornography on his computer.

The one that made Holmes laugh, though, was the reporter who actually *had* done something wrong. The guy had a cocaine addiction, which provided the perfect cover for a hit. Holmes made sure the writer was supplied with a doctored stash of blow. Two days later, the man was found dead of an overdose by the river, sitting in his car.

If anyone else had suspicions regarding Holmes and the deaths of everyone on his board, they kept quiet about it.

He gripped the edges of the podium and looked out at the dozens of eager people. He pinched his lips together as if hesitating for a moment and then began his speech.

"Life gives us many challenges. We are tasked with things that often we believe are too difficult for us to bear. Sometimes these trials carry tragedy with them, as is the case with my..." He faltered for a second to add effect. "Pardon me." He cleared his throat and began again. "As is the case with my coworkers and friends on the board.

"First off, I would like to once more extend my condolences to the families of those we lost in that vicious terrorist attack." He looked down at a middle-aged woman in the front row. Her blonde hair cascaded over the shoulders of her $3,000 dress. She dabbed one of her eyes, fighting back a tear. Holmes had to fight back a laugh. The woman had been married to one of the men on the board. Clearly a gold digger, she was twenty-five years younger than her husband. With his death, she'd become even wealthier than before. Holmes would give her time to mourn before he called on her.

He went on. "This company has experienced extraordinary growth over the last five years. Their leadership and abilities to guide us to tremendous success cannot be questioned. Now we are left with the task of trying to find our way through without them."

Stocks had dropped by nearly half once the news of the elevator incident hit the airwaves. Holmes wasn't stupid enough to sell off his stock before the murders. He knew prices would go down, which is why he had Jack sell off every piece of the company he owned and then buy it back tenfold after things bottomed out.

This press conference would send the stock soaring again. But that was only the beginning.

"We are entering a tenuous age for this company, and for the energy sector as well. The energy needs of the world are not decreasing. Yesterday, there were seven billion people on Earth. Today there are eight. Tomorrow, there will be ten. All of them will need fuel to get them through their days. We are committed to providing that energy to the people of the world so that the human race can continue progressing forward into the dawn of a new era."

His crescendo ended with a round of applause from nearly everyone in the room.

When the clapping died down, he put up a hand. "I can tell you this. No terrorist attack is going to stop us. Our resolve is strong. We will continue moving forward in finding new energy resources. In fact, at this very moment we are working on a deal that will more than double our oil reserves from new deposits our researches have discovered."

The crowd oohed and aahed over the comment. Doubling the reserves would mean doubling profits. Several reporters raised their hands simultaneously, eager to be the first to ask about the new deposits and their location.

Holmes ignored their questions and continued. "Our company has faced difficulty before. We will certainly face it again. But I can promise you this, no one will stand in the way of us providing Australia and the world with the energy it needs to move forward. Because if we are not moving forward, we are not progressing. Our number one goal is progress, not just for the company, but for the world."

The crowd roared again.

He put up both hands as if to thank them and then waved as he left the podium and disappeared behind the curtain.

One of his assistants stood close by holding a cell phone in his hand. "It's Mr. Robinson, sir. He said it's urgent."

"Thank you, Kip," Holmes said as he took the phone.

He put the device to his ear and walked down the hall to get out of the assistant's range of hearing. "Good news, this time?"

"Yes, sir. We have the Americans and their friend. We're en route to Yengo National Park. They say that's where we'll find it."

Holmes raised both eyebrows. "That *is* good news. I guess my question would be, why do you still have the Americans?"

"We kept them as an insurance policy. Want to make sure they take us to the right place before we off them."

"Good thinking," Holmes said with a nod. "If Yengo is indeed where the boomerang is located, let me know as soon as you find it. Once we have it, we can approach the tribes about signing the land over to us. We may even be able to get it cheap." He nearly laughed at the idea.

"You'll be the first to know," Jack said.

Holmes hung up the phone and looked out the window at the downtown district of Sydney. People busily rushed around on the sidewalks and in their cars. He allowed himself a broad smile.

Everything was going according to plan.

Chapter 34
Yengo National Park

The passengers in the back of the pickup truck tipped back and forth as the driver steered through the curvy roads. Thick forests of green trees whooshed by along the road.

Sean braced himself with one arm on the truck bed rail. They'd spent the rest of the previous day and all of the night traveling in the back of the pickup. Sleeping wouldn't have been possible except for the injections they'd been given shortly after leaving Flinders.

The drug worked quickly, and before they knew it, the three companions were out cold.

While sleeping hadn't been a bad thing, sleeping in the bed of a pickup truck had consequences.

Tommy groaned next to Sean and rubbed his left shoulder. Reece was next to him, shifting uneasily in an attempt to stretch out his back.

Pretty much every muscle was sore, but Sean wasn't going to let his captors hear him complain. And he wasn't going to let them see any discomfort. One rule he'd always kept in mind was to let the enemy believe he was invincible, unaffected by things that would bring down mere mortals. It put doubts in the enemy's mind when bullets started flying. Doubts led to weaknesses.

"Would it have been too much to ask for you guys to put down a mattress?" Tommy asked.

Sean almost rolled his eyes. Unfortunately, his friend didn't deploy the same mental warfare.

"I mean seriously, my shoulder is killing me?" Tommy went on.

"Your shoulder?" Reece said. "My back is all out of sorts."

Tommy looked around at the passing scenery. Temperatures had cooled significantly from the hot desert, and there was more humidity in the air. He glanced over at Reece. "Where are we?"

Reece peered down the road behind the truck. "From the looks of it, I'd say we're close to Yengo."

"How long were we out?" Tommy asked.

"About sixteen hours," Sean said.

"What? Are you serious?"

"Why do you think your shoulder is so messed up? You've been unconscious in a truck bed for almost a day."

Tommy tossed his head back and forth to shake the cobwebs from his mind. "I do feel a bit groggy."

"That would be the drugs."

"You guys got any more of that stuff?" Reece said to their guards. "Been having a bit of trouble sleeping lately."

The two gunmen said nothing.

Sean chuckled. It was the first time he'd laughed since... He pushed the thought out of his mind. *It's not real,* he told himself.

The truck's driver steered the pickup onto a side road. They passed a wooden sign that identified the area as Yengo Mountain. The ride got bumpier as they climbed the base of the mountain. Sharp curves pushed the occupants left and right and back again. The driver was probably driving a little too fast, but Sean knew they were in a hurry.

While his two friends looked out at the passing view, Sean locked his eyes on the guard nearest him. He stared at the man like he was a piece of meat about to be devoured. At first, the guard returned the icy stare, unflinching. After several minutes, though, Sean could tell the guy was starting to get unsettled. The nervous movements were subtle. A normal person probably wouldn't have noticed. Like they had so many times before, Sean's poker skills of being able to read a person's body language paid off.

The truck made a sharp turn onto gravel and then another quick turn in the other direction as the driver pulled into an empty parking space. Before Sean took his eyes off the guard, he offered one last smirk before he took a look around.

The parking area could hold no more than four or five cars and was surrounded by tall trees. The dense forest reminded the Americans of the Blue Ridge Mountains back home and only parted at a trailhead nearby where the path ascended, disappearing around a bend several hundred feet away. To get to the trailhead, the group would have to walk through a gate that apparently protected the mountain from motorized vehicles.

"I'm glad to see you're awake," Jack said as he stepped around the front of the pickup.

The two guards stood up and let the tailgate down. They hopped to the ground, keeping their weapons on the prisoners.

"Thanks for the accommodations," Sean said. "I haven't slept that hard in ten years."

Jack's eyes narrowed at Sean's sarcasm. Something in the American's tone suggested he wasn't kidding about the sleep.

"Happy to oblige you. And not to worry, soon you'll be sleeping for much longer. Now, if you don't mind, we should get going. Mr. Holmes is eager to receive his prize."

"I'm sure he is."

"And will Mr. Holmes be joining us on this lovely outing?" Reece asked.

"Mr. Holmes has other things commanding his attention at the moment," Jack answered. "Now, get moving." He brandished his pistol and pointed it at Sean.

Sean snorted derisively. "You think that's the first time I've had one of those shoved in my face, kid?" he asked as he got up slowly and made his way to the back of the truck.

"It might be your last."

"Predictable response," Sean said to himself. Bad guys always had the weakest comebacks.

Tommy climbed down next to his friend, still working his shoulder back and forth. "You know if this is the place where the boomerang is hidden, we might need some tools for digging and such," he said. His hope was to delay things by a few hours while Jack's men went to the nearest town to buy supplies.

His hopes were dashed the second he saw two of the guards walk around the front of the pickup, carrying backpacks with shovels, picks, a mattock, and crow bars hanging off the sides.

"Oh," Tommy said, realizing his plan was an instant failure.

The guards handed the packs to the three prisoners.

"So I guess you want us to carry these then?"

"Very astute of you," Jack replied. "Now move."

The climb up Mount Yengo might as well have been Everest for Tommy. While Reece and Sean were accustomed to the rigors of exercise, Tommy's lack of fitness revealed itself after the first four minutes of hiking.

The trail was steep in spite of the twists and turns carving up the mountain. Tommy stopped to catch his breath every five minutes but was ushered ahead with a rifle barrel in his back.

"Don't suppose you boys brought us any water?" Reece asked after they'd been hiking for twenty minutes.

The cool mountain air seemed to disappear in the wake of the group's strenuous hike. Thirst scratched their throats as sweat rolled down their faces.

The guards had bottles of water in mesh holders on the sides of their backpacks but offered none to the prisoners. Instead, they casually took intermittent drinks during the ascent.

"He's right," Tommy said in between gasps for air. "It's...it's important to stay...to stay hydrated. You wouldn't want one of us to die from heat stroke, would you?"

"Pretty sure you're going to be just fine," Jack said. "We'll give you some water when you get to the top."

"I...was...afraid...you'd say that." Tommy grunted and kept moving.

Despite Sean's high fitness level, he too started struggling. Most of his exercise regimen revolved around sprint training, some slow jogs, and hitting the weights a few times each week. He wasn't accustomed to carrying forty pounds of gear up a steep incline. In his youth he'd done a little backpacking here and there, but not enough to make a difference in the here and now.

Thirty minutes into the hike, the forest opened up to a wide meadow that stretched three hundred yards from left to right. It was covered in tall golden grasses atop shorter green fescue. Across the meadow, the forest continued up the mountain, but there was no trail to be found.

Reece stopped in a patch of grass and turned around to face the others. "You guys do realize that no one is to go beyond this point, right?"

Jack stepped forward through the ranks and drew his pistol, leveling it at Reece's abdomen. "Keep going."

"You don't understand, mate. That's Aborigine sacred ground just beyond those trees. Bad juju to go up there."

Sean and Tommy exchanged a curious, sidelong glance. They weren't sure if Reece was serious or just trying to catch a breather. There was no way Jack was going to let them stop now, sacred ground or not.

"You and your friends said what we're looking for is up there on the top of that mountain. Now either you're lying, or you're not. So, I can kill you right now and leave all three of you here for the animals to feast on, or you can lead on."

Reece looked back at the two Americans. He sighed. "Okay, mate. It's your funeral."

"Soon—"

"Soon it will be ours?" Sean cut Jack off before he could finish his sentence. "Clever. Thank you so much for that."

Jack spun around with fury in his eyes. He clenched his jaw and then marched ahead behind Reece.

Sean started moving forward. He didn't look at his friend as he spoke. "You'd think these villains would have some original material every once in a while."

Reece reached the edge of the woods and paused for a second. He looked down one side of the boundary and then the other before glancing back at Sean and Tommy.

He had a genuinely scared look on his face, not from the guns pointed at him but from something else. It was almost as if he believed the place was haunted.

"What's the holdup?" Jack asked. "Get on with it."

"Spirits," Reece said. "Spirits of the ancient ones are here."

He looked like he'd seen a ghost, the color in his skin fading to a pale ash.

"There'll be one more if you don't move."

Reece lifted his foot and set it down on the leaves just beyond the meadow. He let out a sigh of relief and then took another step, then another. Gradually, he picked up speed until he was deep inside the forest once more.

The climb steepened for a short while, pushing the travelers to their maximum capacity. Tommy wavered back and forth as he pressed on. He'd almost reached the point of delirium. Sean knew if he didn't get some water soon, he'd probably collapse. They'd not had anything to drink since yesterday, not that he knew of at least. He doubted their captors had taken the time to give them liquids while they slumbered in a drug-induced sleep.

Tommy tripped on a root and fell to the ground. He stayed down for a minute, his breath coming in heavy, labored groans.

"Get him up," Jack ordered to the guards.

Two of the men rushed to Tommy's sides and picked him up, wedging their forearms under his armpits. Tommy wobbled for a second, and Sean stepped up close behind him.

"Let me take his pack," Sean said.

Tommy tried to protest but couldn't muster the energy.

Jack eyed Sean suspiciously as he considered the offer.

"Fine," he said after half a minute. "Give him his friend's pack."

One of the guards slipped Tommy out of the
bag and dropped it at Sean's feet. The man
stepped back cautiously, keeping his assault
rifle aimed at the former agent. It was the guy
Sean had been staring at in the back of the
truck. Sean tipped his head upward at the guy
and fired the same sardonic smirk as he'd
done before.

The guard swallowed, trying to keep the
stern look on his face. It was too late. The guy
was already beaten. Now all Sean needed was
the cards to play.

Near the top of the mountain, the ground
began to gradually level off. There wasn't
much to see in the way of the surrounding
countryside. The trees and vegetation around
the summit had grown so thick it was nearly
impossible to see off the mountain. A large
rock formation stood in a small clearing on
the other side of the peak. The cleared area
couldn't have been more than forty feet across
on all sides. Smaller rocks littered the ground
near the trees.

Reece slowed his pace as he drew closer to
the clearing and stopped short next to a stand
of skinny trees. He stared into the rough circle
at something in the center.

The others gathered around and
immediately caught sight of what had Reece's
attention. Tommy was still gasping for air, but

he'd recovered enough in the last minute of easy walking to take a look at the anomaly.

A massive flat stone lay across the ground in the middle of the circle. On it was carved a long, skinny figure holding a boomerang over its head. Dark hands surrounded the being, outlined by white.

Sean looked over at Tommy and then at Reece.

"What next?"

Tommy took a cautious step forward and examined the stone. He crouched down to one knee and ran a finger over the smooth surface. He craned his neck and surveyed the area, wondering if there were any other drawings or anything that might be a clue to another step in their journey. He found nothing.

He stood up and turned around to face the group.

"Is this it?" Jack asked, motioning to the big rock with his pistol.

Tommy swallowed. His throat was parched. He needed water badly but managed to say one sentence. "Yeah, I think it might be."

Jack puckered his lips and nodded, scanning the stone from one end to the other. "Okay. Let's get you boys some tools so you can start digging."

Chapter 35
Yengo National Park

If the two Americans thought the climb to the mountain summit was grueling, digging up the enormous stone was the cherry on top. The slab had to weigh a couple of tons. There was no telling how long it had been there, not without some of the standard equipment Tommy usually brought on a dig.

Research suggested that some Aboriginal settlements had been established in Australia as long as forty thousand years ago. While Tommy wasn't sure if the dating was correct, there was no question the Aborigines were some of the earliest people to roam the earth. Now they were looking at a stone that by all rights had been put there at the dawn of human civilization.

Unfortunately for the three companions, digging away the dirt and rock from such a long time ago took an incredible amount of effort. Two hours in, they'd only managed to dig a foot-deep ditch around the slab.

They stopped to take a break for a couple of minutes and get a quick drink. Jack wasn't stupid. He knew enough to know that thirsty workers were slow workers. So he'd allowed regular hydration breaks for his prisoners to make sure they'd keep going at a steady pace.

The blazing summer sun was high in the sky when the men reached the two-foot mark. Tommy's shirt was almost completely soaked from sweat. Sean and Reece, too, were covered in perspiration. Sean's hands and fingers were dotted with blisters from working with the wooden-handled tools. Years of working as a field agent and then as head of IAA security had kept him from doing his fair share of manual labor. As a result, the skin on his hands grew soft over time. Now he was paying the price. Every motion with the shovel or the pick resulted in a painful sting.

Late in the afternoon, the prisoners were exhausted. They'd had no food and barely enough water to keep them safe from heatstroke. Jack and his guards had been content to sit in the shade the entire time, keeping a careful watch on the men doing the digging. Of course, the overseers had plenty of food and water. They flaunted it, carelessly splashing water on the ground and dropping crumbs all over the place.

"Look at them," Tommy grumbled. "Sitting over there in the shade, eating that food right in front of us." He nearly drooled even though the food was just a bunch of granola bars. "I don't suppose you have any ideas?"

Sean focused on the earth at his feet. "At the moment, there isn't much we can do."

"You're like the king of getting out of these kinds of situations, man. Surely you can think of something."

"Sorry, buddy. Sometimes even the best need a little luck."

"I don't think being here is going to bring any of us good luck," Reece said. "We're on sacred land. And we're digging up something that is probably the most sacred thing in the world to the Aborigines. None of that bodes well for us. If there are ancestral spirits around here, they'll not be happy."

"Pretty sure there's no such thing as ancestral spirits," Tommy said as he wiped his forehead. He'd stopped sweating profusely three hours ago when dehydration started setting in.

"Believe what you want, mate. There's a reason Aborigine land goes untouched by the rest of civilization."

Jack stood up from where he was sitting on a small boulder and strode toward the three diggers. "Less talk and more digging, gents. It'll be getting dark here in a few hours. I'd like to have Mr. Holmes's prize before then."

"Maybe you could get down here and dig a few minutes then," Tommy muttered.

"What was that?"

"I said we need more water and maybe something to eat, then."

Jack was holding a packet with a half-eaten granola bar and another full one. "I suppose you do need to eat. You'll probably work faster. Here you go." He took the two bars and tossed them into the dirt at Tommy's feet. "Eat up, and then get back to digging."

Tommy eagerly grabbed the granola from the ground like he'd been tossed a filet mignon. He held the half bar out to Reece, who gratefully accepted and nearly put the entire thing in his mouth at once. Tommy broke the other bar in half and offered it to Sean.

"Here, man. You need to eat."

Sean shook his head. "Not hungry," he said and kept digging.

"You have to be hungry. We haven't had anything to eat all day."

Sean stayed focused on his task. "Go ahead," he said. "Eat it. You're probably starving."

Tommy stared at his friend for a minute, thinking Sean might change his mind. He never did.

While Tommy ate the granola bar, Sean took another swing with his mattock and pulled back the dirt just as he'd done for the majority of the day. He repeated the process once more and froze. He blinked several times to make sure he wasn't seeing things. It was no hallucination.

The giant stone slab was around two feet thick. Sean had reached the dirt beneath the rock almost half an hour before, but that was at the other end of the side he was working. Standing in the center, he could see a gap between the slab and the dirt below.

He swallowed, though nothing but dry air went down his throat. Sean leaned over and gripped the mattock closer to the head. He rode the wave of renewed energy coursing through his body and chipped away vigorously at the dirt. It fell away more easily now, and in minutes he'd opened up a gaping hole nearly two feet across and about that deep.

Tommy finished his granola bar while watching his friend. "You okay?" he asked.

"I think I found it."

Tommy dragged his shovel around to the other side where Sean was working. Reece stopped what he was doing and looked into the cavity.

Jack had walked back to his boulder to sit down. At first he didn't notice the prisoners' being distracted. Seeing the three men staring down at the slab, however, caused renewed irritation to rise up inside him.

"*What* are you three doing? I said to get back to work." He'd just sat down, so getting back up added to his frustration.

"We found something," Sean said. He let the mattock fall to the ground next to his feet.

Jack twisted his head to the side, suspicious it might be a trick. He stepped back toward the rock and motioned for the three prisoners to move away, waving his pistol in the direction he wanted. "Step back." He turned to three of his guards and ordered them to keep a close eye on the captives.

Sean and the others climbed out of their trench and moved into the clear so Jack could get in and have a closer look.

He hopped down into the ditch, bracing himself with one hand atop the stone. He leaned down and looked into the hole, shining a light from his cell phone inside. "There's a stone box in here," he said, brimming with excitement.

Jack grabbed the mattock lying next to him and pulled more dirt away from the opening until there was enough room to belly crawl inside.

The guards and the three prisoners watched as Jack wiggled into the hole to the point where only his legs from the knees down were visible.

"I see something," he said. There was no containing the man's excitement. Reece's eyes were hollow as he stared into the opening. Tommy had a similar expression.

Sean, however, was keeping an eye on the forest. He'd heard something. It was subtle—some leaves rustling, a twig snapping. None of the guards noticed. The trees were so dense, it was difficult to see between the seemingly endless rows.

There, he thought. Something moved. Or was he hallucinating? His stomach ached, and his mouth felt like it was full of chalk. It was possible his mind was playing tricks on him. That sort of thing happened all the time to people stranded in the desert. They thought they saw oases with shade and water. In this case, Sean was seeing what he wanted to see. But it was a ghost, a figment of his imagination. Or was it?

He stole a quick look at the guard nearest him to the left. It was the guy he'd been across from in the back of the truck, the one in whom Sean had planted the seeds of madness.

Over his shoulder, in a hushed tone, Sean whispered, "Do you see the spirits?"

The guy's head twitched, and he clenched his weapon a little tighter. He said nothing.

"Can you hear them? They're coming. They're coming to protect what belongs to them."

The guard blinked rapidly and took a wary step back. "Quiet," he ordered. It was the first time the guy had said anything. His accent was distinctly Eastern European.

Sean's delirium only served to heighten the madness in his tone. "It won't matter how quiet I am, or any of us. We are on sacred land. The spirits are coming."

Tommy looked over his shoulder at his friend, wondering what he was going on about. He only caught the last few words, but his initial thought was that Sean had lost it.

Under the slab, Jack's legs jerked back and forth. "I...I think I've got it!" he shouted. "It's...beautiful. And it's really heavy."

Sean paid no attention to the former rugby player. He was locked in on his victim now.

"Turn around," the nervous man said. "And keep quiet."

Jack wiggled out from under the slab. He was dragging something heavy, straining as he pulled the object from its hiding place. His head appeared last. Once he was clear of the slab, moving the object became easier. He put both hands under the stone and tugged.

At first, the only thing visible to the rest of the men was a yellowish, narrow object about three inches wide. As Jack removed the entire, thing, everyone's eyes widened as the golden boomerang glimmered in the rays of sunlight streaking through the canopy above.

"I can't believe it," Jack said with a huge grin. He grabbed the object at both ends and held it up to the sky. "I can't believe it!"

Tommy noticed the engravings on the boomerang as Jack held it high. He sighed at the thought of this grunt getting his hands on it. They could learn much from what was carved into the precious metal. Not now.

Sean never looked back at Jack holding up the treasure. He was too busy staring into the guard's soul.

"I told you to turn around," the man's voice grew louder.

Suddenly, a deep vibrating tone echoed through the leaves. The guards simultaneously snapped their heads around to find the source of the noise, but they could see nothing.

The sound was joined by a similar one from another part of the woods. The eerie tone sent a chill up Sean's spine. He didn't let the guards know that. Another didgeridoo came to life in yet another part of the forest, completely surrounding the group in the noise.

"I told you the spirits were coming," Sean said to his guard.

Jack lowered the heavy object and looked around. He tried not to panic but couldn't find the ones responsible for the noise. He set the boomerang on top of the slab and pulled out his pistol, waving it around in all directions.

Sean's guard took a step back. His hands clutching the assault rifle trembled. "Turn around," he said in a quivering voice. "Turn around, and shut your mouth."

Sean had no intention of obeying. He used the noise to his advantage. "They're here because we disturbed a sacred place. And now they will make you pay."

"I told you to shut—"

The man's heel struck a root, and he tripped. His arms flailed wildly as he tried to keep his balance. He fell over backward and accidentally fired his weapon, sending a bullet harmlessly into the trees.

Sean pounced like a hungry lion. One step, and he jumped on the man, even before the guard's back hit the ground.

Jack saw what was happening and aimed at the American. Sean was too fast, though, and grabbed his victim by the shirt. With what little strength he had left, Sean rolled the guard over—putting him squarely between himself and Jack's weapon. Jack pulled the trigger rapidly, sending round after round into the human shield's back.

The man's face grimaced with every bullet that sank into his body until one struck his spinal cord. Then his body went totally limp. Sean felt it go heavy but managed to keep the dead man propped up.

The other four guards saw what happened and turned their attention to Sean, momentarily forgetting about Reece and Tommy. The two big men charged the guys closest to them. They both yelled like rabid wolves, driving their shoulders into the guards before they could whip their weapons around and fire.

Tommy plowed his man into the ground, landing on top of the guard with all his weight. The side of the guy's head hit the ground and dazed him for a moment. Tommy summoned the last remnants of his strength and straddled the man's chest. He pummeled the guard's face over and over again with clenched fists, each blow pushing the victim closer and closer to unconsciousness.

Six feet away, Reece had tumbled over his guy and rolled beyond him. The guard stood up and lunged at the big Aussie, who clambered up from the ground and sank a fist deep into the guard's abdomen.

The guy grunted and doubled over, but he stayed on his feet and deflected Reece's next punch, countering with his own to the Aussie's jaw.

Sean heard Jack's gun click. He was out of rounds. It wouldn't take him long to reload. Sean had to act fast. Then he noticed the other two guards taking aim at Tommy as he pounded one of the guards into oblivion.

Sean's instincts kicked in. He grabbed the knife off his human shield's belt and flipped it over. It only took Sean half a second to size up the distance between him and the guard closest to him. From his backside, he twisted his upper body and flung the blade as hard as he could.

The knife zipped through the air. The tip sank deep into tissue to the right of the gunman's shoulder blade. He yelled and fired his weapon wildly into the air as he dropped to the ground.

The last guard turned around and aimed his rifle at Sean. The dead guy Sean had used before wouldn't help him against that weapon.

He saw the gunman's finger tense on the trigger as he was about to pull it and effectively cut Sean in half. Out of nowhere, something struck the man in the neck. It protruded like a dangling white ornament made of a fuzzy material. The guard winced and grabbed at the dart. He looked around desperate to find the new assailant, but the forest was empty.

Then the poison took hold.

He started shaking as the venom worked its way through his blood, aided by the fact that he'd taken the dart squarely in the carotid artery. He clutched his neck with both hands, squeezing it with his fingers to keep the burning from going any farther. It was too late. The venom did its job quickly. The guard dropped to his knees as his throat tightened. His face reddened as he desperately tried to force air into his lungs. The last sound he made before he fell face-first into the dirt was a desperate gurgle.

Sean stole a look around into the trees. He couldn't find the shooter, and there was no trace of the blowgun. If they were an enemy, he'd be next. Something in Sean's mind told him that whoever was in the trees had no intention of hurting him.

Jack reached into his belt and grabbed a fresh magazine. His hands moved fast as Sean sprang up from the ground and charged. One thumb pressed the button that loosed the magazine from its housing. The other hand deftly brought the magazine around and slid it into the base of the weapon. Sean took one more big step, and Jack held the gun down and jerked the slide back to chamber a new round.

Sean flew through the air, yelling like a banshee. Jack raised the weapon and fired. The round whizzed past Sean's head, missing by mere inches.

The second shot never came.

Sean crashed into Jack, his weight driving the big man back against the stone slab. Jack brought the gun around to take another shot. Sean raised his forearm and blocked the move then smashed his fist into his opponent's jaw. Sean followed the blow by grabbing the gun with his other hand and twisting it at an awkward angle. Jack had no choice but to let go or have his fingers broken by the weapon.

But the big rugger wasn't done. Sean held the gun by the barrel, but a swift snap of Jack's boot sent the weapon tumbling through the air and onto the ground a dozen feet away. Sean watched the gun for a second. As he turned his attention back to the massive man, his cheek took the brunt of a heavy fist.

Chapter 36
Yengo National Park

Twenty feet away, Reece grappled with the last guard. He held the barrel as the man squeezed the trigger. The weapon boomed like thunder. Leaves shook on the nearby trees. Dirt exploded on the ground with every bullet strike. Finally the weapon went silent as the two men spun around in a deadly dance.

Reece immediately recognized the gun was no longer a threat. He let go of the weapon and grabbed the guard by the shirt, yanked him forward, and planted his forehead directly into the man's nose.

The man's hand let go of the rifle. It clacked on the ground at Reece's feet. Reece repeated the move, using his strength to pull the guard at him again. This time, the disoriented guard regained his wits enough to lower his head. The two heads came together like rams' horns atop a mountain.

Reece's grip on the man's shirt loosened, and he staggered backward a few steps until he lost his balance and dropped to his butt.

The guard looked up with blank eyes. Dark crimson blood trickled from his nostrils as he wavered in place for a second. Then he toppled over sideways, unconscious before he hit the ground.

The punch Sean took nearly knocked him out of the trench. His lower back barged into the side. Jack rushed him, but Sean was quicker and rolled out onto the ground above.

Jack jumped after him.

Sean snapped his foot out to kick Jack in the face. The attacker snatched Sean's shoe and twisted it to the right, spinning Sean in midair and sending him to the ground.

Again, Sean rolled out of the way as Jack leaped from the ditch and onto the surface. He stomped at Sean's head and missed, then tried again with the same result. Sean tumbled to safety and pushed up to his feet once more.

He sniffled and narrowed his eyes, holding his fists out in a fighting stance with his body twisted slightly. *This is the man who is responsible for her death. Take your revenge.*

Jack charged. Sean stepped forward. Jack jumped into the air, leading with his boot. Sean ducked to the side and chopped the bridge of his right hand squarely into Jack's midsection.

The counter was a good one. But not good enough.

Jack landed on his feet and whirled around, whipping another kick into the middle of Sean's back. Sean grunted from the dull surge of pain. He reacted with a jab. Jack blocked the punch and swung a roundhouse into

Sean's jaw, knocking him sideways a couple of feet.

The world spun in Sean's eyes. He put out both hands to steady his balance. Another fist smashed into his jaw and sent him stumbling backward.

Sean was losing, and he didn't know if he could win. The big former athlete almost seemed as if the blows Sean delivered had no effect. His body was weak from lack of food and water. *No,* he told himself. *It can't end here. Not like this.*

As Jack stalked toward his prey, Sean's blurry mind drifted back to a thought he'd had a moment before. *Could he beat the big former athlete? That's right. Jack's career ended because of a bad knee injury.*

Just feet away from where Sean wavered, Jack pulled a big knife out of his belt and held it out menacingly.

"Time for you to join your sheila," he said with a sinister grin on his face.

He flipped the grip around in his hand and raised the weapon over his shoulder.

Sean clenched every muscle in his body to make the world steady again, and as Jack brought the tip of the blade down at the American's neck, Sean sidestepped, lifted his foot, and jammed his heel down into the side of Jack's knee.

The joint gave way under the force of Sean's weight. Jack buckled and fell to the ground amid a series of howls. He grabbed at the wounded appendage with both hands, his face contorted in agony.

Sean kept his balance enough to bend down and pick up the knife. He looked at it for a second and then stared down at the big man. Tommy and Reece watched from the other side of the clearing as Sean crouched behind Jack and pulled him up onto his backside. The American wrapped his arm around the man's neck and pressed the edge of the blade against the skin. A thin cut opened, oozing droplets of blood.

"Do it," Jack said. "It won't bring her back."

"No," Sean said. "It won't."

He jerked the knife to his right and shoved the man back to the ground.

For a moment, Reece and Tommy thought Sean had slit the man's throat. Then they heard Jack laughing as Sean walked away, back toward the giant stone slab. He tossed the knife into the woods and sighed.

"You don't have the guts, do you, Wyatt? You're just a coward!" Jack clawed at the ground and noticed the pistol he'd lost just moments before. He reached out to the weapon. His fingers dragged across the grip before a nail caught the edge of the magazine and pulled it closer. Jack sat up and raised the pistol, aiming straight at Sean's back.

Tommy saw the threat, and his eyes lit up with fear. "Sssssean!" he shouted.

Sean stopped, though he didn't turn around. He didn't need to. He could feel the gun pointed at him. For a moment, he wondered when the gunshot was coming. Instead, a low thump came from behind. It was followed by a thud on the ground.

Sean slowly twisted his head and looked back over his shoulder. Jack was facedown in the dirt. His body twitched for a few seconds and then became completely still. The knife Sean had tossed into the woods protruded from the back of his neck.

An apparition stood twenty feet behind him.

Adriana smiled.

For a long moment Sean didn't know if his imagination was running wild on him or if what he saw was real. Tears filled his eyes, and he nearly dropped to the ground.

"I..."

"Thought I was dead?" She walked slowly toward him. Her ponytail bobbed with every step.

"How? I couldn't find you in the river."

Reece and Tommy struggled to their feet and stared with unbelieving eyes as Adriana approached Sean.

She stopped close to him.

He reached out and wrapped his arms around her, squeezing her tighter than he'd ever squeezed anything in his life.

"Easy," she said. "Bullet wound, remember?"

"Oh yeah," he said, sniffling. "Sorry."

"It's okay."

He shook his head. "I don't understand. I saw you get shot. You fell in the water."

"I know," she said. "The bullet went right through. I was lucky. Don't get me wrong, I had to get the wound closed. And I should probably see a doctor pretty soon. But I'll be okay."

"Where did you go? I looked all over the river."

"Yes," she nodded, "I'm sorry about that. When I fell back into the water, I thought I was going to die. It only took me a few seconds before I realized the wound wasn't as bad as I suspected. If he'd been using a bigger-caliber bullet, I might not be standing here. I went under the surface and swam back to the waterfall. I hid there and waited.

"It was a trick to plug the wounds. I had to tear off part of my sports bra. Getting the blood to stop in the back was harder due to the angle, but I managed. Will be a while before I use this arm much."

Tommy and Reece had joined them and listened to her tale.

"You three disappeared, so I waited for the shooter and the others to come down. That one over there," she motioned at Jack, "killed the sniper. When they left, I followed them, tracking them all the way here. I had a little help with the wound from some friends. They burned it shut for me, which by the way, is excruciating."

"Friends?" Tommy asked. He still couldn't believe she was standing there in front of them.

Adriana flashed a sly grin and nodded. "Yes." She waved a hand at the forest and suddenly dozens of dark faces marked with white paint appeared. Some of the men held didgeridoos. Others carried boomerangs. "I knew I would need help since I was outnumbered and still not fully recovered. So I found some people I knew wouldn't be happy about bad guys like them desecrating a sacred place. They were more than willing to oblige. Their only stipulation was that they wouldn't harm anyone personally."

The realization hit Reece. "So they were the ones playing the didgeridoos."

"So much for your spirits," Tommy said.

"They offered to help," Adriana continued. "The instruments were their idea."

One of the Aborigine men stepped forward, separating himself from the others. He wore blue jeans and a gray T-shirt. His black hair hung down just below his ears. One white line streaked from his forehead down his nose. His cheeks were covered in dots and white lines.

He stopped six feet away from the group and paused. "Me and the others would like to thank you for your help in putting a stop to whatever these blokes had planned," he said in a sharp Aussie accent.

"You're welcome," Sean said. "They were going to try to use that golden boomerang to force the sale of tribal lands."

The tribesman looked puzzled. "Land? Is that what this was about? There's plenty of land all over the continent."

"Not with oil in it, there's not. Seems that their boss," Sean gave a nod at Jack, "found a good bit of oil in some Aborigine land in South Australia. He figured if he had the sacred boomerang, the owners would be more apt to listen to a proposal."

The tribesman listened and then pursed his lips together. "Well then, it's a good thing you all came along."

Tommy was about to burst from all the questions in his mind. "I'm sorry. I don't mean to be rude, but what are you going to do with the boomerang?"

"Why? You one of them treasure hunters?" the tribesman asked.

"No," Tommy shook his head vehemently. "I run an archaeological agency. Studying ancient cultures is one of my passions."

"Isn't the study of ancient cultures anthropology?"

Sean and Reece both snorted a laugh.

Tommy blushed. "Well...yes, but we do a bit of both."

"I'm just funnin' with ya, mate. To answer your question, we're going to put the boomerang back where it belongs—where the creator put it in the first place. It must stay there until he returns. If you'd like to have a look at it before we return it, be our guest."

Tommy's eyes lit up. "Oh thank you. Thank you so much. I'll just take a few...oh right. No pictures."

The tribesman's eyes gleamed with mischief. "That's right, mate. No pictures."

Chapter 37
Adelaide

"You sure you don't want to stick around a bit longer?" Reece asked as he took a big sip of the golden beer.

He and the other three sat around a patio table overlooking Downtown Adelaide. They'd just finished a big meal at one of the nicer places in town. That didn't stop Reece from having a few rounds.

"We have to get going," Tommy said. "They're clearing out the rubble from our building this week. I'll be meeting with the architects next week to start looking through designs for the new facility."

"What about you two?" Reece said to Sean and Adriana. "Also heading back to the States?"

"Yeah," Sean said with a nod. "Need to get back and recuperate. Plus I want to spend some time alone with her." He squeezed Adriana's hand and offered her a loving smile. He'd almost lost her twice now. Letting go was something he'd put off as long as possible.

Tommy pointed at Reece's glass. "I thought you guys drank Foster's down here."

Reece was in mid-sip and nearly did a spit take. He leaned forward and set the glass down on the table. "Foster's? Are you serious?"

Tommy looked around the table for some help, but he wasn't getting any from his friends. "Is it not what you guys drink?"

"Foster's, Tom, is only brewed to export. No one drinks that stuff around here. I think I've seen one, maybe two pubs my whole life that sell it in Australia."

"Okay, sorry I asked." He put up his hands to surrender.

"Foster's," Reece muttered as he raised the glass to his lips again.

Sean changed the subject. "So what's in store for you, Reece? You gonna pick up a gig with one of the other adventure tour companies or keep doing your own thing?"

Reece set the glass back down once more and swallowed the beer. He smacked his lips and sighed with satisfaction. "Funny you should ask. I took a look at my bank account this morning and there was a ton more money than was there yesterday. I called the bank to ask them what happened. All they would tell me is that a large deposit was made yesterday evening. I thought it was a mistake, but a note on the deposit slip said, 'Thank you, Reece.' I couldn't make out who it was from."

Sean flashed Tommy a questioning glance.

"Wasn't me," Tommy said.

"Then who?" Sean asked.

"I guess we may never know," Reece said. "All I know is, I'm back in business. Going to have to stay here in town while my house is being repaired. Shouldn't take too long."

"And how is Annie?" Tommy asked. "Recovering?"

Reece nodded. "Yeah, she seems to be doing fine. The police went into Holmes's place and found her in one of his many rooms. She said the men didn't do anything to her, and that they gave her food and water during her captivity."

"That's a relief."

"Yeah, no kidding. Though I doubt she'll be doing any snooping around the museum anytime soon."

"No sign of Holmes, though?" Sean asked. He already knew the answer.

The moment they got back to civilization from Yengo Mountain, Reece started making phone calls to his connections in Sydney. With Jack dead, Holmes would feel the house of cards collapsing around him. At the first sign of trouble he'd vanish, probably leaving the country under a fake name. He could go anywhere, be anyone. Men with the kinds of resources Holmes had didn't have a difficult time disappearing.

"Sadly, no," Reece said. "Into thin air with that one. They'll keep looking. He'll turn up eventually."

Sean picked up his glass of water and raised it over the center of the table. "To Reece for all your help. May your new adventures be successful."

The others raised their glasses and clinked them together.

"Thanks, mate," Reece said. "And to *this* adventure finally being over."

Sean took a sip of water and set it on the table surface. He didn't say anything, but a single thought kept running through his mind.

It's not over yet.

Chapter 38
Hong Kong
Two Weeks Later

Bernard Holmes walked into his building bathed in Hong Kong's flashing electric glow. He looked down both ends of the sidewalk—just as he'd done the last few weeks—to make sure nothing out of the ordinary was going on.

The Australian authorities had frozen most of his assets. It was a predictable move on their part. Luckily, he'd taken precautions before things started going south. While the government seized over a billion dollars in property and money, he'd managed to squirrel away just over $300 million—more than enough to buy him a new life. With that kind of money, he'd have a jump start on getting things going again.

His first order of business was to take out the Americans who'd wrecked his plans. Once he got settled into his new place, he'd find a crew of assassins to eliminate Sean Wyatt and the others.

The Hong Kong streets were flooded with people rushing around to get dinner or heading to their favorite hangouts at the end of the week. Holmes had picked up a quick meal from a place that did carryout. He paid cash, as he'd done with everything for the last two weeks. Tracking paper money was nearly impossible if done correctly.

He pushed through the high-rise revolving door and strode across the marble floor, his thousand-dollar shoes clicking on the hard surface with every step. When he reached the elevator, he stopped and pressed the up arrow. The button illuminated a bright red. A digital display over the doors told him the lift was on the ninth floor and on its way down.

Holmes hadn't had any trouble finding a place to lie low. He had a few unscrupulous associates in Hong Kong's real estate market. When he offered an exorbitant amount of cash for a condo downtown, they had the perfect location.

It was a penthouse villa on the fortieth floor. The condo featured an incredible view of the city, complete with a hot tub overlooking downtown.

The elevator dinged, and the doors opened.

Holmes got in and pressed the *40* button on the panel. A moment later, the doors closed and he was whisked away toward the top of the building. He remembered back to a time when elevators were long, slow rides. This one, however, was more like an express lift. Getting from the ground floor to the fortieth took about a minute.

He watched the numbers passing quickly on another display over the doors. Suddenly, when the number hit *30*, the elevator slowed. At *32* it came to a full stop between floors.

Holmes frowned. He reached out and pressed the *40* repeatedly. Nothing happened.

"You have to be kidding me," he grumbled.

The phone in his jacket pocket started ringing. He'd just bought the device the week before, and no one had the number. Like with everything else, he'd paid cash and used his alias to register the phone on the network.

He took it out and looked at the screen. It was a local number, but no one he recognized. Why would he? The only Hong Kong number he vaguely remembered was the friend who'd arranged for the condo.

Holmes pressed one of the buttons on the side of the phone to silence it. He slid it back into his pocket and started hitting the number again on the elevator panel. The phone started ringing again.

He looked at the screen once more and saw it was the same number. He hit the green button and put the device to his ear. "I'm sorry, you have the wrong number," he said.

He lowered the device, but before he could end the call, he heard a voice on the other line. "Do I?"

The man was American.

Holmes's frown deepened as he put the phone back to his ear. "Who is this? How did you get this number?"

"Let's just say for most people, you'd be a hard man to find, Mr. Holmes."

He knows my name. He knows where I am. Those were just a couple of the hundreds of panicked thoughts rushing through Holmes's mind.

"Who is this?" he asked. He reached out and pressed some of the other numbers on the panel. The elevator remained still.

"You've been bad, Mr. Holmes. You killed innocent people."

Holmes tried to suppress his irritation, but it leaked out anyway. "Look, whoever you are, I don't know what kind of game you're trying to play here, but you're messing with the wrong guy. If you know what's good for you, you'll disappear. Or I'll make that happen myself."

"Like you did with your board of directors in Sydney?"

The question sent a chill down Holmes's spine. *How did they know? How did they find me?*

"Before you start spouting off a bunch of lies about that, you should just save it. I know everything. I know about your plan to take control of the company. I know how you killed those twelve men. I even know about the museum director you had executed."

Holmes did a 180 in less than two seconds. "Listen. I don't know who you are, but let's get together and talk about this. Okay? We can meet and discuss what you want. That's what all this is about, right? You want money? I can give it to you. I have millions. You can have it."

He started mashing the buttons faster now as his desperation reached its zenith. He banged on the elevator doors, loud enough for the man on the other end to hear.

"No one is going to help you, Mr. Holmes. That floor is full of offices. And no one is at work right now. You're all alone. And no, it's not about money. It's about taking one more piece of garbage out of this world."

A loud boom shook the elevator from above. Holmes's feet left the floor as the lift dropped. He struck the mirrored ceiling and then heard the emergency brakes engage just above his head. He crashed to the floor, smashing his bag of rice and chicken in the process.

Holmes picked himself up off the floor. Relief flooded his emotions, replacing the terror that had momentarily taken hold. *I'm alive. I'm alive!*

He stood up and brushed some rice off his expensive suit. The phone was on the floor beneath the panel. He tentatively bent down and picked it up, feeling a sharp pain in his knee from the fall. It was probably just a bruise. He'd be okay in a few days.

"So that was your plan? Kill me in an elevator? Don't get me wrong. I appreciate the sense of irony you have about all this, but it looks like you forgot the emergency brakes."

"Did I?"

A renewed sense of horror overwhelmed Holmes. He tried to wedge his fingers into the seam between the doors, but they wouldn't move.

"Look, I'll give you whatever you want. Okay? Just let me out of this thing, and I'll take care of it." He took a step back and looked up at the number on the display. It read 27.

"Sorry, Mr. Holmes. I have to be going now. Goodbye."

"No. No, wait!" The call ended.

Holmes flinched as he waited for the elevator to drop again, but it didn't. Instead, he was consumed by the eerie silence in the confined space. He swallowed and slowed his breathing. After standing still for nearly a minute, he started laughing. "He mucked it up," he said out loud. "Well done, whoever you are."

He pressed some of the buttons again, with the same result. Then he noticed the red emergency button. "I was rather hoping to avoid the fireman, but it beats waiting around in here." His finger depressed the button.

Four rapid explosions came in quick succession from the roof above. One of them blew a hole through the corner of the ceiling.

Holmes's eyes widened at the realization. Terrified, he screamed as the elevator's last brake blew out.

The lift dropped again, plummeting down the shaft.

Holmes hit the mirror above once more. He stared down at the floor as the display to his right showed the numbers falling almost two at a time.

Half a block away, Sean Wyatt stepped out of a noodle bar with a bag of takeout. He heard the thunderous crash come from the building across the street a few hundred feet away. The ground vibrated for a moment, and everyone around him on the sidewalk looked around, wondering if it was an earthquake. They only gave it a second's thought.

Sean pressed the green button on his phone and put the device to his ear.

Two seconds later, Emily answered. "Yeah?"

"Just wanted to say thanks for tracking him down for me. I appreciate it."

"Anytime. We can't have those types running around, can we?"

Sean had called Emily about Holmes before he'd been captured by Jack Robinson. He knew the man was up to something. When

Holmes left the country, it was Emily who'd tracked him to Hong Kong.

"The fewer, the better," Sean said. "Gotta go. I'll talk to you when I get back stateside."

He ended the call as he rounded a corner into an alley. Bending down fluidly, he dropped the phone into a storm drain and kept moving. He walked into a cloud of steam that poured out of pipes on a nearby wall. Sirens blared in the distance, echoing down the canyon of buildings in the city as Sean Wyatt disappeared into the mist.

Thank You

I just wanted to take a moment to say thank you for choosing to spend your time reading my work. I put one of these little notes at the end of all my books because I know that you could have spent your money and time on something else, but you chose this book.

I am honored and hope you enjoyed it.

Please swing by one of your favorite online retailers and leave an honest review. Those reviews help authors because they let other readers know if the book is something they might enjoy. Plus, reviews help readers decide on what to read next. It's a win-win.

So thank you once more for reading me. I appreciate it and look forward to entertaining you again.

Ernest

Author's Note

I thought I'd do things a little differently this time and work backward from the end of the story.

The legend about Baiame is a real Aboriginal myth. It's one of many creation stories Australian natives celebrate. The stone on Yengo Mountain is purported to be there, but since people are not permitted beyond a certain point due to the sacred nature of the summit, it is unclear whether it exists or not.

Aborigines are an incredible people with a diverse history and a many fascinating belief systems. While I did try to represent their culture correctly and with strong accuracy, there were things I had to add to suit the stories needs. For example, on one spot, a blowgun is used. This is not necessarily a traditional weapon, even though they were used in the past. Blowguns, in fact, are outlawed in Australia for hunting purposes.

The golden boomerang was a concoction of my imagination. When I saw the rock art at Milbrodale, I couldn't help but wonder what the significance of the two boomerangs might be. Seemed to make sense that the creator gave one as a gift to the people of Australia.

All of the rock art I mentioned in this story exists. It's all real, and although I did tweak some of the meanings a little to fit the story, every place in this novel can be visited. Keep in mind that most of these locations have a spiritual significance to the Aboriginal people, so if you do go, be respectful.

Aboriginal tribes do have a fairly common belief that big rock formations are spirits or ancestors. Just one more reason to not go traipsing around like a crazed tourist if you go on a walkabout.

The snake I mentioned earlier in the book—the Mulga—is extremely venomous. They don't frequently bite humans unless someone provokes them (usually drunk people).

The piece about Foster's not being consumed in Australia is also true. Their beers of choice are Victoria Bitter or Toohey's, with a few others mixed in. So if you go down under and are looking for a pint, don't ask for the export.

The museum at the beginning of the story is a figment of my imagination. Though Sydney does have wonderful museums, this one does not exist. I used it purely for the purpose of this tale.

R.H. Mathews was a real person. He was a fascinating man and had a keen interest in anthropology revolving around the Aborigine people. He befriended many tribesmen during his later years and is now considered one of the foremost experts of his time on Aboriginal history and culture. While his secret coded note was my creation, it is entirely possible that Mathews discovered something of historical significance related to ancient Aboriginal beliefs.

Get Free Books

If you haven't joined the Ernest Dempsey VIP reader list, you should. You'll get two free, full-length novels, plus a couple of novellas just for signing up. On top of that, you get exclusive updates on new releases—and VIP pricing when the new books come out. It doesn't cost anything to be a member, so what are you waiting for?

Visit http://ernestdempsey.net to learn how to get your free digital books today.

Other Sean Wyatt Thrillers by Ernest Dempsey
(In order)

The Secret of the Stones
The Cleric's Vault
The Last Chamber
The Grecian Manifesto
The Norse Directive
Game of Shadows
The Jerusalem Creed
The Samurai Cipher
The Cairo Vendetta

War of Thieves Box Set
(An Adriana Villa Adventure)

Dedication

For my brother, Erik. Thanks for always making me laugh and inspiring me to work harder every day. See you under the shady tree, weirdo.

Acknowledgements

None of my stories would be possible without the great input I get from incredible readers all over the globe. My advance reader group is such an incredibly unselfish and supportive team. I couldn't do any of this without them.

My editors, Anne Storer and Jason Whited, must also be thanked for their amazing work and guidance in crafting these stories. They make everything so much better for the reader.

Last but not least, I need to give a big thank you to Elena at L1 Graphics for the incredible cover art she always delivers, along with beautiful social media artwork.

Prologue
1
2
3
4
5
6
7
8
9
10
11
12
13
14
15
16
17
18
19
20
21
22
23
24
25
26
27
28
29
30

Copyright ©2016 Ernest Dempsey
Ernestdempsey.net
All rights reserved.
Published in the United States of America by Enclave Publishing.
ISBN 978-1-944647-12-4

Made in the USA
San Bernardino, CA
06 February 2020